P9-CMN-776

MEASURE FOR MEASURE

The RSC Shakespeare

Edited by Jonathan Bate and Eric Rasmussen

Chief Associate Editors: Héloïse Sénéchal and Jan Sewell

Associate Editors: Trey Jansen, Eleanor Lowe, Lucy Munro,
Dee Anna Phares

Measure for Measure

Textual editing: Eric Rasmussen

Introduction and "Shakespeare's Career in the Theater": Jonathan Bate

Commentary: Charlotte Scott and Héloïse Sénéchal

Scene-by-Scene Analysis: Esme Miskimmin

In Performance: Karin Brown (RSC stagings) and Jan Sewell (overview)

Playing *Measure for Measure* (interviews by Jonathan Bate and
Kevin Wright):
Trevor Nunn, Josette Simon, Roger Allam

Editorial Advisory Board

Gregory Doran, Chief Associate Director,
Royal Shakespeare Company

Jim Davis, Professor of Theatre Studies, University of Warwick, UK

Charles Edelman, Senior Lecturer, Edith Cowan University,
Western Australia

Lukas Erne, Professor of Modern English Literature,
Université de Genève, Switzerland

Jacqui O'Hanlon, Director of Education, Royal Shakespeare Company

Akiko Kusunoki, Tokyo Woman's Christian University, Japan

Ron Rosenbaum, author and journalist, New York, USA

James Shapiro, Professor of English and Comparative Literature,
Columbia University, USA

Tiffany Stern, Professor and Tutor in English, University of Oxford, UK

The RSC Shakespeare

William Shakespeare

MEASURE FOR MEASURE

Edited by Jonathan Bate and Eric Rasmussen

Introduction by Jonathan Bate

The Modern Library
New York

2010 Modern Library Paperback Edition

Copyright © 2007, 2010 by The Royal Shakespeare Company

All rights reserved.

Published in the United States by Modern Library, an imprint of
The Random House Publishing Group, a division of
Random House, Inc., New York.

MODERN LIBRARY and the TORCHBEARER Design are registered trademarks
of Random House, Inc.

"Royal Shakespeare Company," "RSC," and the RSC logo are trademarks
or registered trademarks of The Royal Shakespeare Company.

The version of *Measure for Measure* and the corresponding footnotes
that appear in this volume were originally published in *William Shakespeare:
Complete Works*, edited by Jonathan Bate and Eric Rasmussen, published
in 2007 by Modern Library, an imprint of The Random House
Publishing Group, a division of Random House, Inc.

ISBN 978-0-8129-6928-3
eBook ISBN 978-1-58836-875-1

Printed in the United States of America

www.modernlibrary.com

CONTENTS

CONTENTS

INTRODUCTION

"JUDGE NOT, THAT YE BE NOT JUDGED"

The most widely read book in Shakespeare's England was the "Geneva" translation of the Bible. Because of this, the title of *Measure for Measure* would have been readily recognized by the play's original audience as an allusion to the opening verses of the seventh chapter of St. Matthew's Gospel:

> Judge not, that ye be not judged.
> For with what judgement ye judge, ye shall be judged, and with
> what measure ye mete, it shall be measured to you again.
> And why see'st thou the mote, that is in thy brother's eye, and
> perceivest not the beam that is in thine own eye?

The running head summarizing the content of this page in the Geneva Bible reads "Christ's doctrine—God's providence." Of all Shakespeare's plays, *Measure for Measure* is the one in which the dramatization of Christian doctrine and the motions of divine providence are most prominent.

It is actually unusual for Shakespeare to take his own title quite so seriously. *Measure* was written soon after *Twelfth Night*, with its throwaway subtitle *or What You Will*, and around the same time as *All's Well That Ends Well*, which pointedly modifies its own title in the climactic line "All yet *seems* well." Here, by contrast, the moral of the action is spelled out explicitly. Angelo sees the mote in Claudio's eye (getting his girlfriend Juliet pregnant before marrying her, albeit after becoming engaged to her) and fails to perceive the beam in his own (dumping his girlfriend Mariana upon discovering that she hasn't got any money). He judges Claudio, but the duke contrives to judge him by his own measure:

"An Angelo for Claudio, death for death!"
Haste still pays haste, and leisure answers leisure,
Like doth quit like, and measure still for measure.

The Geneva Bible included interpretative glosses in its margins. Beside the "measure for measure" verses appeared the admonition "hypocrites hide their own faults, and seek not to amend them, but are curious to reprove other men's." That could as well be an instant character sketch of Angelo. He is more than once described as "precise," a term applied to no other character in Shakespeare. It was a word that often went with "puritan," as may be seen from the way in which Shakespeare's acquaintance John Florio defined the phrase *Gabba santi* in his Anglo-Italian dictionary: "a precise dissembling puritan, an hypocrite." Shakespeare was always guarded about the Roman Catholicism that was in his blood—was there a family connection with a certain Isabella Shakespeare, abbess of a nunnery not far from Stratford-upon-Avon?—but there is no doubt that he had little time for the puritans who stood on the opposite edge of the religious spectrum.

Despite the steer given by the title, the play is much more tangled than the old drama on which it was based, George Whetstone's *History of Promos and Cassandra*, which showed "the unsufferable abuse of a lewd magistrate," "the virtuous behaviour of a chaste lady," and "the perfect magnanimity of a noble king in checking vice and favouring virtue," all for the purpose of revealing "the ruin and overthrow of dishonest practices" and "the advancement of upright dealing." Shakespeare took Whetstone's basic plotline and principal characters—the indecent proposal, the hypocritical dealing of the lawgiver, the beautiful gentlewoman asked to give up her chastity in return for her brother's life, the ruler who returns and sorts everything out—but greatly complicated the moral vision. Whetstone's character of Promos has two anguished soliloquies in which he reflects on his desire for Cassandra. They offer a structural anticipation of Angelo's self-questioning "What's this? What's this? Is this her fault or mine? / The tempter or the tempted, who sins most? Ha?" and "When I would pray and think, I think and pray / To several subjects." Whetstone, however, lacks Shakespeare's gift of writing soliloquy with meditative pauses, shifts between argument and emotion, and rhetorical twists that create the illusion that the character is having the thought as he speaks rather than speechifying on a predetermined theme.

Promos' dilemma is set up in terms of a simple opposition between reason and desire; with Angelo, on the other hand, it is the force of Isabella's reason—her powers of linguistic persuasion—that inflames his desire. He wants her not because she's beautiful or even because she is on the verge of taking a vow of perpetual chastity, but because he loves to see her mind and tongue at work. "She speaks, and 'tis such sense / That my sense breeds with it." Here rational sense is the very thing that stirs sensuality. In his book *The Structure of Complex Words* (1951), the critic William Empson brilliantly demonstrated how a movement between the different senses of the word "sense" comes to the core of the play.

In a good production, sexual chemistry crackles between Angelo and Isabella even as she resists him. Being a man who is used to getting his way, he does not realize how much he loves it when he does not. Two strong wills strain against each other. As we watch, there is a little part of us that anticipates—or even hopes—that they will end up marrying each other in the manner of Shakespeare's other sparring couples, Petruchio and Kate, Berowne and Rosaline, Beatrice and Benedick.

Intriguingly, the Mariana plotline is Shakespeare's key innovation in the plot: Whetstone's play and the various sixteenth-century Italian versions of the story do not have the "bed trick" and they end with the king or duke punishing the Angelo figure by having him marry the Isabella figure (in order to repair her honor) before being executed. The Isabella figure then intervenes and professes her love for the man who has abused her; he is pardoned and they live happily ever after. Shakespeare transposes these turns onto Mariana and saves Angelo from execution. Mercy prevails over justice: it should be remembered that the "measure for measure" passage in St. Matthew's Gospel is at the heart of the Sermon on the Mount, in which Jesus lays out his moral code, sharply distinguishing his new covenant of forgiveness from the harsher "eye for an eye" law of the Old Testament.

The introduction of Mariana into the story displaces the marriage plot from Isabella, seemingly leaving her free to return to the nunnery and take her final vows. But the play ends with the wholly unexpected twist of the duke's proposal. In one way, it is a fitting union. Having made the wrong choice of deputy (Escalus would have done the job much better), the duke makes the right choice of wife: Isabella will bring to his household the moral fiber that has been lacking, without any of Angelo's hypocrisy. Her "ghostly father" will become her husband and the Mother Superior of the nunnery will have to do without her: the monastic virtues will be brought from the contemplative to the active life, from the cloister to the secular state, in a manner characteristic of the sixteenth-century Protestant Reformation. In another way, though, it is an astonishing ending. This has not been a courtship comedy. And is there not a little touch of moral blackmail in the proposal? Angelo's proposition was: sleep with me and I will save your brother's life. The duke's is: I have saved your brother's life, so marry me.

It has sometimes been argued that Shakespeare was becoming bored with comedy's conventional happy ending in multiple marriages. Perhaps this is a parody of a comic ending. He certainly turned away from comedy in the next few years of his writing career. Strikingly, Isabella does not respond to the proposal. Does she fall into the duke's arms with silent and submissive joy? Or look puzzled? Or aghast? Some productions of the play leave the ending open, with a kind of freeze-frame effect. It is not unknown—though without textual warrant—for Isabella to look the duke up and down, then turn away and march back to the sisterhood.

"THE OLD FANTASTICAL DUKE OF DARK CORNERS"

The puzzle over the ending is bound up with broader interpretative anxieties about the duke. He may be regarded as a God-like figure, benignly controlling the world of the play from behind the scenes. But is it healthy for a human to take on the role of divine providence? Angelo is a moral hypocrite, but it should not be forgotten that the origin of the word "hypocrite" is the Greek term for an actor. It is the duke who is the role player, the actor. Does he have the right to impersonate a friar and hear the confessions of Claudio and Mariana? "Confess" is another of the play's key words, used in both its spiritual and judicial senses.

The part of Lucio is considerably bigger than that of Angelo. Where Angelo is a false-seeming angel crested with the devil's horn, Lucio plays a seductive Lucifer to the duke's God. To adapt what William Blake said of John Milton's *Paradise Lost*, Shakespeare was a true poet and of the devil's party without (perhaps) knowing it. Lucio speaks deep truths in light language: the extinction of sexual desire would require the gelding and spaying of all the youth of the city; the duke *is* in certain senses a creature of "dark corners." It is almost the first law of the Shakespearean universe that the voice of the devil's advocate should not be silenced. "I am a kind of burr," says Lucio, "I shall stick."

The first recorded performance of *Measure for Measure* took place on December 26, 1604, as part of the royal Christmas festivities. It was, then, one of the first plays written by Shakespeare for his new monarch. Within weeks of Queen Elizabeth's death in 1603, Shakespeare's acting company had been renamed the King's Men. Over the next ten years they played at court between a dozen and twenty times a year, far more often than any other company. Though the duke is by no means an allegorical representation of King James, the play reveals Shakespeare moving into territory that fascinated the king: a concern with slander and reputation, an anatomy of the secret springs of power as opposed to a public display of majesty in the style of Queen Elizabeth's pageants and processions ("I love the people, / But do not like to stage me to their eyes"), a demonstration of the intricacies of theological and moral debate (one of James's first acts on arriving in London was to convene a conference at Hampton Court in which he participated in the contentions of high and low churchmen over such matters as the estate of holy matrimony and the question of who could legitimately perform the Sacraments). The king would therefore have been the ideal spectator for such set pieces as the duke's rhetorical mortification of Claudio ("Be absolute for death"). An acute ironist himself, he would have enjoyed the irony whereby Claudio is instantly persuaded by the duke's richly rendered argument, only to change his position a few minutes later when his sister tells him of Angelo's offer—at which point he voices a speech about the horrors of bodily decay and spiritual damnation that is the very antithesis of the duke's argument against life.

Though the play is set in Vienna, the brothels in the "suburbs" or "liberties" of the city evoke the London in which it was performed, where theater and the sex trade stood side by side on the south bank of the Thames. The malapropisms of Constable Elbow, meanwhile, are in the vein of very English humor associated with Dogberry in *Much Ado About Nothing* and Mistress Quickly in *The Merry Wives of Windsor*. At the same time, the play has the whiff of both sexual license and political intrigue that the Elizabethans and Jacobeans associated with Italy. The duke's plan to get Angelo to do his dirty work for him could be read as a political strategy deriving from the pages of Machiavelli. There is a striking analogy with the strategy adopted by another duke, one of the Borgias, who is commended in the seventh chapter of *The Prince*, Machiavelli's handbook on the art of ruthless and pragmatic statecraft:

When the duke occupied the Romagna he found it under the rule of weak masters, who rather plundered their subjects than ruled them, and gave them more cause for disunion than for union, so that the country was full of robbery, quarrels, and every kind of violence; and so, wishing to bring back peace and obedience to authority, he considered it necessary to give it a good governor. Thereupon he promoted Messer Ramiro d'Orco [de Lorqua], a swift and cruel man, to whom he gave the fullest power. This man in a short time restored peace and unity with the greatest success. Afterwards the duke considered that it was not advisable to confer such excessive authority, for he had no doubt but that he would become odious, so he set up a court of judgment in the country, under a most excellent president, wherein all cities had their advocates. And because he knew that the past severity had caused some hatred against himself, so, to clear himself in the minds of the people, and gain them entirely to himself, he desired to show that, if any cruelty had been practiced, it had not originated with him, but in the natural sternness of the minister. Under this pretence he took Ramiro, and one morning caused him to be executed and left on the piazza at Cesena with the block and a bloody knife at his side. The barbarity of this spectacle caused the people to be at once satisfied and dismayed.

The duke of *Measure for Measure* might be considered to have employed his deputy Angelo in a similar way, with the difference that, this being a comedy, he marries him off rather than executes him at the end of the play.

A drama is always a species of trial, in which actions, motives, and ideas are tested before the jury of an audience. The Duke of Vienna—like Duke Prospero of Milan in *The Tempest*—is a dramatist engaged upon a test. How is unbridled carnal license best restrained, in order to save society from the ravages of sexual disease and the burden of unwanted children? By extreme puritanism of the kind advocated by Angelo? This solution is tested and found severely wanting. What does the duke offer in its place? In theory the answer is a middle road between justice and mercy, license and restraint. The technical term for this third way is "temperance," a key virtue in classical ethics. The duke, says Escalus, is "A gentleman of all temperance."

Temperance, however, depends on everyone behaving reasonably and obeying the rule of moderation. What Shakespeare recognizes—as the duke does not—is that people simply cannot be relied upon to show perpetual temperance. So it is that at the very center of the action we find the extraordinary bit-part of Barnardine, the man who announces that he will not be executed today, thank you very much, because he has a hangover. The whole of the duke's plot nearly collapses because of him. It is only salvaged by the palpably improbable device of inventing the pirate Ragozine who just happens to look like Claudio and to die at the right moment. Barnardine, wrote the great nineteenth-century essayist William Hazlitt, "is a fine antithesis to the morality and the hypocrisy of the other characters of the play."

SHAKESPEAREAN MORALITY

Hazlitt was unusual among critics of his time in admiring *Measure for Measure*. Many eighteenth- and nineteenth-century readers had severe reservations about the play. Dr. Samuel Johnson greatly admired some of its sentiments, for instance the duke's speech to Claudio, readying him for death:

> . . . Thou hast nor youth, nor age,
> But, as it were, an after-dinner's sleep
> Dreaming on both . . . .

This is exquisitely imagined. When we are young we busy ourselves in forming schemes for succeeding time, and miss the gratifications that are before us; when we are old we amuse the languor of age with the recollection of youthful pleasures or performances; so that our life, of which no part is filled with the business of the present time, resembles our dreams after dinner, when the events of the morning are mingled with the designs of the evening. (Johnson's 1765 edition of Shakespeare)

But Johnson was puzzled by the ending—"It is somewhat strange, that Isabel is not made to express either gratitude, wonder or joy at the sight of her brother . . . After the pardon of two murderers Lucio might be treated by the good Duke with less harshness; but perhaps the Poet intended to show, what is too often seen, that men easily forgive wrongs which are not committed against themselves"—and he felt that overall "the grave scenes, if a few passages be excepted, have more labour than elegance. The plot is rather intricate than artful."

At the end of the nineteenth century the impassioned poet and critic A. C. Swinburne took a very different view. He suggested that *Measure for Measure* had long been an unpopular play not because, as certain French commentators had suggested, the cant and hypocrisy of Angelo presented too raw a portrayal of "the huge national vice of England," but because the failure to punish Angelo baffled the sense of natural justice. This, Swinburne noted, was Samuel Taylor Coleridge's reason for disliking the play: "The expression is absolutely correct and apt: justice is not merely evaded or ignored or even defied: she is both in the older and the newer sense of the word directly and deliberately baffled; buffeted, outraged, insulted, struck in the face" (Swinburne, *A Study of Shakespeare*, 1880). A deliberately outrageous and insulting play: what Shakespeare had done to expectations about justice in *Measure for Measure* is what Swinburne did to Victorian morality in his scandalously sexual *Poems and Ballads* of 1866. That is why *Measure* was one of the plays that he valued the most.

The changing fortunes of *Measure for Measure* coincided with the shift from Victorianism to aestheticism. Victorian Shakespeare was ushered in by Thomas and Henrietta Bowdler a generation before the young queen came to the throne. *Measure for Measure* was the one play that defeated their project to create a *Family Shakespeare* suitable for reading aloud in the home. They bowdlerized what they took to be obscenities out of all the other plays, but a sex-free *Measure for Measure* proved an impossibility: "the indecent expressions with which many of the scenes abound, are so interwoven with the story, that it is extremely difficult to separate the one from the other. Feeling my own inability to render this play sufficiently correct for family-reading, I have thought it advisable to print it (without presuming to alter a single word) from the published copy, as performed at the Theatre Royal, Covent Garden" (prefatory note in *The Family Shakespeare*, 1818).

It was the aesthetes Algernon Swinburne and Walter Pater who overturned the bowdlerian legacy in the 1870s—and they did so by making *Measure for Measure* into a central and characteristic, as opposed to a marginal and awkward, Shakespearean play. Walter Pater's 1874 essay on the play was stylistically inspired by Swinburne's criticism, but its original publication predated Swinburne's specifically Shakespearean musings. The essay was reprinted as the centerpiece of Pater's "art for art's sake" manifesto *Appreciations, with an Essay on Style* (1889). Pater read the play in terms of the disruption of northern European puritanism by what he called "southern passion." Richard Wagner had done something similar in Germany back in the 1830s: when turning the play into his early opera *Das Liebesverbot* ("the ban on love") he had shifted the action to Palermo.

Pater's method of shifting the play southward was to link it to its Italian sources. But he also made extraordinary high claims. In *Measure for Measure*, says Pater, Shakespeare works out "a morality so characteristic that the play might well pass for the central expression of his moral judgements." The play is "hardly less indicative than *Hamlet* even, of Shakespeare's reason, of his power of moral interpretation." No one hitherto, except perhaps, by implication, Richard Wagner, had seen the centrality of *Measure for Measure* to the mind of Shakespeare.

Pater argues that the play deals not with the problems of one exceptional individual, as *Hamlet* does, but with "the central paradox of human nature." It brings before us "a group of persons, attractive, full of desire, vessels of the genial, seed-bearing powers of nature . . . but bound by the tyranny of nature and circumstance." The characters are seen as embodiments of the force of life itself. Central to the sense of fully lived life is a consciousness of the power of death: Pater sees Claudio's "Ay, but to die . . . to lie in cold obstruction and to rot" as perhaps the most eloquent of all Shakespeare's words. He finds the plea for life everywhere in the play, not least in Barnardine's line "Truly, sir, I am a poor fellow that would live." Such is Shakespeare's elemental sympathy that even the meanest characters "are capable of many friendships and of a true dignity in danger, giving each other a sympathetic, if transitory, regret—one sorry that another should be so foolishly lost at a game of tick-tack." The need to seize the day is shown negatively in the way that "in their yearning for untainted enjoyment, [the characters] are really discounting their days." Pater notes here that this sentiment inspired Tennyson's great lyric poem on Mariana at the moated grange.

Pater ends his essay by returning to the idea that *Measure for Measure* offers in its ethics "an epitome of Shakespeare's moral judgments." He contrasts it with Whetstone's original and the older type of morality play in which the drama exemplifies some rough and ready moral lesson. In *Measure for Measure*, as its title suggests, the ethical vision is shaped by the very structure of the play. This is in accordance with Pater's key aesthetic principle: "that artistic law which demands the predominance of form everywhere over the mere matter or subject handled." The morality of *Measure for Mea-*

sure is that of poetic, not political or theological justice. What the play teaches us is that human beings all have "mixed motives," that our "real intents" are "improvised" by circumstance and that virtue and vice are often copresent in unexpected places:

> The action of the play, like the action of life itself for the keener observer, develops in us the conception of this poetical justice, and the yearning to realize it, the true justice of which Angelo knows nothing, because it lies for the most part beyond the limits of any acknowledged law. The idea of justice involves the idea of rights . . . The recognition of his rights therefore . . . is the recognition of that which the person, in his inmost nature, really is; and as sympathy alone can discover that which really is in matters of feeling and thought, true justice is in its essence a finer knowledge through love.

For Pater, poetry is the highest form of sympathy. It is therefore the route to that true—and truly modern—form of justice that is built on the need to recognize all persons as they really are in their inmost nature. In interpreting *Measure for Measure* thus, Pater reads Shakespeare as a moralist ahead of his time, a playwright who profoundly anticipates a theory of justice more characteristic of the modern era than the early modern: "each person is to have an equal right to the most extensive scheme of equal basic liberties compatible with a similar scheme of liberties for others" (first principle in John Rawls, *A Theory of Justice*, 1971).

ABOUT THE TEXT

Shakespeare endures through history. He illuminates later times as well as his own. He helps us to understand the human condition. But he cannot do this without a good text of the plays. Without editions there would be no Shakespeare. That is why every twenty years or so throughout the last three centuries there has been a major new edition of his complete works. One aspect of editing is the process of keeping the texts up to date—modernizing the spelling, punctuation, and typography (though not, of course, the actual words), providing explanatory notes in the light of changing educational practices (a generation ago, most of Shakespeare's classical and biblical allusions could be assumed to be generally understood, but now they can't).

Because Shakespeare did not personally oversee the publication of his plays, with some plays there are major editorial difficulties. Decisions have to be made as to the relative authority of the early printed editions, the pocket format "Quartos" published in Shakespeare's lifetime and the elaborately produced "First Folio" text of 1623, the original "Complete Works" prepared for the press after his death by Shakespeare's fellow actors, the people who knew the plays better than anyone else. *Measure for Measure*, however, exists only in a Folio text that is reasonably well printed. However, the surviving text may represent a theatrical adaptation postdating Shakespeare's retirement, possibly overseen by Thomas Middleton. The extent of Middleton's involvement is debated by scholars. There are a number of inconsistencies, puzzles, and textual anomalies. Why, for instance, does Juliet appear on stage in three scenes but only speak in one of them? Why is the duke unnamed in the play, but called Vincentio in the list of roles attached to it? Why are his remarks about how "might and greatness" or "place and greatness" cannot escape censure split into two very short soliloquies at different points in the action (3.2, where the sentiments are relevant, and 4.1, where they are not)? Why does Mariana's song "Take, O, take those lips away" also appear, with an additional stanza, in John Fletcher's play *Rollo*

Duke of Normandy of *The Bloody Brother* (written between 1617 and 1620)? Some editors have considered the array of such problems to be little more than the result of minor tinkering with the script in the two decades between its first performance and publication in the Folio, while others have argued for wholesale revision on Middleton's part. The Oxford *Collected Works of Thomas Middleton* (2007) actually prints a "genetic text" of the play by "William Shakespeare, adapted by Thomas Middleton," with many passages printed in bold type to indicate possible authorship by Middleton, who is said to have changed the play's location to Vienna, for political reasons, from an allegedly Italian setting in Shakespeare's original (conjecturally Ferrara).

Shakespearean textual debates of this kind go in cycles: the Cambridge editor in the 1920s proposed an elaborate theory of revision; the Arden editor in the 1970s thought that the text was close to its Shakespearean original; the late twentieth- and early twenty-first-century Oxford editors have seen more Middleton than ever before. For the purpose of our edition, which is fidelity to the Folio, we print a modernized version of the 1623 text and leave speculation to others.

The following notes highlight various aspects of the editorial process and indicate conventions used in the text of this edition:

Lists of Parts are supplied in the First Folio for only six plays, one of which is *Measure for Measure*, so the list at the beginning of the play is adapted from that in the First Folio. Capitals indicate that part of the name which is used for speech headings in the script (thus "The DUKE, unnamed in play, but 'Vincentio' in Folio list of roles").

Locations are provided by the Folio for only two plays, of which *Measure for Measure* is not one. Eighteenth-century editors, working in an age of elaborately realistic stage sets, were the first to provide detailed locations ("*another part of the city*"). Given that Shakespeare wrote for a bare stage and often with an imprecise sense of place, we have relegated locations to the explanatory notes at the foot of the page. They are given at the beginning of each scene where the imaginary location is different from the one before. In the case of *Measure for Measure*, the entire action is set in and around Vienna.

Act and Scene Divisions were provided in the Folio in a much more thoroughgoing way than in the Quartos. Sometimes, however, they were erroneous or omitted; corrections and additions supplied by editorial tradition are indicated by square brackets. Five-act division was based on a classical model, and act breaks provided the opportunity to replace the candles in the indoor Blackfriars playhouse which the King's Men used after 1608, but Shakespeare did not necessarily think in terms of a five-part structure of dramatic composition. The Folio convention is that a scene ends when the stage is empty. Nowadays, partly under the influence of film, we tend to consider a scene to be a dramatic unit that ends with either a change of imaginary location or a significant passage of time within the narrative. Shakespeare's fluidity of composition accords well with this convention, so in addition to act and scene numbers we provide a *running scene* count in the right margin at the beginning of each new scene, in the typeface used for editorial directions. Where there is a scene break caused by a momentarily bare stage, but the location does not change and extra time does not pass, we use the convention *running scene continues*. There is inevitably a degree of editorial judgment in making such calls, but the system is very valuable in suggesting the pace of the plays.

Speakers' Names are often inconsistent in Folio. We have regularized speech headings, but retained an element of deliberate inconsistency in entry directions, in order to give the flavor of Folio. Thus POMPEY is always so-called in his speech headings, but "*Clown*" in entry directions.

Verse is indicated by lines that do not run to the right margin and by capitalization of each line. The Folio printers sometimes set verse as prose, and vice versa (either out of misunderstanding or for reasons of space). We have silently corrected in such cases, although in some instances there is ambiguity, in which case we have leaned toward the preservation of Folio layout. Folio sometimes uses contraction ("turnd" rather than "turned") to indicate whether or not the final "-ed" of a past participle is sounded, an area where there is variation for the sake of the five-beat iambic pentameter rhythm. We use the convention of a grave accent to indicate sounding (thus "turnèd" would be two syllables), but would urge actors not to overstress. In cases where one speaker ends with a verse half line and the next begins with the other half of the pentameter, editors since the late eighteenth century have indented the second line. We have abandoned this convention, since the Folio does not use it, nor did actors' cues in the Shakespearean theater. An exception is made when the second speaker actively interrupts or completes the first speaker's sentence.

Spelling is modernized, but older forms are very occasionally maintained where necessary for rhythm or aural effect.

Punctuation in Shakespeare's time was as much rhetorical as grammatical. "Colon" was originally a term for a unit of thought in an argument. The semicolon was a new unit of punctuation (some of the Quartos lack them altogether). We have modernized punctuation throughout, but have given more weight to Folio punctuation than many editors, since, though not Shakespearean, it reflects the usage of his period. In particular, we have used the colon far more than many editors: it is exceptionally useful as a way of indicating how many Shakespearean speeches unfold clause by clause in a developing argument that gives the illusion of enacting the process of thinking in the moment. We have also kept in mind the origin of punctuation in classical times as a way of assisting the actor and orator: the comma suggests the briefest of pauses for breath, the colon a middling one, and a full stop or period a longer pause. Semicolons, by contrast, belong to an era of punctuation that was only just coming in during Shakespeare's time and that is coming to an end now: we have accordingly only used them where they occur in our copy texts (and not always then). Dashes are sometimes used for parenthetical interjections where the Folio has brackets. They are also used for interruptions and changes in train of thought. Where a change of addressee occurs within a speech, we have used a dash preceded by a period (or occasionally another form of punctuation).

Often the identity of the respective addressees is obvious from the context. When it is not, this has been indicated in a marginal stage direction.

Entrances and Exits are fairly thorough in Folio, which has accordingly been followed as faithfully as possible. Where characters are omitted or corrections are necessary, this is indicated by square brackets (e.g. "[*and Attendants*]"). *Exit* is sometimes silently normalized to *Exeunt* and *Manet* anglicized to "remains." We trust Folio positioning of entrances and exits to a greater degree than most editors.

Editorial Stage Directions such as stage business, asides, indications of addressee and of characters' position on the gallery stage are only used sparingly in Folio. Other editions mingle directions of this kind with original Folio and Quarto directions, sometimes marking them by means of square brackets. We have sought to distinguish what could be described as *directorial* interventions of this kind from Folio-style directions (either original or supplied) by placing them in the right margin in a different typeface. There is a degree of subjectivity about which directions are of which kind, but the procedure is intended as a reminder to the reader and the actor that Shakespearean stage directions are often dependent upon editorial inference alone and are not set in stone. We also depart from editorial tradition in sometimes admitting uncertainty and thus printing permissive stage directions, such as an **Aside?** (often a line may be equally effective as an aside or as a direct address—it is for each production or reading to make its own decision) or a **may exit** or a piece of business placed between arrows to indicate that it may occur at various different moments within a scene.

Line Numbers in the left margin are editorial, for reference and to key the explanatory and textual notes.

Explanatory Notes at the foot of each page explain allusions and gloss obsolete and difficult words, confusing phraseology, occasional major textual cruces, and so on. Particular attention is given to non-standard usage, bawdy innuendo, and technical terms (e.g. legal and military language). Where more than one sense is given, commas indicate shades of related meaning, slashes alternative or double meanings.

Textual Notes at the end of the play indicate major departures from the Folio. They take the following form: the reading of our text is given in bold and its source given after an equals sign, with "F2" a reading that derives from the Second Folio of 1632 and "Ed" one that is derived from the subsequent editorial tradition. The rejected Folio ("F") reading is then given. Thus, for example, "**3.1.143 penury** = F2. F = perjury." This indicates that at Act 3 Scene 1 line 143 the Folio compositor erroneously printed "perjury," which the Second Folio corrected to "penury."

MAJOR PARTS: (*with percentage of lines/number of speeches/scenes on stage*) Duke (30%/194/9), Isabella (15%/129/8), Lucio (11%/111/5), Angelo (11%/83/5), Escalus (7%/78/5), Provost (6%/65/7), Pompey (6%/60/4), Claudio (4%/35/4), Elbow (2%/28/2), Mariana (2%/24/3), Overdone (1%/15/2).

LINGUISTIC MEDIUM: 65% verse, 35% prose.

DATE: Performed at court December 26, 1604, probably written earlier the same year.

SOURCES: Main plot from George Whetstone's two-part play *Promos and Cassandra* (1578) and the novella in Giraldi Cinthio's *Hecatommithi* (1565) that was Whetstone's source; the bed trick was a common romance motif, though not in these sources; the "disguised duke" motif appears in a number of contemporaneous plays, such as John Marston's *The Malcontent* and Thomas Middleton's *The Phoenix* (both c.1603).

TEXT: The 1623 Folio is the only early text. It was typeset from a transcript by the scribe Ralph Crane, though the nature of Crane's copy is not clear. The absence of swear words from the play's seamy underbelly suggests a theatrical script from after the 1606 Act against profanity. The song at the beginning of Act 4 also occurs (with a second stanza) in *Rollo Duke of Normandy* by John Fletcher and others (1616–19). It has been suggested that the song, perhaps together with the ensuing dialogue between the duke and Mariana, was introduced as part of a revision of the play in which a five-act structure was imposed. The soliloquy "O place and greatness" (4.1.60) has often been regarded as an interpolation. The duke is unnamed in the text, but called Vincentio in Crane's list of parts. These, and other minor inconsistencies and loose ends, have led to the supposition that the Folio text is a theatrical adaptation—in which some have detected the hand of Thomas Middleton—as opposed to a pure Shakespearean original.

MEASURE FOR MEASURE

LIST OF PARTS

The DUKE, unnamed in play, but
   'Vincentio' in Folio list of roles

ANGELO, the Deputy

ESCALUS, an ancient lord

CLAUDIO, a young gentleman

LUCIO, a fantastic

Two other like GENTLEMEN

PROVOST

THOMAS AND PETER, two friars
   (probably the same character,
   with misremembered name)

A JUSTICE

VARRIUS, a lord, friend to the duke

ELBOW, a simple constable

FROTH, a foolish gentleman

POMPEY, the clown, servant to
   Mistress Overdone

ABHORSON, an executioner

BARNARDINE, a dissolute prisoner

ISABELLA, sister to Claudio

MARIANA, betrothed to Angelo

JULIET, beloved of Claudio

FRANCISCA, a nun

MISTRESS OVERDONE, a bawd

BOY, singer attending Mariana

Lords, Officers, Citizens, Servants,
   Messenger, Attendants

The Scene: Vienna

List of parts   fantastic extravagant, showy dresser/person with fanciful ideas   PROVOST
officer in charge of the arrest, custody, and punishment of offenders   ISABELLA sometimes
"Isabel" for sake of meter   JULIET sometimes "Julietta" for sake of meter   bawd pimp

Act 1 Scene 1

Enter Duke, Escalus, Lords [and Attendants]

DUKE   Escalus.

ESCALUS   My lord.

DUKE   Of government the properties to unfold
     Would seem in me t'affect speech and discourse,
5   Since I am put to know that your own science
     Exceeds, in that, the lists of all advice
     My strength can give you. Then no more remains
     But that to your sufficiency as your worth is able,
     And let them work. The nature of our people,
10   Our city's institutions, and the terms
     For common justice, you're as pregnant in
     As art and practice hath enrichèd any
     That we remember. There is our commission,   *Hands him a paper*
     From which we would not have you warp. Call hither,
15   I say, bid come before us Angelo.   *[Exit an Attendant]*
     What figure of us think you he will bear?
     For you must know, we have with special soul
     Elected him our absence to supply;
     Lent him our terror, dressed him with our love,
20   And given his deputation all the organs
     Of our own power. What think you of it?

1.1 *Location: with the exception of Act 4 Scenes 1 and 5, the entire play is set in Vienna, moving between the duke's palace, the street, the monastery, the nunnery, the prison and, in the final scene, the city gates*   **3 properties** particulars, qualities   **unfold** explain   **4 seem . . . t'affect** make it appear that I loved/make it seem as if I wished to display   **5 put to know** obliged to acknowledge   **science** knowledge   **6 that** i.e. knowledge of the properties of government   **lists** limits   **7 strength** mental capacity   **8 But . . . work** unclear, possibly because certain words have been omitted accidentally; the general sense seems to be "other than to rely on the workings of your ability (**sufficiency**) and worth"   **10 institutions** customs/laws   **terms** conditions/sessions of the law court   **11 pregnant** knowledgeable   **12 art and practice** learning and experience   **14 warp** deviate   **16 What . . . bear?** How do you think he will represent me?/How will he perform as my substitute?   **figure** duke's stamp on a coin or seal   **17 special soul** inner conviction, particular consideration   **18 supply** occupy as a substitute   **19 terror** supreme authority, power to punish   **dressed . . . love** furnished him with our ability to grant favors/invested him with our favor   **20 deputation** position as deputy   **organs** instruments

ESCALUS   If any in Vienna be of worth
To undergo such ample grace and honour,
It is Lord Angelo.

25   DUKE   Look where he comes.

Enter Angelo

ANGELO   Always obedient to your grace's will,
I come to know your pleasure.

DUKE   Angelo,
There is a kind of character in thy life
30   That to th'observer doth thy history
Fully unfold. Thyself and thy belongings
Are not thine own so proper as to waste
Thyself upon thy virtues, they on thee.
Heaven doth with us as we with torches do,
35   Not light them for themselves: for if our virtues
Did not go forth of us, 'twere all alike
As if we had them not. Spirits are not finely touched
But to fine issues, nor nature never lends
The smallest scruple of her excellence
40   But, like a thrifty goddess, she determines
Herself the glory of a creditor,
Both thanks and use. But I do bend my speech
To one that can my part in him advertise.
Hold therefore, Angelo.
45   In our remove be thou at full ourself:

---

23 undergo sustain **grace** favor **26 Angelo** from the word "angel," a celestial being as well as a gold coin bearing the image of the Archangel Michael **27 pleasure** wishes
29 character distinctive mark/personal trait/individual handwriting **30 history** life story/record **31 unfold** narrate/reveal **belongings** attributes **32 Are . . . proper** do not belong to you exclusively (i.e. you have a duty to the public good to share your talents) **waste . . . thee** i.e. you cannot squander your virtues for purely personal ends or waste your personal efforts purely on cultivating your virtues **36 of** from (i.e. in public service) **37 Spirits** souls/temperaments **touched** created/put to the test or stamped, like coins **38 But . . . issues** except to do fine deeds/except, like coins, to be refined and put into circulation
39 scruple tiny amount **40 thrifty** frugal, economical **determines . . . use** appoints herself the privileges of a creditor, namely both gratitude for the loan and financial interest (use puns on the sense of "actively using nature's gifts") **42 bend** direct **43 my . . . advertise** instruct me **44 Hold** wait a moment/be steadfast, or "take what I am about to offer you" **45 remove** absence **at full** in every respect

Mortality and mercy in Vienna
Live in thy tongue and heart. Old Escalus,
Though first in question, is thy secondary.
Take thy commission.   *Offers a paper*

50 ANGELO   Now, good my lord,
Let there be some more test made of my mettle,
Before so noble and so great a figure
Be stamped upon it.

DUKE   No more evasion.
55 We have with a leavenèd and preparèd choice
Proceeded to you: therefore take your honours.   *Angelo takes*
Our haste from hence is of so quick condition   *paper*
That it prefers itself and leaves unquestioned
Matters of needful value. We shall write to you,
60 As time and our concernings shall importune,
How it goes with us, and do look to know
What doth befall you here. So, fare you well:
To th'hopeful execution do I leave you
Of your commissions.

65 ANGELO   Yet give leave, my lord,
That we may bring you something on the way.

DUKE   My haste may not admit it,
Nor need you, on mine honour, have to do
With any scruple. Your scope is as mine own,
70 So to enforce or qualify the laws
As to your soul seems good. Give me your hand,
I'll privily away. I love the people,
But do not like to stage me to their eyes:
Though it do well, I do not relish well

---

46 Mortality (power to impose) the death penalty   **48 first in question** first under consideration/senior   **secondary** deputy   **51 mettle** character/spirit; puns on "metal" (of a coin)   **52 figure** image   **55 leavened** carefully considered/matured (like dough left to rise)   **57 quick condition** urgent a nature   **58 prefers itself** takes precedence   **unquestioned** unexamined   **59 needful value** necessary importance   **60 concernings** affairs   **importune** urge   **61 look** expect   **63 th'hopeful** the promising   **65 leave** permission   **66 bring you something** accompany you a little   **67 admit** allow   **68 have . . . scruple** concern yourself with any doubt   **70 qualify** moderate   **72 privily** secretly   **73 stage me** publicly display myself   **74 do well** is fitting/politically appropriate/pleasing to the crowd

<table>
<tr><td>75</td><td></td><td>Their loud applause and aves vehement,</td><td></td></tr>
<tr><td></td><td></td><td>Nor do I think the man of safe discretion</td><td></td></tr>
<tr><td></td><td></td><td>That does affect it. Once more, fare you well.</td><td></td></tr>
<tr><td></td><td>ANGELO</td><td>The heavens give safety to your purposes!</td><td></td></tr>
<tr><td></td><td>ESCALUS</td><td>Lead forth and bring you back in happiness!</td><td></td></tr>
<tr><td>80</td><td>DUKE</td><td>I thank you. Fare you well.</td><td>Exit</td></tr>
<tr><td></td><td>ESCALUS</td><td>I shall desire you, sir, to give me leave</td><td></td></tr>
<tr><td></td><td></td><td>To have free speech with you; and it concerns me</td><td></td></tr>
<tr><td></td><td></td><td>To look into the bottom of my place.</td><td></td></tr>
<tr><td></td><td></td><td>A power I have, but of what strength and nature</td><td></td></tr>
<tr><td>85</td><td></td><td>I am not yet instructed.</td><td></td></tr>
<tr><td></td><td>ANGELO</td><td>'Tis so with me. Let us withdraw together,</td><td></td></tr>
<tr><td></td><td></td><td>And we may soon our satisfaction have</td><td></td></tr>
<tr><td></td><td></td><td>Touching that point.</td><td></td></tr>
<tr><td></td><td>ESCALUS</td><td>I'll wait upon your honour.</td><td>Exeunt</td></tr>
</table>

Act 1 Scene 2

running scene 2

Enter Lucio and two other Gentlemen

	LUCIO	If the duke with the other dukes come not to composition with the King of Hungary, why then all the dukes fall upon the king.
	FIRST GENTLEMAN	Heaven grant us its peace, but not the King of
5		Hungary's!
	SECOND GENTLEMAN	Amen.
	LUCIO	Thou concludest like the sanctimonious pirate, that went to sea with the Ten Commandments, but scraped one out of the table.
10	SECOND GENTLEMAN	'Thou shalt not steal'?
	LUCIO	Ay, that he razed.

---

75 aves welcoming shouts   **76 safe discretion** sound judgment   **77 affect** cultivate, like
79 Lead may they lead you   **82 concerns . . . place** is important to me to establish the full
extent of my position   **88 Touching** regarding   **1.2   Lucio** from the Italian for "light"
(bright/of loose morals)   **2 composition** settlement   **3 fall upon** attack   **4 peace . . .
Hungary's** plays on the notion of a "hungry peace," during which jobless soldiers struggled to
feed themselves   **7 sanctimonious** outwardly pious   **9 table** thin stone or wood slab
inscribed with the Ten Commandments   **11 razed** erased

FIRST GENTLEMAN   Why, 'twas a commandment to command the captain and all the rest from their functions: they put forth to steal. There's not a soldier of us all that, in the thanksgiving
15   before meat, do relish the petition well that prays for peace.

SECOND GENTLEMAN   I never heard any soldier dislike it.

LUCIO   I believe thee; for I think thou never wast where grace was said.

SECOND GENTLEMAN   No? A dozen times at least.

20   FIRST GENTLEMAN   What, in metre?

LUCIO   In any proportion or in any language.

FIRST GENTLEMAN   I think, or in any religion.

LUCIO   Ay, why not? Grace is grace, despite of all controversy: as for example, thou thyself art a wicked
25   villain, despite of all grace.

FIRST GENTLEMAN   Well, there went but a pair of shears between us.

LUCIO   I grant, as there may between the lists and the velvet. Thou art the list.

30   FIRST GENTLEMAN   And thou the velvet. Thou art good velvet; thou'rt a three-piled piece, I warrant thee. I had as lief be a list of an English kersey as be piled, as thou art piled, for a French velvet. Do I speak feelingly now?

LUCIO   I think thou dost, and indeed, with most painful
35   feeling of thy speech. I will, out of thine own confession, learn to begin thy health, but, whilst I live, forget to drink after thee.

---

13 from their functions to desist from their occupations   **put forth** set out   **15 meat** a meal   **petition** entreaty   **20 metre** verse   **21 proportion** form   **24 controversy** refers to religious dispute over the nature of God's **grace** (mercy), in particular the puritan-Catholic controversy over whether one's soul was saved by one's actions in life or by grace alone   **26 there . . . us** i.e. we are both cut from the same cloth   **28 lists** plain fabric edging   **31 three-piled piece** trebly thick, of high-quality material/sufferer from hemorrhoids   **lief** willingly   **32 kersey** plain, coarsely woven cloth   **piled** luxuriously thick/bald (a symptom of syphilis)   **33 French velvet** fancy garment (plays on the fact that syphilis was known as the "French disease," and syphilitic scars were sometimes covered with velvet patches)   **feelingly** aptly/ painfully   **34 painful feeling** conviction/pain caused by oral syphilitic ulcers   **35 confession** admission   **36 begin . . . thee** toast your health, but remember not to drink after you (since the cup will be contaminated)

FIRST GENTLEMAN   I think I have done myself wrong, have I not?

SECOND GENTLEMAN   Yes, that thou hast, whether thou art
40   tainted or free.

Enter Bawd [Mistress Overdone]

LUCIO   Behold, behold, where Madam Mitigation comes! I
have purchased as many diseases under her roof as come to—

SECOND GENTLEMAN   To what, I pray?

LUCIO   Judge.

45 SECOND GENTLEMAN   To three thousand dolours a year.

FIRST GENTLEMAN   Ay, and more.

LUCIO   A French crown more.

FIRST GENTLEMAN   Thou art always figuring diseases in me, but
thou art full of error, I am sound.

50 LUCIO   Nay, not as one would say, healthy: but so sound as
things that are hollow; thy bones are hollow, impiety has
made a feast of thee.

FIRST GENTLEMAN   How now! Which of your   *To Mistress Overdone*
hips has the most profound sciatica?

55 MISTRESS OVERDONE   Well, well. There's one yonder arrested and
carried to prison was worth five thousand of you all.

SECOND GENTLEMAN   Who's that, I pray thee?

MISTRESS OVERDONE   Marry, sir, that's Claudio, Signior Claudio.

FIRST GENTLEMAN   Claudio to prison? 'Tis not so.

60 MISTRESS OVERDONE   Nay, but I know 'tis so. I saw him arrested,
saw him carried away, and, which is more, within these
three days his head to be chopped off.

LUCIO   But, after all this fooling, I would not have it so. Art
thou sure of this?

65 MISTRESS OVERDONE   I am too sure of it. And it is for getting
Madam Julietta with child.

---

38 done myself wrong misrepresented myself/laid myself open to mockery   **40 tainted or
free** infected or healthy   **Overdone** her name implies that she is a worn-out prostitute (to
"do" was slang for "to have sex")   **41 Mitigation** i.e. one who relieves (mitigates) sexual desire
44 Judge guess   **45 dolours** lamentations/silver coins   **47 French crown** gold coin (plays on
baldness caused by syphilis)   **48 figuring** calculating/imagining   **50 sound** healthy/
echoingly resonant   **51 bones are hollow** brittle bones were a symptom of late syphilis
impiety lust, sin   **54 profound** acute   **sciatica** pain in the upper hip, thought to be a
symptom of syphilis   **58 Marry** by the Virgin Mary   **63 after** despite

LUCIO   Believe me, this may be: he promised to meet me
    two hours since, and he was ever precise in promise-keeping.
SECOND GENTLEMAN   Besides, you know, it draws something near
70   to the speech we had to such a purpose.
FIRST GENTLEMAN   But most of all agreeing with the proclamation.
LUCIO   Away! Let's go learn the truth of it.

Exeunt [Lucio and Gentlemen]

MISTRESS OVERDONE   Thus, what with the war, what with the
    sweat, what with the gallows and what with poverty, I am
75   custom-shrunk.

Enter Clown [Pompey]

    How now? What's the news with you?
POMPEY   Yonder man is carried to prison.
MISTRESS OVERDONE   Well, what has he done?
POMPEY   A woman.
80   MISTRESS OVERDONE   But what's his offence?
POMPEY   Groping for trouts in a peculiar river.
MISTRESS OVERDONE   What, is there a maid with child by him?
POMPEY   No, but there's a woman with maid by him. You
    have not heard of the proclamation, have you?
85   MISTRESS OVERDONE   What proclamation, man?
POMPEY   All houses in the suburbs of Vienna must be
    plucked down.
MISTRESS OVERDONE   And what shall become of those in the city?
POMPEY   They shall stand for seed: they had gone down too,
90   but that a wise burgher put in for them.

---

68 **precise** scrupulous   69 **draws . . . purpose** is relevant to the conversation we had on that
topic   71 **proclamation** public declaration/legal prohibition   74 **sweat** sweating-sickness/
induction of sweating as a treatment for syphilis   75 **custom-shrunk** lacking in customers
Pompey his name has (ironic) connotations of "pomp and splendor"; Pompey the Great was a
famous Roman general of the first century BC   77 **Yonder man** i.e. Claudio   78 **done**
Pompey's response puns on the sense of "had sex with"   81 **Groping . . . river** i.e. sex
(literally, a reference to catching fish by hand)   **peculiar** privately owned, with play on
female private parts   82 **maid** young unmarried woman/virgin (plays on the sense of "type
of fish")   86 **houses . . . suburbs** brothels, almost always situated in city suburbs
89 **stand for seed** like plants, remain unharvested so that they may generate another crop
(**stand** plays on the sense of "have an erection" and **seed** on "semen")   90 **burgher** citizen
put in bid/interceded

MISTRESS OVERDONE   But shall all our houses of resort in the suburbs be pulled down?

POMPEY   To the ground, mistress.

MISTRESS OVERDONE   Why, here's a change indeed in the
95   commonwealth! What shall become of me?

POMPEY   Come, fear you not: good counsellors lack no clients. Though you change your place, you need not change your trade: I'll be your tapster still. Courage! There will be pity taken on you; you that have worn your eyes almost out
100   in the service, you will be considered.

MISTRESS OVERDONE   What's to do here, Thomas tapster? Let's withdraw.

POMPEY   Here comes Signior Claudio, led by the provost to prison, and there's Madam Juliet.   *Exeunt*

Act 1 Scene 3   *running scene 2 continues*

Enter Provost, Claudio, Juliet, Officers; Lucio and the two Gentlemen [follow]

CLAUDIO   Fellow, why dost thou show me thus to th'world?
Bear me to prison, where I am committed.

PROVOST   I do it not in evil disposition,
But from Lord Angelo by special charge.

5   CLAUDIO   Thus can the demigod Authority
Make us pay down for our offence by weight
The words of heaven; on whom it will, it will,
On whom it will not, so. Yet still 'tis just.

LUCIO   Why, how now, Claudio? Whence comes this
10   restraint?

---

91 **resort** regular visiting   96 **counsellors** advisers/lawyers   98 **tapster** waiter, barman
99 **worn . . . service** worked so long and hard in the business/become almost blind from
syphilis through sexually servicing so many men   101 **Thomas** generic name for a **tapster**
1.3   3 evil disposition malice   **6 down** immediately   **weight** in full (literally, weighing
rather than counting coins, in order to ensure their true value)   **7 The . . . heaven** according
to the Bible (specifically Romans 9:15, in which God says "I will have mercy on him to whom I
will show mercy")   **9 Whence . . . restraint?** Why have you been arrested?

CLAUDIO	From too much liberty, my Lucio, liberty:
	As surfeit is the father of much fast,
	So every scope by the immoderate use
	Turns to restraint. Our natures do pursue,
15	Like rats that ravin down their proper bane,
	A thirsty evil, and when we drink we die.
LUCIO	If I could speak so wisely under an arrest, I would
	send for certain of my creditors: and yet, to say the truth, I
	had as lief have the foppery of freedom as the morality of
20	imprisonment. What's thy offence, Claudio?
CLAUDIO	What but to speak of would offend again.
LUCIO	What, is't murder?
CLAUDIO	No.
LUCIO	Lechery?
25	CLAUDIO Call it so.
PROVOST	Away, sir. You must go.
CLAUDIO	One word, good friend. Lucio, a word with you.
LUCIO	A hundred, if they'll do you any good.
	Is lechery so looked after?
30	CLAUDIO Thus stands it with me: upon a true contract
	I got possession of Julietta's bed.
	You know the lady, she is fast my wife,
	Save that we do the denunciation lack
	Of outward order. This we came not to
35	Only for propagation of a dower
	Remaining in the coffer of her friends,
	From whom we thought it meet to hide our love
	Till time had made them for us. But it chances

---

11 **liberty** freedom/sexual license   12 **surfeit** excess, overindulgence   **fast** starvation/
restraint   13 **scope** opportunity, freedom   15 **ravin . . . bane** eagerly devour their particular
poison (ratsbane, usually arsenic oxide)   16 **thirsty** thirst-provoking (rat poison dehydrates
rodents)   18 **creditors** i.e. those who would arrest him (for debt)   19 **lief** willingly   **foppery**
folly   **morality** wisdom   29 **looked after** vigilantly pursued, watched out for   30 **true
contract** i.e. both parties declared their intention to marry, in the presence of witnesses
32 **fast** firmly   33 **Save** except   **denunciation** official declaration   34 **outward** public/legal
35 **propagation of a dower** increase/production of a dowry   36 **friends** relatives/protectors
37 **meet** right   38 **made . . . us** made them into our allies

The stealth of our most mutual entertainment
40   With character too gross is writ on Juliet.

LUCIO   With child, perhaps?

CLAUDIO   Unhappily, even so.
And the new deputy now for the duke —
Whether it be the fault and glimpse of newness,
45   Or whether that the body public be
A horse whereon the governor doth ride,
Who, newly in the seat, that it may know
He can command, lets it straight feel the spur:
Whether the tyranny be in his place,
50   Or in his eminence that fills it up,
I stagger in — but this new governor
Awakes me all the enrollèd penalties
Which have, like unscoured armour, hung by th'wall
So long that nineteen zodiacs have gone round
55   And none of them been worn; and, for a name,
Now puts the drowsy and neglected act
Freshly on me. 'Tis surely for a name.

LUCIO   I warrant it is: and thy head stands so tickle on thy
shoulders that a milkmaid, if she be in love, may sigh it off.
60   Send after the duke and appeal to him.

CLAUDIO   I have done so, but he's not to be found.
I prithee, Lucio, do me this kind service:
This day my sister should the cloister enter
And there receive her approbation.
65   Acquaint her with the danger of my state,
Implore her, in my voice, that she make friends
To the strict deputy: bid herself assay him.

39 mutual entertainment lovemaking   40 character too gross writing that is only too large,
obvious   44 glimpse of newness brief dazzling of new power   45 body public state/
populace   47 that so that   48 straight straightaway   49 in his place inherent in his official
position   50 his . . . up the pride of the man who occupies that position   51 stagger in am
uncertain about   52 Awakes me revives (me is emphatic)   enrollèd legally recorded
53 unscoured unpolished, rusty   54 zodiacs years   55 them i.e. the armor/laws   for a
name to gain a reputation   58 tickle precariously   63 cloister nunnery   64 approbation
probationary period as a novice (one in the early stages of becoming a nun)   67 To with
assay assault/test/tempt

I have great hope in that, for in her youth
There is a prone and speechless dialect,
70   Such as move men. Beside, she hath prosperous art
When she will play with reason and discourse,
And well she can persuade.

LUCIO   I pray she may; as well for the encouragement of
the like, which else would stand under grievous imposition,
75   as for the enjoying of thy life, who I would be sorry should be
thus foolishly lost at a game of tick-tack. I'll to her.

CLAUDIO   I thank you, good friend Lucio.

LUCIO   Within two hours.

CLAUDIO   Come, officer, away!   *Exeunt*

Act 1 Scene 4   *running scene 3*

Enter Duke and Friar Thomas

DUKE   No, holy father, throw away that thought:
Believe not that the dribbling dart of love
Can pierce a complete bosom. Why I desire thee
To give me secret harbour hath a purpose
5   More grave and wrinkled than the aims and ends
Of burning youth.

FRIAR THOMAS   May your grace speak of it?

DUKE   My holy sir, none better knows than you
How I have ever loved the life removed,
10   And held in idle price to haunt assemblies
Where youth and cost and witless bravery keeps.
I have delivered to Lord Angelo —

---

69 **prone** ready/gentle, tractable, submissive   **speechless dialect** silent communication
(body language)   70 **move** affects/arouses   **prosperous art** successful rhetorical skill
71 **discourse** rationality, understanding   74 **the like** others guilty of the same offense
grievous imposition serious accusation/penalty   76 **game of tick-tack** form of backgammon
involving the placing of pegs in holes, hence a euphemism for sex   1.4   1 **that thought**
apparently the friar thinks that the duke wishes to conceal himself in the monastery as part of
some amorous plan   2 **dribbling dart** random arrow (of Cupid)   3 **complete** whole,
accomplished, perfect   4 **harbour** refuge   5 **wrinkled** i.e. mature   9 **removed** secluded
10 **in idle price** at little worth   **assemblies** large social gatherings   11 **cost** extravagance
witless bravery keeps foolish bravado is to be found

A man of stricture and firm abstinence —
My absolute power and place here in Vienna,
15   And he supposes me travelled to Poland,
For so I have strewed it in the common ear,
And so it is received. Now, pious sir,
You will demand of me why I do this.

FRIAR THOMAS   Gladly, my lord.

20   DUKE   We have strict statutes and most biting laws,
The needful bits and curbs to headstrong weeds,
Which for this fourteen years we have let slip,
Even like an o'ergrown lion in a cave
That goes not out to prey. Now, as fond fathers,
25   Having bound up the threat'ning twigs of birch,
Only to stick it in their children's sight
For terror, not to use, in time the rod
Becomes more mocked than feared: so our decrees,
Dead to infliction, to themselves are dead,
30   And liberty plucks justice by the nose,
The baby beats the nurse, and quite athwart
Goes all decorum.

FRIAR THOMAS   It rested in your grace
To unloose this tied-up justice when you pleased:
35   And it in you more dreadful would have seemed
Than in Lord Angelo.

DUKE   I do fear, too dreadful.
Sith 'twas my fault to give the people scope,
'Twould be my tyranny to strike and gall them
40   For what I bid them do, for we bid this be done,
When evil deeds have their permissive pass

---

13 **stricture** severity, self-restraint   16 **strewed** spread   18 **demand** ask   21 **bits and curbs**
parts of harnesses used to control horses   **weeds** people who are of no use in society (some
editors emend to "steeds" so as to maintain the equine imagery)   22 **let slip** unloosed/allowed
to go unchecked   23 **o'ergrown** old/fat and inactive   24 **fond** foolish/doting   25 **twigs of
birch** used for beating disobedient children   27 **rod** cane   29 **Dead . . . dead** not being
enforced, have become redundant   30 **liberty . . . nose** freedom/license contemptuously
mocks the law   31 **athwart** in the wrong direction   32 **decorum** propriety, social order
35 **dreadful** awe-inspiring/terrible   38 **Sith** since   39 **gall** vex, harass   41 **permissive pass**
authorization

And not the punishment. Therefore indeed, my father,
I have on Angelo imposed the office,
Who may in th'ambush of my name strike home,
45   And yet my nature never in the fight
To do in slander. And to behold his sway,
I will, as 'twere a brother of your order,
Visit both prince and people: therefore, I prithee,
Supply me with the habit and instruct me
50   How I may formally in person bear me
Like a true friar. More reasons for this action
At our more leisure shall I render you;
Only, this one: Lord Angelo is precise,
Stands at a guard with envy, scarce confesses
55   That his blood flows, or that his appetite
Is more to bread than stone. Hence shall we see,
If power change purpose, what our seemers be.   *Exeunt*

Act 1 Scene 5

running scene 4

Enter Isabella and Francisca, a nun

ISABELLA   And have you nuns no further privileges?
FRANCISCA   Are not these large enough?
ISABELLA   Yes, truly. I speak not as desiring more,
But rather wishing a more strict restraint
5   Upon the sisterhood, the votarists of Saint Clare.
LUCIO   Ho? Peace be in this place!   *Within*
ISABELLA   Who's that which calls?
FRANCISCA   It is a man's voice. Gentle Isabella,
Turn you the key, and know his business of him;

---

43 office role/responsibility   **44 in th'ambush** under the cover or authority of   **home** to the center of the target   **45 my . . . slander** not incite hatred toward me   **46 sway** power, influence   **47 brother . . . order** i.e. disguised as a Franciscan friar   **48 prince** i.e. Angelo, as the reigning authority   **49 habit** clothing/friar's outfit   **50 formally** outwardly   **bear me** conduct myself   **53 precise** punctilious, morally strict   **54 at . . . with** on guard toward (fencing term)   **envy** malice   **scarce . . . stone** i.e. barely admits that he is human   **57 purpose** intention, attitude   **1.5**   **5 votarists** those bound by religious vows   **Saint Clare** religious order set up by Saint Clare in 1212, sworn to observe poverty and silence

10   You may, I may not: you are yet unsworn.
      When you have vowed, you must not speak with men
      But in the presence of the prioress.
      Then, if you speak, you must not show your face,
      Or, if you show your face, you must not speak.
15   He calls again. I pray you, answer him.   [*Exit*]

ISABELLA   Peace and prosperity! Who is't that calls?
[*Enter Lucio*]

LUCIO   Hail, virgin, if you be, as those cheek-roses
      Proclaim you are no less. Can you so stead me
      As bring me to the sight of Isabella,
20   A novice of this place and the fair sister
      To her unhappy brother Claudio?

ISABELLA   Why her unhappy brother? Let me ask,
      The rather for I now must make you know
      I am that Isabella and his sister.

25 LUCIO   Gentle and fair, your brother kindly greets you.
      Not to be weary with you, he's in prison.

ISABELLA   Woe me! For what?

LUCIO   For that which, if myself might be his judge,
      He should receive his punishment in thanks:
30   He hath got his friend with child.

ISABELLA   Sir, make me not your story.

LUCIO   'Tis true.
      I would not, though 'tis my familiar sin
      With maids to seem the lapwing and to jest,
35   Tongue far from heart, play with all virgins so.
      I hold you as a thing enskied and sainted
      By your renouncement, an immortal spirit,

---

10 unsworn have not yet taken a nun's vows   **12 prioress** head of the nunnery   **17 cheek-roses** rosy/blushing cheeks   **18 stead** assist   **20 novice** one in the early stages of becoming a nun, yet to take her vows   **21 unhappy** miserable/unlucky   **23 rather for** more so because   **25 kindly** with brotherly affection   **26 weary** tedious   **29 thanks** gratitude/approval   **30 friend** lover   **31 your story** the subject of your mockery   **33 familiar** usual (plays on the sense of "overly intimate")   **34 lapwing** plover (bird associated with amorous intrigue and deceit)   **35 Tongue . . . heart** i.e. my words contradicting my intentions   **play** jest (with sexual connotations)   **36 enskied** in the skies, heavenly   **37 By your renouncement** because of your rejection of the material world (you are)

And to be talked with in sincerity,
As with a saint.

40 ISABELLA   You do blaspheme the good in mocking me.

LUCIO   Do not believe it. Fewness and truth, 'tis thus:
Your brother and his lover have embraced.
As those that feed grow full, as blossoming time
That from the seedness the bare fallow brings
45 To teeming foison, even so her plenteous womb
Expresseth his full tilth and husbandry.

ISABELLA   Someone with child by him? My cousin Juliet?

LUCIO   Is she your cousin?

ISABELLA   Adoptedly, as school-maids change their names
50 By vain though apt affection.

LUCIO   She it is.

ISABELLA   O, let him marry her.

LUCIO   This is the point.
The duke is very strangely gone from hence,
55 Bore many gentlemen, myself being one,
In hand and hope of action: but we do learn
By those that know the very nerves of state,
His giving-out were of an infinite distance
From his true-meant design. Upon his place,
60 And with full line of his authority,
Governs Lord Angelo, a man whose blood
Is very snow-broth: one who never feels
The wanton stings and motions of the sense,
But doth rebate and blunt his natural edge
65 With profits of the mind, study and fast.
He — to give fear to use and liberty,

---

40 You . . . me in mocking/flattering me, you defame what is truly holy   41 Fewness in few
words   42 embraced i.e. had sex   44 seedness act of sowing seeds   bare fallow
uncultivated land   45 teeming foison plentiful harvest   46 Expresseth reveals   tilth and
husbandry plowing and cultivation (with sexual connotations)   47 cousin relative/close
friend   50 vain . . . affection silly though natural fondness   55 Bore . . . hand misleadingly
kept many men, including me, waiting in   58 giving-out utterances   59 true-meant design
real intentions   Upon in   60 line scope   62 snow-broth melted snow   63 wanton
uncontrolled/lascivious   motions urges   sense senses   64 rebate blunt (as of a
weapon)/suppress   edge blade/keen desire   65 profits improvements   fast fasting
66 use (disreputable) habit

Which have for long run by the hideous law,
As mice by lions — hath picked out an act,
Under whose heavy sense your brother's life
70 Falls into forfeit. He arrests him on it,
And follows close the rigour of the statute
To make him an example. All hope is gone,
Unless you have the grace by your fair prayer
To soften Angelo: and that's my pith of business
75 'Twixt you and your poor brother.

ISABELLA   Doth he so seek his life?

LUCIO   Has censured him already,
And, as I hear, the provost hath a warrant
For's execution.

80 ISABELLA   Alas, what poor ability's in me
To do him good?

LUCIO   Assay the power you have.

ISABELLA   My power? Alas, I doubt—

LUCIO   Our doubts are traitors,
85 And make us lose the good we oft might win
By fearing to attempt. Go to Lord Angelo,
And let him learn to know, when maidens sue,
Men give like gods: but when they weep and kneel,
All their petitions are as freely theirs
90 As they themselves would owe them.

ISABELLA   I'll see what I can do.

LUCIO   But speedily,

ISABELLA   I will about it straight,
No longer staying but to give the mother
95 Notice of my affair. I humbly thank you:
Commend me to my brother. Soon at night
I'll send him certain word of my success.

---

67 hideous frightening   **69 heavy sense** severe meaning   **70 Falls into forfeit** has to be
given up   **73 grace** good fortune/favor   **74 pith** essence   **77 censured** condemned
82 Assay try   **87 sue** plead   **88 give** yield/offer   **89 petitions . . . them** requests are granted
as fully as the maidens themselves would wish   **94 mother** mother superior, head of the
nunnery   **96 Soon at night** early in the evening   **97 my success** the outcome of my
attempts

LUCIO	I take my leave of you.
ISABELLA	Good sir, adieu.

Exeunt [separately]

Act 2 Scene 1

Enter Angelo, Escalus, Servants, [and a] Justice

ANGELO   We must not make a scarecrow of the law,
Setting it up to fear the birds of prey,
And let it keep one shape, till custom make it
Their perch and not their terror.

5   ESCALUS   Ay, but yet
Let us be keen, and rather cut a little
Than fall and bruise to death. Alas, this gentleman
Whom I would save had a most noble father.
Let but your honour know —

10   Whom I believe to be most strait in virtue —
That, in the working of your own affections,
Had time cohered with place or place with wishing,
Or that the resolute acting of your blood
Could have attained th'effect of your own purpose,

15   Whether you had not sometime in your life
Erred in this point which now you censure him,
And pulled the law upon you.

ANGELO   'Tis one thing to be tempted, Escalus,
Another thing to fall. I not deny,

20   The jury passing on the prisoner's life,
May in the sworn twelve have a thief or two
Guiltier than him they try. What's open made to justice,
That justice seizes. What knows the laws
That thieves do pass on thieves? 'Tis very pregnant,

2.1   **2 fear** frighten   **3 custom** familiarity   **6 keen** shrewd/sharp   **cut a little** i.e. proceed
gradually (in the restriction of crime)   **7 fall** let fall (wide-ranging or heavy punishments)
bruise crush   **10 strait** rigorous   **11 affections** emotions/desires   **13 that . . . purpose** if
the determined acting out of your passion could have obtained the desired outcome (i.e. sex)
16 Erred . . . which made the mistake for which   **20 passing** delivering a verdict   **21 sworn**
twelve the twelve members of a jury sworn in under a legal oath   **22 open made** made visible
23 What who   **24 pregnant** obvious (that)

25   The jewel that we find, we stoop and take't
    Because we see it, but what we do not see
    We tread upon, and never think of it.
    You may not so extenuate his offence
    For I have had such faults, but rather tell me,
30   When I, that censure him, do so offend,
    Let mine own judgement pattern out my death,
    And nothing come in partial. Sir, he must die.

Enter Provost

ESCALUS   Be it as your wisdom will.

ANGELO   Where is the provost?

35 **PROVOST**   Here, if it like your honour.

ANGELO   See that Claudio
    Be executed by nine tomorrow morning.
    Bring him his confessor, let him be prepared,
    For that's the utmost of his pilgrimage.   *[Exit Provost]*

40 **ESCALUS**   Well, heaven forgive him, and forgive us all.   *Aside*
    Some rise by sin, and some by virtue fall.
    Some run from breaks of ice, and answer none,
    And some condemnèd for a fault alone.

Enter Elbow [and] Officers [with] Froth [and] Clown [Pompey]

ELBOW   Come, bring them away: if these be good people in
45 a commonweal that do nothing but use their abuses in
common houses, I know no law. Bring them away.

ANGELO   How now, sir, what's your name? And what's the
matter?

ELBOW   If it please your honour, I am the poor duke's
50 constable, and my name is Elbow: I do lean upon justice, sir,

---

28 extenuate lessen   **29 For** because   **31 judgement pattern out** sentence (on Claudio)
act as a precedent for   **32 nothing . . . partial** let nothing intervene in my favor   **35 like**
please   **38 prepared** i.e. for death (by confessing his sins and receiving the last rites)
39 utmost . . . pilgrimage limit of his life's journey   **42 run . . . ice** flee cracks in ice underfoot,
or perhaps "get away with breaches of chastity," but Folio spelling "brakes" has led to
uncertainty and editorial speculation   **answer none** are not made responsible for their sins
43 a fault alone a single fault   *Froth* connotations of empty-headedness and insubstantiality,
perhaps also "head of ale" and conceivably suggestive of semen   **45 use . . . houses** engage
in their vices in brothels   **49 poor duke's** duke's poor   **50 lean** rely (perhaps with a play on
his name)

and do bring in here before your good honour two notorious benefactors.

ANGELO   Benefactors? Well, what benefactors are they? Are they not malefactors?

55   ELBOW   If it please your honour, I know not well what they are, but precise villains they are, that I am sure of, and void of all profanation in the world that good Christians ought to have.

ESCALUS   This comes off well: here's a wise officer.   *To Angelo*

60   ANGELO   Go to, what quality are they of? Elbow is your name? Why dost thou not speak, Elbow?

POMPEY   He cannot, sir: he's out at elbow.

ANGELO   What are you, sir?

ELBOW   He, sir? A tapster, sir, parcel-bawd, one that serves a
65   bad woman, whose house, sir, was, as they say, plucked down in the suburbs: and now she professes a hot-house, which, I think, is a very ill house too.

ESCALUS   How know you that?

ELBOW   My wife, sir, whom I detest before heaven and your
70   honour—

ESCALUS   How? Thy wife?

ELBOW   Ay, sir: whom, I thank heaven, is an honest woman—

ESCALUS   Dost thou detest her therefore?

ELBOW   I say, sir, I will detest myself also, as well as she, that
75   this house, if it be not a bawd's house, it is pity of her life, for it is a naughty house.

ESCALUS   How dost thou know that, constable?

---

52 **benefactors** malapropism for "malefactors"   56 **precise** malapropism for "precious" (i.e. "out-and-out")   **void** devoid   57 **profanation** either Elbow really means "reverence" or this is a malapropism for "profession"   59 **comes off well** is well spoken   60 **Go to** expression of dismissive impatience   **quality** rank, position   62 **out at elbow** disconcerted/speechless/ ragged   64 **parcel-bawd** part-time pimp   **serves** works for/serves drinks to/serves sexually   65 **house** i.e. brothel   66 **professes** makes a profession of/claims to run (perhaps playing on the sense of "makes vows to a religious order")   **hot-house** bathhouse (effectively another brothel)   69 **detest** malapropism for "protest" (i.e. "declare")   75 **pity . . . life** a great pity/ bad thing for her/pity she should live   76 **naughty** wicked

ELBOW   Marry, sir, by my wife, who, if she had been a woman
cardinally given, might have been accused in fornication,
80   adultery and all uncleanliness there.

ESCALUS   By the woman's means?

ELBOW   Ay, sir, by Mistress Overdone's means: but as she spit
in his face, so she defied him.

POMPEY   Sir, if it please your honour, this is not so.

85   ELBOW   Prove it before these varlets here, thou honourable
man, prove it.

ESCALUS   Do you hear how he misplaces?   *Aside to Angelo*

POMPEY   Sir, she came in great with child, and longing —
saving your honour's reverence — for stewed prunes. Sir, we
90   had but two in the house, which at that very distant time
stood, as it were, in a fruit-dish, a dish of some three-pence
— your honours have seen such dishes, they are not China
dishes, but very good dishes—

ESCALUS   Go to, go to: no matter for the dish, sir.

95   POMPEY   No, indeed, sir, not of a pin: you are therein in the
right. But to the point. As I say, this Mistress Elbow, being, as
I say, with child, and being great-bellied, and longing, as I
said, for prunes, and having but two in the dish, as I said,
Master Froth here, this very man, having eaten the rest, as I
100   said, and, as I say, paying for them very honestly, for, as you
know, Master Froth, I could not give you three-pence again.

FROTH   No, indeed.

POMPEY   Very well: you being then, if you be remembered,
cracking the stones of the foresaid prunes—

105   FROTH   Ay, so I did indeed.

---

79 **cardinally** malapropism for "carnally"   80 **uncleanliness** moral impurity   81 **the
woman's means** Mistress Overdone's doing (Elbow responds to the sense of "by her agent,
Pompey")   83 **his** i.e. Pompey's   85 **varlets . . . honourable** Elbow gets his terms the wrong
way around   **varlets** knaves   87 **misplaces** misuses language, gets his word order mixed up
89 **saving . . . reverence** i.e. begging your pardon/if you will excuse my language   **stewed
prunes** often available in brothels, they were used to treat syphilis, and here function as a
euphemism for scrotum; **stewed** puns on "stews" (i.e. a brothel)   90 **distant** for "instant" or
"present"   91 **stood** plays on the sense of "were erect"   **fruit-dish** euphemism for vagina
95 **not . . . pin** it is not worth a trifle (**pin** plays on the sense of "penis")   96 **point** with phallic
connotations   101 **again** back   104 **stones** puns on the sense of "testicles"

POMPEY   Why, very well: I telling you then, if you be
remembered, that such a one and such a one were past cure
of the thing you wot of, unless they kept very good diet, as I
told you—

110   FROTH   All this is true.

POMPEY   Why, very well, then—

ESCALUS   Come, you are a tedious fool. To the purpose: what
was done to Elbow's wife, that he hath cause to complain of?
Come me to what was done to her.

115   POMPEY   Sir, your honour cannot come to that yet.

ESCALUS   No, sir, nor I mean it not.

POMPEY   Sir, but you shall come to it, by your honour's leave.
And, I beseech you, look into Master Froth here, sir, a man of
fourscore pound a year, whose father died at Hallowmas.

120   Was't not at Hallowmas, Master Froth?

FROTH   All-hallond eve.

POMPEY   Why, very well, I hope here be truths. He, sir, sitting,
as I say, in a lower chair, sir, 'twas in the Bunch of Grapes,
where indeed you have a delight to sit, have you not?

125   FROTH   I have so, because it is an open room and good for
winter.

POMPEY   Why, very well, then. I hope here be truths.

ANGELO   This will last out a night in Russia,
When nights are longest there. I'll take my leave

130   And leave you to the hearing of the cause,
Hoping you'll find good cause to whip them all.   *Exit [Angelo]*

ESCALUS   I think no less. Good morrow to your lordship.—
Now, sir, come on: what was done to Elbow's wife, once more?

POMPEY   Once, sir? There was nothing done to her once.

135   ELBOW   I beseech you, sir, ask him what this man did to my
wife.

108 thing . . . of i.e. syphilis   wot know   114 Come me come (me is emphatic)   done
Pompey's response plays on the sense of "had sex"   118 look into consider   119 fourscore
pound £80 (a good income)   Hallowmas November 1, All Saints' Day   121 All-hallond eve
October 31, All Hallows' Eve (Halloween)   123 lower chair unclear; probably a low-slung
seat, or easy chair   Bunch of Grapes the name of a tavern or room in a tavern   125 open
public (with a fire)   128 last . . . Russia i.e. take a very long time   130 cause case
131 cause reason   134 done plays on the sexual sense

POMPEY   I beseech your honour, ask me.

ESCALUS   Well, sir, what did this gentleman to her?

POMPEY   I beseech you, sir, look in this gentleman's face.
140   Good Master Froth, look upon his honour, 'tis for a good
          purpose. Doth your honour mark his face?

ESCALUS   Ay, sir, very well.

POMPEY   Nay, I beseech you, mark it well.

ESCALUS   Well, I do so.

145 POMPEY   Doth your honour see any harm in his face?

ESCALUS   Why, no.

POMPEY   I'll be supposed upon a book, his face is the worst
          thing about him. Good, then, if his face be the worst thing
          about him, how could Master Froth do the constable's wife
150   any harm? I would know that of your honour.

ESCALUS   He's in the right. Constable, what say you to it?

ELBOW   First, an it like you, the house is a respected house;
          next, this is a respected fellow, and his mistress is a respected
          woman.

155 POMPEY   By this hand, sir, his wife is a more respected person
          than any of us all.

ELBOW   Varlet, thou liest, thou liest, wicked varlet! The time
          is yet to come that she was ever respected with man, woman
          or child.

160 POMPEY   Sir, she was respected with him before he married
          with her.

ESCALUS   Which is the wiser here? Justice or Iniquity? Is this
          true?

ELBOW   O thou caitiff! O thou varlet! O thou wicked
165   Hannibal! I respected with her before I was married to her? If
          ever I was respected with her, or she with me, let not your

---

141 **mark** note   147 **supposed** malapropism for "deposed" (i.e. sworn)   **book** i.e. the Bible
148 **if . . . harm** i.e. if his face is the worst thing about him, and is in fact harmless, how could
any other part of him (i.e. his penis) be effective   152 **an it like** if it please   **respected**
malapropism for "suspected"   158 **respected** Elbow understands "suspected" (of having had
sex)   162 **Justice or Iniquity** personified characters in morality plays   164 **caitiff** wretch,
villain   165 **Hannibal** probably a mistake for "cannibal"; Hannibal was a Carthaginian
general who fought the Romans in the third century BC

worship think me the poor duke's officer. Prove this, thou
wicked Hannibal, or I'll have mine action of battery on thee.

ESCALUS   If he took you a box o'th'ear, you might have your
170   action of slander too.

ELBOW   Marry, I thank your good worship for it. What is't
your worship's pleasure I shall do with this wicked caitiff?

ESCALUS   Truly, officer, because he hath some offences in him
that thou wouldst discover if thou couldst, let him continue
175   in his courses till thou know'st what they are.

ELBOW   Marry, I thank your worship for it.—   To Pompey
Thou see'st, thou wicked varlet, now, what's come upon thee:
thou art to continue now, thou varlet, thou art to continue.

ESCALUS   Where were you born, friend?
180   FROTH   Here in Vienna, sir.

ESCALUS   Are you of fourscore pounds a year?

FROTH   Yes, an't please you, sir.

ESCALUS   So. What trade are you of, sir?

POMPEY   A tapster, a poor widow's tapster.

185   ESCALUS   Your mistress' name?

POMPEY   Mistress Overdone.

ESCALUS   Hath she had any more than one husband?

POMPEY   Nine, sir: Overdone by the last.

ESCALUS   Nine? Come hither to me, Master Froth. Master
190   Froth, I would not have you acquainted with tapsters: they
will draw you, Master Froth, and you will hang them. Get
you gone, and let me hear no more of you.

FROTH   I thank your worship. For mine own part, I never
come into any room in a tap-house, but I am drawn in.

195   ESCALUS   Well, no more of it, Master Froth, farewell.—

[Exit Froth]

---

168 **action of battery** lawsuit for assault, but a mistake for **slander** as Escalus notices
169 **took** gave   174 **discover** reveal   175 **courses** way of life   178 **continue** Elbow seems to
think this means "be punished" or "be restrained"   182 **an't** if it   188 **Overdone . . . last** she
got the name Overdone from her last husband/she became sexually worn out after her ninth
husband   191 **draw** corrupt/draw in/drag to execution/drain of money (plays on the sense of
drawing ale from a barrel)   **hang them** caused them to be hanged/curse them   194 **tap-
house** tavern   **but** unless

Come you hither to me, Master Tapster. What's   *To Pompey*
your name, Master Tapster?

POMPEY   Pompey.

ESCALUS   What else?

200 POMPEY   Bum, sir.

ESCALUS   Troth, and your bum is the greatest thing about
you, so that in the beastliest sense you are Pompey the Great.
Pompey, you are partly a bawd, Pompey, howsoever you
colour it in being a tapster, are you not? Come, tell me true, it
205   shall be the better for you.

POMPEY   Truly, sir, I am a poor fellow that would live.

ESCALUS   How would you live, Pompey? By being a bawd?
What do you think of the trade, Pompey? Is it a lawful trade?

POMPEY   If the law would allow it, sir.

210 ESCALUS   But the law will not allow it, Pompey, nor it shall not
be allowed in Vienna.

POMPEY   Does your worship mean to geld and splay all the
youth of the city?

ESCALUS   No, Pompey.

215 POMPEY   Truly, sir, in my poor opinion, they will to't then. If
your worship will take order for the drabs and the knaves,
you need not to fear the bawds.

ESCALUS   There is pretty orders beginning, I can tell you: it is
but heading and hanging.

220 POMPEY   If you head and hang all that offend that way but
for ten year together, you'll be glad to give out a commission
for more heads: if this law hold in Vienna ten year, I'll rent
the fairest house in it after three-pence a bay. If you live to see
this come to pass, say Pompey told you so.

---

202 **beastliest** crudest/most brutish   **Pompey the Great** famous Roman general
204 **colour it in** conceal it   206 **would live** wants to earn a living   212 **geld and splay**
castrate (the men) and spay (the women)   215 **to't** continue   216 **take . . . knaves** find
employment for whores and their clients   217 **fear** worry about   218 **pretty orders**
considerable laws   219 **but . . . hanging** exclusively beheading and hanging   221 **glad . . .**
heads have to give an order for more people (**heads** may also play on "maidenheads"—i.e.
young women)   222 **hold** remains valid/is observed   223 **after** at the rate of   **bay** room/
space under a gable (i.e. extremely cheaply)

225 ESCALUS   Thank you, good Pompey, and, in requital of your
prophecy, hark you: I advise you, let me not find you before
me again upon any complaint whatsoever, no, not for
dwelling where you do. If I do, Pompey, I shall beat you to
your tent, and prove a shrewd Caesar to you: in plain
230 dealing, Pompey, I shall have you whipped. So, for this time,
Pompey, fare you well.

POMPEY   I thank your worship for your good counsel—
but I shall follow it as the flesh and fortune shall   *Aside*
better determine.

235 Whip me? No, no, let carman whip his jade:
The valiant heart's not whipped out of his trade.   *Exit*

ESCALUS   Come hither to me, Master Elbow, come hither,
Master Constable. How long have you been in this place of
constable?

240 ELBOW   Seven year and a half, sir.

ESCALUS   I thought by the readiness in the office you had
continued in it some time. You say, seven years together?

ELBOW   And a half, sir.

ESCALUS   Alas, it hath been great pains to you. They do you
245 wrong to put you so oft upon't. Are there not men in your
ward sufficient to serve it?

ELBOW   Faith, sir, few of any wit in such matters: as they are
chosen, they are glad to choose me for them. I do it for some
piece of money, and go through with all.

250 ESCALUS   Look you bring me in the names of some six or
seven, the most sufficient of your parish.

ELBOW   To your worship's house, sir?

ESCALUS   To my house. Fare you well.   *[Exit Elbow]*
What's o'clock, think you?   *To Justice*

---

225 **requital of** repayment for   228 **beat . . . you** Julius Caesar defeated Pompey the Great at
the battle of Pharsalia, in 48 BC   229 **shrewd** artful/severe   230 **dealing** terms
233 **flesh . . . determine** my body and opportunity dictate   235 **carman** the driver of a cart
jade worn-out horse   238 **place** position   241 **readiness** eagerness/speed   244 **pains**
trouble   245 **put . . . upon't** make you perform the task for so long/work you so hard
246 **ward** district of a city   **sufficient** competent (enough)   247 **wit** intelligence
249 **go . . . all** carry out all the duties of my position

255	JUSTICE	Eleven, sir.
	ESCALUS	I pray you home to dinner with me.
	JUSTICE	I humbly thank you.
	ESCALUS	It grieves me for the death of Claudio,
		But there's no remedy.
260	JUSTICE	Lord Angelo is severe.
	ESCALUS	It is but needful.

ESCALUS
Mercy is not itself that oft looks so,
Pardon is still the nurse of second woe:
But yet, poor Claudio! There is no remedy.
255 Come, sir.   *Exeunt*

Act 2 Scene 2

running scene 5 continues

Enter Provost [and a] Servant

SERVANT   He's hearing of a cause: he will come straight, I'll
tell him of you.

PROVOST   Pray you, do.— I'll know   [*Exit Servant*]
His pleasure, maybe he will relent. Alas,
5   He hath but as offended in a dream!
All sects, all ages smack of this vice, and he
To die for't?

Enter Angelo

ANGELO   Now, what's the matter, provost?

PROVOST   Is it your will Claudio shall die tomorrow?

10   ANGELO   Did not I tell thee yea? Hadst thou not order?
Why dost thou ask again?

PROVOST   Lest I might be too rash.
Under your good correction, I have seen
When, after execution, judgement hath
15   Repented o'er his doom.

---

255 **Eleven . . . dinner** lunch was usually eaten before midday   261 **needful** necessary
262 **Mercy . . . woe** i.e. being merciful may in fact encourage further wrongdoing
2.2   1 He's i.e. Angelo   **4 pleasure** intention   **5 He** i.e. Claudio   **but as offended** only
done wrong as if   **6 sects** types of people   **smack** have a flavor of, partake in   **12 Lest** in
case   **13 Under . . . correction** correct me if I am wrong   **15 Repented . . . doom** regretted
the sentence he had imposed

ANGELO   Go to, let that be mine.
Do you your office, or give up your place,
And you shall well be spared.

PROVOST   I crave your honour's pardon.

20   What shall be done, sir, with the groaning Juliet?
She's very near her hour.

ANGELO   Dispose of her
To some more fitter place, and that with speed.

[Enter Servant]

SERVANT   Here is the sister of the man condemned

25   Desires access to you.

ANGELO   Hath he a sister?

PROVOST   Ay, my good lord, a very virtuous maid,
And to be shortly of a sisterhood,
If not already.

30   ANGELO   Well, let her be admitted.   [Exit Servant]
See you the fornicatress be removed.
Let her have needful but not lavish means.
There shall be order for't.

Enter Lucio and Isabella

PROVOST   'Save your honour!

35   ANGELO   Stay a little while.——   To Provost
You're welcome: what's your will?   To Isabella

ISABELLA   I am a woeful suitor to your honour,
Please but your honour hear me.

ANGELO   Well, what's your suit?

40   ISABELLA   There is a vice that most I do abhor,
And most desire should meet the blow of justice,
For which I would not plead, but that I must,
For which I must not plead, but that I am
At war 'twixt will and will not.

45   ANGELO   Well, the matter?

---

16 mine my role/my problem   18 you . . . spared we will manage perfectly well without
you/you will be spared the fear of error   20 groaning i.e. in labor   21 hour time to give birth
22 Dispose of make arrangements for   28 sisterhood order of nuns   31 fornicatress i.e.
Juliet   33 order authorization   37 suitor petitioner, supplicant   44 will . . . not wanting and
not wanting to   45 matter subject/point

ISABELLA	I have a brother is condemned to die:		

ISABELLA   I have a brother is condemned to die:
    I do beseech you, let it be his fault,
    And not my brother.

PROVOST   Heaven give thee moving graces!   *Aside*

50 ANGELO   Condemn the fault and not the actor of it?
    Why, every fault's condemned ere it be done:
    Mine were the very cipher of a function,
    To fine the faults whose fine stands in record,
    And let go by the actor.

55 ISABELLA   O, just but severe law!
    I had a brother, then. Heaven keep your honour.

LUCIO   Give't not o'er so. To him again, entreat him,   *Aside to*
    Kneel down before him, hang upon his gown.   *Isabella*
    You are too cold. If you should need a pin,
60   You could not with more tame a tongue desire it.
    To him, I say!

ISABELLA   Must he needs die?   *To Angelo*

ANGELO   Maiden, no remedy.

ISABELLA   Yes, I do think that you might pardon him,
65   And neither heaven nor man grieve at the mercy.

ANGELO   I will not do't.

ISABELLA   But can you, if you would?

ANGELO   Look what I will not, that I cannot do.

ISABELLA   But might you do't, and do the world no wrong,
70   If so your heart were touched with that remorse
    As mine is to him?

ANGELO   He's sentenced, 'tis too late.

LUCIO   You are too cold.   *Aside to Isabella*

ISABELLA   Too late? Why, no, I that do speak a word
75   May call it back again. Well, believe this:
    No ceremony that to great ones 'longs,

---

47 **his . . . brother** let the evil deed be condemned rather than Claudio himself   49 **moving** persuasive   51 **every . . . done** i.e. all faults are wrong, by their very nature, therefore they must be condemned even before they can be committed   52 **the . . . function** a meaningless role   53 **fine** punish   **fine . . . record** punishments are set down by the law   54 **by** unpunished   57 **Give't . . . so** do not give up so easily   59 **pin** i.e. worthless trifle   67 **would** wanted to   68 **what** whatever   70 **remorse** compassion   76 **'longs** belongs, is fitting

Not the king's crown, nor the deputed sword,
The marshal's truncheon, nor the judge's robe,
Become them with one half so good a grace
80   As mercy does.
If he had been as you and you as he,
You would have slipped like him, but he, like you,
Would not have been so stern.

ANGELO   Pray you, be gone.

85 ISABELLA   I would to heaven I had your potency,
And you were Isabel. Should it then be thus?
No, I would tell what 'twere to be a judge,
And what a prisoner.

LUCIO   Ay, touch him, there's the vein.   *Aside to Isabella*

90 ANGELO   Your brother is a forfeit of the law,
And you but waste your words.

ISABELLA   Alas, alas!
Why, all the souls that were were forfeit once,
And he that might the vantage best have took
95   Found out the remedy. How would you be,
If he, which is the top of judgement, should
But judge you as you are? O, think on that,
And mercy then will breathe within your lips
Like man new made.

100 ANGELO   Be you content, fair maid,
It is the law, not I, condemn your brother.
Were he my kinsman, brother, or my son,
It should be thus with him. He must die tomorrow.

ISABELLA   Tomorrow? O, that's sudden! Spare him, spare him!
105   He's not prepared for death. Even for our kitchens
We kill the fowl of season: shall we serve heaven

---

77 **deputed sword** sword of justice entrusted to rulers or their deputies as a symbol of office
78 **marshal** senior military officer   **truncheon** military staff symbolizing command
79 **Become** suits   **grace** virtue   81 **as you** in your position   85 **potency** power   87 **tell**
assert   89 **vein** proper course to follow   90 **a forfeit of** subject to   92 **were** ever existed
before Christ offered redemption   94 **he** i.e. God   **vantage** opportunity (to condemn
mankind for original sin)   99 **new made** i.e. reborn through Christian salvation, or through
Christ's redemption of mankind   106 **kill . . . season** kill the birds when they are in the best
condition to be eaten

With less respect than we do minister
To our gross selves? Good, good my lord, bethink you;
Who is it that hath died for this offence?
There's many have committed it.

LUCIO   Ay, well said.   *Aside to Isabella*

ANGELO   The law hath not been dead, though it hath slept:
Those many had not dared to do that evil,
If the first that did th'edict infringe
Had answered for his deed. Now 'tis awake,
Takes note of what is done, and, like a prophet,
Looks in a glass that shows what future evils,
Either now, or by remissness new-conceived,
And so in progress to be hatched and born,
Are now to have no successive degrees,
But ere they live to end.

ISABELLA   Yet show some pity.

ANGELO   I show it most of all when I show justice:
For then I pity those I do not know,
Which a dismissed offence would after gall,
And do him right that, answering one foul wrong,
Lives not to act another. Be satisfied;
Your brother dies tomorrow; be content.

ISABELLA   So you must be the first that gives this sentence,
And he, that suffers. O, it is excellent
To have a giant's strength, but it is tyrannous
To use it like a giant.

LUCIO   That's well said.   *Aside to Isabella*

ISABELLA   Could great men thunder
As Jove himself does, Jove would ne'er be quiet,
For every pelting, petty officer

---

107 **minister** attend to/supply   108 **gross** inferior/mortal   **bethink you** consider
113 **Those . . . deed** the many people who have engaged in extramarital sex would not have
done so if the first person to break the law had been punished   117 **glass** mirror/crystal
118 **now** now in existence   **remissness new-conceived** moral laxity freshly contemplated
(though not yet carried out)   119 **hatched and born** planned and executed   120 **successive
degrees** further stages of development   121 **ere** before   **end** die   125 **dismissed**
overlooked/unpunished   **gall** harm/vex   135 **Jove** in Roman mythology, king of the gods;
his weapon was the thunderbolt   **quiet** at peace   136 **pelting** paltry

                Would use his heaven for thunder,
                Nothing but thunder! Merciful heaven,
                Thou rather with thy sharp and sulphurous bolt
140   Splits the unwedgeable and gnarlèd oak
                Than the soft myrtle: but man, proud man,
                Dressed in a little brief authority,
                Most ignorant of what he's most assured —
                His glassy essence — like an angry ape
145   Plays such fantastic tricks before high heaven
                As makes the angels weep, who, with our spleens,
                Would all themselves laugh mortal.

        LUCIO   O, to him, to him, wench: he will relent.   *Aside to*
                He's coming, I perceive't.   *Isabella*
150   PROVOST   Pray heaven she win him.   *Aside*
        ISABELLA   We cannot weigh our brother with ourself.
                Great men may jest with saints, 'tis wit in them,
                But in the less foul profanation.

        LUCIO   Thou'rt i'th'right, girl, more o'that.   *Aside to Isabella*
155   ISABELLA   That in the captain's but a choleric word,
                Which in the soldier is flat blasphemy.

        LUCIO   Art avised o'that? More on't.   *Aside to Isabella*
        ANGELO   Why do you put these sayings upon me?
        ISABELLA   Because authority, though it err like others,
160   Hath yet a kind of medicine in itself
                That skins the vice o'th'top. Go to your bosom,
                Knock there, and ask your heart what it doth know
                That's like my brother's fault. If it confess
                A natural guiltiness such as is his,

---

139 **sharp . . . bolt** i.e. lightning   140 **unwedgeable** incapable of being split   **oak** a tree that
was sacred to Jove   141 **myrtle** evergreen shrub symbolic of love   142 **brief** temporal,
earthly   143 **assured** confident about   144 **glassy** vain/fragile/translucent/reflected
145 **fantastic** illusory/grotesque/capricious/foolish   146 **with our spleens** if they had human
spleens (thought to be the seat of laughter)   147 **laugh mortal** laugh themselves into being
human/laugh themselves to death   149 **coming** coming around   151 **weigh . . . ourself**
judge others by the same standards we employ for ourselves   152 **jest with** joke about/speak
lightly of   **wit** mental sharpness   153 **in . . . profanation** in inferior men it is blasphemy
155 **choleric** hot-tempered   156 **flat** downright   157 **avised** aware   158 **put** force
161 **skins** covers up, like a film of skin over an ulcer   164 **natural guiltiness** inherent
tendency to sin/guilt over normal affections

165   Let it not sound a thought upon your tongue
    Against my brother's life.

ANGELO   She speaks, and 'tis such sense   *Aside*
    That my sense breeds with it.— Fare you well.   *Starts to go*

ISABELLA   Gentle my lord, turn back.

170 ANGELO   I will bethink me. Come again tomorrow.

ISABELLA   Hark how I'll bribe you: good my lord, turn back.

ANGELO   How? Bribe me?

ISABELLA   Ay, with such gifts that heaven shall share with you.

LUCIO   You had marred all else.   *Aside to Isabella*

175 ISABELLA   Not with fond sicles of the tested gold,
    Or stones whose rates are either rich or poor
    As fancy values them, but with true prayers
    That shall be up at heaven and enter there
    Ere sunrise, prayers from preservèd souls,
180   From fasting maids whose minds are dedicate
    To nothing temporal.

ANGELO   Well, come to me tomorrow.

LUCIO   Go to, 'tis well; away!   *Aside to Isabella*

ISABELLA   Heaven keep your honour safe.

185 ANGELO   Amen.   *Aside*
    For I am that way going to temptation,
    Where prayers cross.

ISABELLA   At what hour tomorrow
    Shall I attend your lordship?

190 ANGELO   At any time 'fore noon.

ISABELLA   'Save your honour!

    [*Exeunt Isabella, Lucio and Provost*]

ANGELO   From thee, even from thy virtue.
    What's this? What's this? Is this her fault or mine?

---

165 **sound** declare   167 **sense** reason   168 **sense** senses/sexual impulses   **breeds** grows
(with connotations of pregnancy and, possibly, erection)   174 **You . . . else** i.e. a material
bribe would have undone all your previous good work   175 **fond** foolish, trivial   **sicles**
shekels, silver coins   **tested** genuine   176 **stones** jewels   **rates** value   177 **fancy** whim,
arbitrariness   **true** faithful, constant   179 **preservèd** protected (in the nunnery)
180 **fasting maids** i.e. nuns   **dedicate** dedicated   181 **temporal** worldly   187 **cross** are in
conflict, thwart one another   191 **'Save** God save

The tempter or the tempted, who sins most? Ha?
195   Not she — nor doth she tempt — but it is I
That, lying by the violet in the sun,
Do as the carrion does, not as the flower,
Corrupt with virtuous season. Can it be
That modesty may more betray our sense
200   Than woman's lightness? Having waste ground enough,
Shall we desire to raze the sanctuary
And pitch our evils there? O, fie, fie, fie!
What dost thou? Or what art thou, Angelo?
Dost thou desire her foully for those things
205   That make her good? O, let her brother live!
Thieves for their robbery have authority
When judges steal themselves. What, do I love her,
That I desire to hear her speak again,
And feast upon her eyes? What is't I dream on?
210   O cunning enemy, that to catch a saint
With saints dost bait thy hook! Most dangerous
Is that temptation that doth goad us on
To sin in loving virtue: never could the strumpet,
With all her double vigour, art and nature,
215   Once stir my temper, but this virtuous maid
Subdues me quite. Ever till now,
When men were fond, I smiled and wondered how.   *Exit*

Act 2 Scene 3   *running scene 6*

Enter [separately] Duke [disguised as a friar] and Provost

DUKE   Hail to you, provost — so I think you are.
PROVOST   I am the provost. What's your will, good friar?

196 **violet** flower associated with chastity   197 **carrion** dead, putrefying flesh   198 **Corrupt . . .
season** rot under the wholesome sun (which causes violets to flourish)   199 **modesty**
chastity   200 **lightness** promiscuity, lasciviousness   **waste ground** wasteland   201 **raze
the sanctuary** obliterate the holy places   202 **pitch** build   204 **foully** i.e. immorally/sexually
210 **enemy** i.e. the devil   214 **double vigour** twofold power, enhanced energy   **art and nature**
skills of seduction and inherent sexuality   215 **stir my temper** disturb my temperament/
equilibrium, inflame my desire   217 **fond** infatuated/loving/foolish   **2.3   1 so . . . are** the
duke remembers that he is in disguise and, as a friar, would not know the provost

DUKE   Bound by my charity and my blest order,
            I come to visit the afflicted spirits
5   Here in the prison. Do me the common right
            To let me see them and to make me know
            The nature of their crimes, that I may minister
            To them accordingly.

PROVOST   I would do more than that, if more were needful.

Enter Juliet

10   Look, here comes one: a gentlewoman of mine,
            Who, falling in the flaws of her own youth,
            Hath blistered her report. She is with child,
            And he that got it, sentenced: a young man
            More fit to do another such offence
15   Than die for this.

DUKE   When must he die?

PROVOST   As I do think, tomorrow.
            I have provided for you, stay awhile,   *To Juliet*
            And you shall be conducted.

20   DUKE   Repent you, fair one, of the sin you carry?

JULIET   I do, and bear the shame most patiently.

DUKE   I'll teach you how you shall arraign your conscience
            And try your penitence, if it be sound
            Or hollowly put on.

25   JULIET   I'll gladly learn.

DUKE   Love you the man that wronged you?

JULIET   Yes, as I love the woman that wronged him.

DUKE   So then it seems your most offenceful act
            Was mutually committed?

30   JULIET   Mutually.

DUKE   Then was your sin of heavier kind than his.

JULIET   I do confess it, and repent it, father.

---

3 **Bound** obliged   **blest order** religious order   5 **common right** right of a priest to visit
condemned people/right of any citizen   10 **of mine** in my charge   11 **flaws** gusts of
passion/faults/cracks   12 **blistered her report** tarnished her reputation   13 **got** conceived
19 **conducted** escorted   21 **bear** endure (plays on the sense of "bear a child")   22 **arraign**
interrogate   23 **try** test   **if** to see whether   **sound** genuine   24 **hollowly** insincerely
31 **heavier** more severe/more sorrowful/heavier with the weight of a baby

DUKE   'Tis meet so, daughter, but lest you do repent
              As that the sin hath brought you to this shame,
35   Which sorrow is always toward ourselves, not heaven,
              Showing we would not spare heaven as we love it,
              But as we stand in fear—

JULIET   I do repent me, as it is an evil,
              And take the shame with joy.

40 DUKE   There rest.
              Your partner, as I hear, must die tomorrow,
              And I am going with instruction to him.
              Grace go with you, *Benedicite*.   *Exit*

JULIET   Must die tomorrow! O injurious love,
45   That respites me a life, whose very comfort
              Is still a dying horror!

PROVOST   'Tis pity of him.   *Exeunt*

Act 2 Scene 4

running scene 7

Enter Angelo

ANGELO   When I would pray and think, I think and pray
              To several subjects. Heaven hath my empty words,
              Whilst my invention, hearing not my tongue,
              Anchors on Isabel: heaven in my mouth,
5   As if I did but only chew his name,
              And in my heart the strong and swelling evil
              Of my conception. The state whereon I studied
              Is like a good thing, being often read,
              Grown seared and tedious: yea, my gravity,

33 **meet so** proper that you do so   **lest** in case   34 **As that** because   35 **toward ourselves** selfish   37 **we . . . fear** i.e. we tend to repent out of fear of God rather than love for him   38 **as** because   40 **There rest** maintain that attitude   42 **instruction** moral guidance   43 *Benedicite* bless you   44 **injurious** harmful   45 **respites** grants   46 **still** constantly   47 **'Tis . . . him** he is to be pitied   **2.4**   2 **several** various   3 **invention** thoughts/imagination   4 **Anchors** fixes   **heaven** probably substituted for "God" as a result of prohibition on naming the deity   7 **conception** thought/plan (perhaps with connotations of pregnancy)   **state** affairs of government   9 **seared** dried up   **gravity** authority/respectability

10   Wherein — let no man hear me — I take pride,
      Could I with boot change for an idle plume
      Which the air beats for vain. O place, O form,
      How often dost thou with thy case, thy habit,
      Wrench awe from fools and tie the wiser souls
15   To thy false seeming? Blood, thou art blood.
      Let's write good angel on the devil's horn —
      'Tis not the devil's crest.

Enter [a] Servant

                               How now? Who's there?

SERVANT   One Isabel, a sister, desires access to you.

20 **ANGELO**   Teach her the way.   [*Exit Servant*]
                          O heavens,
      Why does my blood thus muster to my heart,
      Making both it unable for itself,
      And dispossessing all my other parts
25   Of necessary fitness?
      So play the foolish throngs with one that swoons,
      Come all to help him, and so stop the air
      By which he should revive: and even so
      The general, subject to a well-wished king,
30   Quit their own part and in obsequious fondness
      Crowd to his presence, where their untaught love
      Must needs appear offence.

Enter Isabella

                           How now, fair maid?

ISABELLA   I am come to know your pleasure.

---

11 **boot** advantage   **change** exchange   **idle plume** frivolous feather (worn in hats)   **12 for vain** (in punishment) for vanity/to no purpose (plays on "weather vane")   **place** rank   **form** ceremony, dignity   **13 case, thy habit** clothing/outward appearance   **14 tie . . . seeming** bind even the wiser people to a faith in the trappings of authority   **15 Blood** sexual desire/human frailty   **16 Let's** even if we were to   **angel** plays on Angelo's name   **17 'Tis . . . crest** i.e. it would still not change the devil's evil nature   **crest** identifying feature on a coat of arms   **20 Teach** show   **22 muster** to rush to, collect in   **23 unable for itself** incapable   **24 dispossessing** depriving   **26 throngs** crowds   **29 general** people   **well-wished** well-liked   **30 part** role   **obsequious fondness** fawning foolishness/dutiful affection   **31 untaught** indecorous, ignorant

35	ANGELO	That you might know it would much better *Aside?*
		please me
		Than to demand what 'tis.— Your brother cannot live.
	ISABELLA	Even so. Heaven keep your honour. *She starts to go*
	ANGELO	Yet may he live awhile, and it may be
40		As long as you or I: yet he must die.
	ISABELLA	Under your sentence?
	ANGELO	Yea.
	ISABELLA	When, I beseech you? That in his reprieve,
		Longer or shorter, he may be so fitted
45		That his soul sicken not.
	ANGELO	Ha! Fie, these filthy vices! It were as good
		To pardon him that hath from nature stolen
		A man already made, as to remit
		Their saucy sweetness that do coin heaven's image
50		In stamps that are forbid: 'tis all as easy
		Falsely to take away a life true made
		As to put mettle in restrainèd means
		To make a false one.
	ISABELLA	'Tis set down so in heaven, but not in earth.
55	ANGELO	Say you so? Then I shall pose you quickly.
		Which had you rather, that the most just law
		Now took your brother's life, or, to redeem him,
		Give up your body to such sweet uncleanness
		As she that he hath stained?
60	ISABELLA	Sir, believe this,
		I had rather give my body than my soul.
	ANGELO	I talk not of your soul. Our compelled sins
		Stand more for number than for account.

---

35 That . . . 'tis I would rather you gave me what I desire, than ask what it is (plays on the sexual connotations of **know** and **pleasure**)   **38 Even so** so be it   **43 reprieve** time before his execution   **44 fitted** prepared spiritually   **47 from . . . made** i.e. murdered a man   **48 remit** pardon   **49 saucy sweetness** lecherous pleasures   **coin . . . forbid** i.e. forge illegitimate children in God's image   **50 stamps** instruments for impressing images on coins   **51 Falsely** wrongly   **true** legitimately   **52 mettle** substance/metal/semen   **restrainèd means** forbidden molds   **54 'Tis . . . earth** the sins of murder and conceiving illegitimate children may be judged equally sinful in heaven, but they are not by humans   **55 pose you** present you with a problem/question you   **62 Our . . . account** sins we commit out of necessity are recorded, but we are not made to pay for them

ISABELLA   How say you?

65   ANGELO   Nay, I'll not warrant that, for I can speak
Against the thing I say. Answer to this:
I, now the voice of the recorded law,
Pronounce a sentence on your brother's life.
Might there not be a charity in sin
70   To save this brother's life?

ISABELLA   Please you to do't,
I'll take it as a peril to my soul,
It is no sin at all, but charity.

ANGELO   Pleased you to do't at peril of your soul,
75   Were equal poise of sin and charity.

ISABELLA   That I do beg his life, if it be sin,
Heaven let me bear it. You granting of my suit,
If that be sin, I'll make it my morn prayer
To have it added to the faults of mine,
80   And nothing of your answer.

ANGELO   Nay, but hear me.
Your sense pursues not mine: either you are ignorant,
Or seem so crafty, and that's not good.

ISABELLA   Let me be ignorant, and in nothing good,
85   But graciously to know I am no better.

ANGELO   Thus wisdom wishes to appear most bright
When it doth tax itself, as these black masks
Proclaim an enshield beauty ten times louder
Than beauty could, displayed. But mark me,
90   To be receivèd plain, I'll speak more gross:
Your brother is to die.

ISABELLA   So.

---

65 warrant guarantee   71 Please if it please   72 I'll . . . soul I'll risk the punishment of my
soul (by saying)   75 poise balance   78 morn morning   80 answer responsibility
82 sense understanding/intention (plays on sense of "sensual inclination")   ignorant
unaware   83 seem so crafty are cunningly pretending to be so (some editors emend to
"craftily")   85 But graciously except with grace and humility   87 tax rebuke   masks worn
to shield the complexion from the sun (perhaps also with suggestion of nuns' habits)
88 enshield concealed   89 mark pay attention to   90 receivèd understood   gross bluntly

ANGELO   And his offence is so, as it appears,
Accountant to the law upon that pain.

95   ISABELLA   True.

ANGELO   Admit no other way to save his life —
As I subscribe not that, nor any other,
But in the loss of question — that you, his sister,
Finding yourself desired of such a person,
100   Whose credit with the judge, or own great place,
Could fetch your brother from the manacles
Of the all-building law, and that there were
No earthly mean to save him, but that either
You must lay down the treasures of your body
105   To this supposed, or else to let him suffer:
What would you do?

ISABELLA   As much for my poor brother as myself:
That is, were I under the terms of death,
Th'impression of keen whips I'd wear as rubies,
110   And strip myself to death, as to a bed
That longing have been sick for, ere I'd yield
My body up to shame.

ANGELO   Then must your brother die.

ISABELLA   And 'twere the cheaper way.
115   Better it were a brother died at once,
Than that a sister by redeeming him
Should die for ever.

ANGELO   Were not you then as cruel as the sentence
That you have slandered so?

120   ISABELLA   Ignomy in ransom and free pardon
Are of two houses. Lawful mercy
Is nothing kin to foul redemption.

---

93 appears is evident/is set down (in law)   94 Accountant accountable   pain penalty (of death)   96 Admit suppose   97 subscribe not agree to neither   98 in . . . question unclear; perhaps "for the sake of argument"   100 credit influence/reputation   great place powerful position   102 all-building on which everything is founded (some editors emend to "all-binding")   104 treasures . . . body i.e. virginity   105 supposed hypothetical man   108 terms sentence   109 impression marks   keen biting/eager   110 strip whip/bare myself   117 die for ever i.e. suffer eternal damnation   120 Ignomy . . . houses shameful bargaining for pardon and unconditional release are entirely different matters   122 nothing kin unrelated

ANGELO   You seemed of late to make the law a tyrant,
And rather proved the sliding of your brother
125   A merriment than a vice.

ISABELLA   O pardon me, my lord, it oft falls out
To have what we would have, we speak not what we mean.
I something do excuse the thing I hate,
For his advantage that I dearly love.

130 ANGELO   We are all frail.

ISABELLA   Else let my brother die,
If not a fedary, but only he
Owe and succeed thy weakness.

ANGELO   Nay, women are frail too.

135 ISABELLA   Ay, as the glasses where they view themselves,
Which are as easy broke as they make forms.
Women? Help heaven! Men their creation mar
In profiting by them. Nay, call us ten times frail,
For we are soft as our complexions are,
140   And credulous to false prints.

ANGELO   I think it well.
And from this testimony of your own sex —
Since I suppose we are made to be no stronger
Than faults may shake our frames — let me be bold.
145   I do arrest your words. Be that you are,
That is, a woman; if you be more, you're none.
If you be one, as you are well expressed
By all external warrants, show it now,
By putting on the destined livery.

---

124 **sliding** sinfulness   125 **merriment** lighthearted matter   126 **oft falls out** often happens
127 **would** wish to   128 **something** somewhat   131 **Else** otherwise   132 **not a fedary** no
accomplice   133 **Owe . . . weakness** owns and inherits the moral frailty that you speak of
136 **as . . . forms** can be destroyed as easily as they can reflect images   137 **Help heaven!**
Heaven help them!   **Men . . . them** men debase their inherent superiority by abusing
women/men ruin women, who created them, by abusing them   140 **credulous . . . prints**
susceptible to forged imprints (i.e. ready believers of male falsehood)   141 **think it well** agree
143 **suppose** propose   144 **Than . . . frames** than the weaknesses that we are prey to
145 **that** what   146 **none** not a woman (as you define one)   147 **well . . . warrants** clearly
reveal yourself to be by your outward appearance   149 **livery** uniform (of womanly frailty)

150 ISABELLA   I have no tongue but one. Gentle my lord,
Let me entreat you speak the former language.

ANGELO   Plainly conceive I love you.

ISABELLA   My brother did love Juliet,
And you tell me that he shall die for't.

155 ANGELO   He shall not, Isabel, if you give me love.

ISABELLA   I know your virtue hath a licence in't,
Which seems a little fouler than it is,
To pluck on others.

ANGELO   Believe me, on mine honour,
160 My words express my purpose.

ISABELLA   Ha! Little honour to be much believed,
And most pernicious purpose! Seeming, seeming!
I will proclaim thee, Angelo, look for't.
Sign me a present pardon for my brother,
165 Or with an outstretched throat I'll tell the world aloud
What man thou art.

ANGELO   Who will believe thee, Isabel?
My unsoiled name, th'austereness of my life,
My vouch against you, and my place i'th'state,
170 Will so your accusation overweigh,
That you shall stifle in your own report
And smell of calumny. I have begun,
And now I give my sensual race the rein:
Fit thy consent to my sharp appetite,
175 Lay by all nicety and prolixious blushes
That banish what they sue for. Redeem thy brother
By yielding up thy body to my will,

---

150 **but one** i.e. a truthful one (two tongues would be deceitful)   151 **speak . . . language** use
the plainer language employed earlier/return to the matters discussed previously   152 **conceive**
understand (perhaps with sexual connotations)   156 **licence** freedom of authority (perhaps
with play on sense of "licentiousness")   158 **To pluck on** as a means of testing   162 **pernicious**
destructive   **Seeming** deceptive behavior   163 **proclaim** denounce   164 **present** immediate
165 **outstretched** wide open   166 **What** what kind of   168 **austereness** strictness
169 **vouch** testimony   171 **stifle** suffocate   **report** story/reputation   172 **calumny** slander
173 **sensual . . . rein** allow my desires to run freely   175 **by** aside   **prolixious** time-wasting
176 **banish . . . for** eliminate the very feelings they aim to arouse

Or else he must not only die the death,
But thy unkindness shall his death draw out
180   To ling'ring sufferance. Answer me tomorrow,
Or, by the affection that now guides me most,
I'll prove a tyrant to him. As for you,
Say what you can; my false o'erweighs your true.   *Exit*

ISABELLA   To whom should I complain? Did I tell this,
185   Who would believe me? O perilous mouths,
That bear in them one and the self-same tongue,
Either of condemnation or approof,
Bidding the law make curtsy to their will,
Hooking both right and wrong to th'appetite,
190   To follow as it draws! I'll to my brother.
Though he hath fallen by prompture of the blood,
Yet hath he in him such a mind of honour
That, had he twenty heads to tender down
On twenty bloody blocks, he'd yield them up
195   Before his sister should her body stoop
To such abhorred pollution.
Then Isabel, live chaste, and brother, die;
More than our brother is our chastity.
I'll tell him yet of Angelo's request,
200   And fit his mind to death, for his soul's rest.   *Exit*

Act 3 Scene 1   *running scene 8*

Enter Duke [disguised], Claudio and Provost

DUKE   So then you hope of pardon from Lord Angelo?
CLAUDIO   The miserable have no other medicine
But only hope:
I've hope to live, and am prepared to die.

---

179 **unkindness** cruelty/unnatural behavior/lack of sisterly feeling   **180 sufferance** torment
181 **affection** passion   184 **Did I** were I to   187 **approof** approval   188 **make curtsy**
submit, bow   190 **draws** demands/leads   191 **prompture** urging   **blood** sexual desire
193 **tender down** lay down in payment   194 **blocks** execution blocks   **198 More** worth
more   200 **fit** prepare

5 DUKE   Be absolute for death: either death or life
    Shall thereby be the sweeter. Reason thus with life:
    If I do lose thee, I do lose a thing
    That none but fools would keep. A breath thou art,
    Servile to all the skyey influences
10   That dost this habitation where thou keep'st
    Hourly afflict. Merely, thou art death's fool,
    For him thou labour'st by thy flight to shun,
    And yet runn'st toward him still. Thou art not noble,
    For all th'accommodations that thou bear'st
15   Are nursed by baseness. Thou'rt by no means valiant,
    For thou dost fear the soft and tender fork
    Of a poor worm. Thy best of rest is sleep,
    And that thou oft provok'st, yet grossly fear'st
    Thy death, which is no more. Thou art not thyself,
20   For thou exists on many a thousand grains
    That issue out of dust. Happy thou art not,
    For what thou hast not, still thou striv'st to get,
    And what thou hast, forget'st. Thou art not certain,
    For thy complexion shifts to strange effects
25   After the moon. If thou art rich, thou'rt poor,
    For like an ass, whose back with ingots bows,
    Thou bear'st thy heavy riches but a journey,
    And death unloads thee. Friend hast thou none,
    For thine own bowels which do call thee sire,
30   The mere effusion of thy proper loins,
    Do curse the gout, serpigo and the rheum
    For ending thee no sooner. Thou hast nor youth, nor age,

3.1 **5 absolute** resolved **9 Servile** subject/obedient **skyey influences** planetary/
meteorological influences **10 habitation** world/dwelling/body **keep'st** reside **11 Merely**
entirely **fool** plaything/dupe **12 For . . . still** you strive to flee death and yet are always
running toward it **14 accommodations** civilized comforts/clothing **15 Are . . . baseness**
spring from lowly origins **16 fork** forked tongue **17 worm** snake **of rest** way to rest
18 provok'st summon **grossly** excessively/foolishly **19 no more** i.e. than sleep
21 issue . . . dust grow from the earth **23 certain** consistent **24 complexion** disposition
strange new/unusual **25 After** in accordance with/in imitation of **26 ingots** gold bars
29 bowels i.e. children **sire** father **30 mere effusion** very product **proper** own
31 serpigo spreading skin disease **rheum** catarrh/head cold **32 nor** neither

But as it were an after-dinner's sleep
Dreaming on both, for all thy blessèd youth
35 Becomes as agèd, and doth beg the alms
Of palsied eld. And when thou art old and rich,
Thou hast neither heat, affection, limb, nor beauty
To make thy riches pleasant. What's yet in this
That bears the name of life? Yet in this life
40 Lie hid more thousand deaths; yet death we fear,
That makes these odds all even.

CLAUDIO   I humbly thank you.
To sue to live, I find I seek to die,
And, seeking death, find life. Let it come on.

45 ISABELLA   What, ho! Peace here, grace and good   *Within*
company.

PROVOST   Who's there? Come in. The wish deserves a welcome.

DUKE   Dear sir, ere long I'll visit you again.   *To Claudio*

CLAUDIO   Most holy sir, I thank you.

Enter Isabella

50 ISABELLA   My business is a word or two with Claudio.

PROVOST   And very welcome. Look, signior, here's your sister.

DUKE   Provost, a word with you.   *Duke and Provost talk apart*

PROVOST   As many as you please.

DUKE   Bring me to hear them speak, where I may be
55 concealed.   *Provost and Duke withdraw and hide themselves*

CLAUDIO   Now, sister, what's the comfort?   *Provost may exit*

ISABELLA   Why,
As all comforts are: most good, most good indeed.
Lord Angelo, having affairs to heaven,
60 Intends you for his swift ambassador,
Where you shall be an everlasting leiger;

---

33 **after-dinner's** i.e. early afternoon   35 **as agèd** i.e. like an elderly beggar   **alms Of** money
from   36 **palsied eld** old age, afflicted by palsy (disease characterized by trembling)
37 **heat, affection, limb** passion, love, agility   39 **bears . . . of** is worthy of being called
41 **makes . . . even** i.e. levels all differences   43 **To sue** in pleading   44 **it** i.e. death   47 **wish**
i.e. of peace, grace and good company   59 **affairs to** business with   61 **leiger** resident
ambassador

Therefore your best appointment make with speed,
Tomorrow you set on.

CLAUDIO   Is there no remedy?

65 ISABELLA   None, but such remedy as, to save a head,
To cleave a heart in twain.

CLAUDIO   But is there any?

ISABELLA   Yes, brother, you may live;
There is a devilish mercy in the judge,
70   If you'll implore it, that will free your life,
But fetter you till death.

CLAUDIO   Perpetual durance?

ISABELLA   Ay, just, perpetual durance, a restraint,
Though all the world's vastidity you had,
75   To a determined scope.

CLAUDIO   But in what nature?

ISABELLA   In such a one as, you consenting to't,
Would bark your honour from that trunk you bear,
And leave you naked.

80 CLAUDIO   Let me know the point.

ISABELLA   O, I do fear thee, Claudio, and I quake,
Lest thou a feverous life shouldst entertain,
And six or seven winters more respect
Than a perpetual honour. Dar'st thou die?
85   The sense of death is most in apprehension,
And the poor beetle that we tread upon
In corporal sufferance finds a pang as great
As when a giant dies.

CLAUDIO   Why give you me this shame?

90   Think you I can a resolution fetch

---

62 **appointment** preparation   63 **set on** begin (your journey)   66 **cleave** split   **twain**
two   71 **fetter** enchain   72 **Perpetual durance** life imprisonment   73 **just** exactly
74 **Though . . . had** even if you had freedom to roam the entire world   **vastidity** vastness
75 **determined scope** limited range   76 **in what nature** of what sort   78 **bark** strip   **trunk**
body/tree trunk   82 **feverous** feverish   **entertain** cherish, harbor   83 **more respect** value
more   85 **sense** fearful awareness   **apprehension** anticipation   87 **corporal sufferance**
physical pain   89 **Why . . . shame?** Why do you dishonor me in this way?   90 **resolution**
strength of purpose   **fetch** derive

From flow'ry tenderness? If I must die,
I will encounter darkness as a bride,
And hug it in mine arms.

ISABELLA   There spake my brother: there my father's grave
95   Did utter forth a voice. Yes, thou must die.
Thou art too noble to conserve a life
In base appliances. This outward-sainted deputy,
Whose settled visage and deliberate word
Nips youth i'th'head and follies doth enew
100   As falcon doth the fowl, is yet a devil:
His filth within being cast, he would appear
A pond as deep as hell.

CLAUDIO   The prenzie Angelo?

ISABELLA   O, 'tis the cunning livery of hell,
105   The damned'st body to invest and cover
In prenzie guards! Dost thou think, Claudio,
If I would yield him my virginity
Thou mightst be freed?

CLAUDIO   O heavens, it cannot be.

110   ISABELLA   Yes, he would give't thee, from this rank offence,
So to offend him still. This night's the time
That I should do what I abhor to name,
Or else thou diest tomorrow.

CLAUDIO   Thou shalt not do't.

115   ISABELLA   O, were it but my life,
I'd throw it down for your deliverance
As frankly as a pin.

CLAUDIO   Thanks, dear Isabel.

---

91 flow'ry tenderness elaborately worded offers of comfort   92 encounter meet/engage with
sexually   97 In base appliances through dishonorable remedies   outward-sainted
seemingly holy   98 settled visage fixed countenance   deliberate carefully considered/
calculating   99 Nips youth i'th'head grasps youth by the neck, like a bird of prey   enew
drive into the water, as a falcon does its victim   101 cast vomited up/cleansed by draining
103 prenzie unclear meaning; possibly an obscure heraldic term (the register of livery, invest,
guards); perhaps a misprint for "precise" (puritanical), "priestly," or "princely" (meant
ironically)   105 invest dress   106 guards trimmings on the front of a rich garment   Dost
thou think would you believe   110 he . . . still in exchange for this foul sin he would give you
the freedom to continue breaking the law   116 deliverance release   117 frankly freely

| | ISABELLA | Be ready, Claudio, for your death tomorrow. |
| 120 | CLAUDIO | Yes. Has he affections in him, |

That thus can make him bite the law by th'nose,
When he would force it? Sure it is no sin,
Or of the deadly seven, it is the least.

ISABELLA   Which is the least?

125   CLAUDIO   If it were damnable, he being so wise,
Why would he for the momentary trick
Be perdurably fined? O Isabel!

ISABELLA   What says my brother?

CLAUDIO   Death is a fearful thing.

130   ISABELLA   And shamèd life a hateful.

CLAUDIO   Ay, but to die, and go we know not where,
To lie in cold obstruction and to rot,
This sensible warm motion to become
A kneaded clod; and the delighted spirit

135   To bathe in fiery floods, or to reside
In thrilling region of thick-ribbèd ice,
To be imprisoned in the viewless winds,
And blown with restless violence round about
The pendent world: or to be worse than worst

140   Of those that lawless and incertain thought
Imagine howling — 'tis too horrible!
The weariest and most loathèd worldly life
That age, ache, penury and imprisonment
Can lay on nature is a paradise

145   To what we fear of death.

ISABELLA   Alas, alas!

CLAUDIO   Sweet sister, let me live.
What sin you do to save a brother's life,

120 affections lust   121 bite . . . th'nose i.e. mock, insult the law   122 force enforce (plays on the sense of "violate")   126 trick trifle/whim/sexual act   127 perdurably fined eternally punished   132 obstruction state of death   133 sensible warm motion feeling, living, body   134 kneaded clod compacted lump of earth   delighted capable of delight   136 thrilling bitterly cold   region separate part of the universe   thick-ribbèd formed into ridges   137 viewless invisible   139 pendent hanging in space   140 lawless and incertain frenzied and uncertain   143 penury poverty   144 nature human nature, powers of endurance   145 To compared to

Nature dispenses with the deed so far
150   That it becomes a virtue.

ISABELLA   O you beast!
O faithless coward! O dishonest wretch!
Wilt thou be made a man out of my vice?
Is't not a kind of incest to take life
155   From thine own sister's shame? What should I think?
Heaven shield my mother played my father fair,
For such a warpèd slip of wilderness
Ne'er issued from his blood. Take my defiance!
Die, perish! Might but my bending down
160   Reprieve thee from thy fate, it should proceed.
I'll pray a thousand prayers for thy death,
No word to save thee.

CLAUDIO   Nay, hear me, Isabel.

ISABELLA   O, fie, fie, fie!
165   Thy sin's not accidental, but a trade.
Mercy to thee would prove itself a bawd,
'Tis best that thou diest quickly.

CLAUDIO   O, hear me, Isabella!   *The Duke comes forward*

DUKE   Vouchsafe a word, young sister, but one word.

170   ISABELLA   What is your will?

DUKE   Might you dispense with your leisure, I would by and by have some speech with you: the satisfaction I would require is likewise your own benefit.

ISABELLA   I have no superfluous leisure, my stay must be stolen
175   out of other affairs, but I will attend you awhile.   *She walks apart*

DUKE   Son, I have overheard what hath passed between you and your sister. Angelo had never the purpose to corrupt

---

149 **Nature** human nature/nature itself   **dispenses** pardons   151 **beast** i.e. creature lacking judgment or compassion   152 **dishonest** shameful   153 **made a man** given life or prosperity   156 **shield** ensure/forbid   **played . . . fair** was faithful   157 **warpèd . . . wilderness** twisted seedling/offspring of licentiousness   158 **defiance** rejection/contempt 159 **but** merely   **bending down** praying (on bended knees)   165 **accidental** a one-off event **trade** habitual practice   166 **prove itself** turn out to be   169 **Vouchsafe** permit 171 **dispense . . . leisure** give up your time   **by and by** soon   172 **satisfaction** recompense 173 **likewise . . . benefit** as much to your advantage as mine   175 **attend** wait for 177 **purpose** intention

her; only he hath made an assay of her virtue to practise his
judgement with the disposition of natures. She, having the
180   truth of honour in her, hath made him that gracious denial
which he is most glad to receive. I am confessor to Angelo,
and I know this to be true. Therefore prepare yourself to
death: do not satisfy your resolution with hopes that are
fallible. Tomorrow you must die, go to your knees and make
185   ready.

CLAUDIO   Let me ask my sister pardon. I am so out of love with
life that I will sue to be rid of it.

DUKE   Hold you there. Farewell.   [*Exit Claudio*]
Provost, a word with you.   *Provost enters or comes forward*

190   PROVOST   What's your will, father?

DUKE   That now you are come, you will be gone. Leave me
awhile with the maid. My mind promises with my habit no
loss shall touch her by my company.

PROVOST   In good time.   *Exit*

Isabella comes forward

195   DUKE   The hand that hath made you fair hath made you
good: the goodness that is cheap in beauty makes beauty
brief in goodness; but grace, being the soul of your
complexion, shall keep the body of it ever fair. The assault
that Angelo hath made to you, fortune hath conveyed to my
200   understanding; and, but that frailty hath examples for his
falling, I should wonder at Angelo. How will you do to
content this substitute, and to save your brother?

ISABELLA   I am now going to resolve him. I had rather my
brother die by the law than my son should be unlawfully
205   born. But, O, how much is the good duke deceived in Angelo!
If ever he return and I can speak to him, I will open my lips
in vain, or discover his government.

---

178 only . . . assay he has merely tested   practise . . . natures test his ability to judge
personality   180 gracious virtuous   182 to for   183 satisfy your resolution maintain your
determination   188 Hold you there preserve that state of mind   192 habit friar's clothing
(that)   193 touch affect, harm   196 goodness . . . goodness if those who are beautiful do
not value virtue, their beauty will not last   197 grace divine virtue   198 complexion
disposition   200 frailty . . . falling there are other comparable examples of such wrongdoing
202 substitute deputy   203 resolve answer   207 discover his government reveal his conduct

DUKE   That shall not be much amiss. Yet, as the matter
now stands, he will avoid your accusation: he made trial of
210   you only. Therefore fasten your ear on my advisings: to the
love I have in doing good a remedy presents itself. I do make
myself believe that you may most uprighteously do a poor
wronged lady a merited benefit, redeem your brother from
the angry law, do no stain to your own gracious person, and
215   much please the absent duke, if peradventure he shall ever
return to have hearing of this business.

ISABELLA   Let me hear you speak further. I have spirit to do
anything that appears not foul in the truth of my spirit.

DUKE   Virtue is bold, and goodness never fearful. Have you
220   not heard speak of Mariana, the sister of Frederick, the great
soldier who miscarried at sea?

ISABELLA   I have heard of the lady, and good words went with
her name.

DUKE   She should this Angelo have married, was affianced
225   to her by oath, and the nuptial appointed: between which
time of the contract and limit of the solemnity, her brother
Frederick was wrecked at sea, having in that perished vessel
the dowry of his sister. But mark how heavily this befell to
the poor gentlewoman: there she lost a noble and renowned
230   brother, in his love toward her ever most kind and natural:
with him, the portion and sinew of her fortune, her
marriage-dowry: with both, her combinate husband, this
well-seeming Angelo.

ISABELLA   Can this be so? Did Angelo so leave her?

235   DUKE   Left her in her tears, and dried not one of them with
his comfort, swallowed his vows whole, pretending in her
discoveries of dishonour: in few, bestowed her on her own

---

209 avoid refute   210 advisings advice   211 I . . . believe I am convinced   212 uprighteously
uprightly, righteously   213 merited worthy/deserved   215 peradventure perhaps
217 spirit courage   218 spirit soul   221 miscarried had an accident/died/went missing
224 affianced betrothed   225 nuptial appointed wedding arranged   226 contract
engagement   limit . . . solemnity appointed time of the ceremony   228 heavily grievously
befell to fell out for/affected   230 natural brotherly   231 sinew mainstay   232 combinate
betrothed   237 dishonour sexual misconduct   few short   bestowed . . . lamentation
married her to her own grief

lamentation, which she yet wears for his sake: and he, a
marble to her tears, is washed with them, but relents not.

240 ISABELLA   What a merit were it in death to take this poor maid
from the world? What corruption in this life that it will let
this man live! But how out of this can she avail?

DUKE   It is a rupture that you may easily heal, and the cure
of it not only saves your brother, but keeps you from
245 dishonour in doing it.

ISABELLA   Show me how, good father.

DUKE   This forenamed maid hath yet in her the
continuance of her first affection: his unjust unkindness —
that in all reason should have quenched her love — hath,
250 like an impediment in the current, made it more violent and
unruly. Go you to Angelo, answer his requiring with a
plausible obedience, agree with his demands to the point.
Only refer yourself to this advantage: first, that your stay
with him may not be long, that the time may have all
255 shadow and silence in it, and the place answer to
convenience. This being granted in course, and now
follows all: we shall advise this wronged maid to stead up
your appointment, go in your place. If the encounter
acknowledge itself hereafter, it may compel him to her
260 recompense; and here, by this is your brother saved, your
honour untainted, the poor Mariana advantaged, and the
corrupt deputy scaled. The maid will I frame and make fit for
his attempt. If you think well to carry this as you may, the
doubleness of the benefit defends the deceit from reproof.
265 What think you of it?

ISABELLA   The image of it gives me content already, and I trust
it will grow to a most prosperous perfection.

---

238 yet still   242 avail benefit   248 continuance . . . affection i.e. still loves Angelo
250 impediment . . . current obstacle in the flow of a river   251 requiring request
252 plausible believable/ingratiating   to the point to the letter   253 refer . . . advantage ask
for these advantageous conditions   255 answer to convenience be opportune/suit your
convenience   256 course due course   257 stead up carry out   258 encounter meeting/
sexual interaction   259 acknowledge reveals   her recompense redress   262 scaled
weighed up   frame prepare   fit ready   263 carry manage   264 doubleness two-fold
nature   reproof blame   266 image idea   267 perfection completion

DUKE   It lies much in your holding up. Haste you speedily
to Angelo: if for this night he entreat you to his bed, give him
270   promise of satisfaction. I will presently to Saint Luke's, there
at the moated grange resides this dejected Mariana. At that
place call upon me, and dispatch with Angelo, that it may be
quickly.

ISABELLA   I thank you for this comfort. Fare you well, good
275   father.   *Exit*

Enter Elbow [and] Officers [with Pompey, the] Clown

ELBOW   Nay, if there be no remedy for it, but that you will
needs buy and sell men and women like beasts, we shall have
all the world drink brown and white bastard.

DUKE   O heavens, what stuff is here?

280   POMPEY   'Twas never merry world since of two usuries the
merriest was put down, and the worser allowed by order of
law a furred gown to keep him warm; and furred with fox
and lamb-skins too, to signify that craft, being richer than
innocency, stands for the facing.

285   ELBOW   Come your way, sir. Bless you, good father friar.

DUKE   And you, good brother father. What offence hath
this man made you, sir?

ELBOW   Marry, sir, he hath offended the law; and, sir, we
take him to be a thief too, sir, for we have found upon him,
290   sir, a strange picklock, which we have sent to the deputy.

DUKE   Fie, sirrah, a bawd, a wicked bawd!
The evil that thou causest to be done,
That is thy means to live. Do thou but think
What 'tis to cram a maw or clothe a back
295   From such a filthy vice. Say to thyself,

---

268 **holding up** ability to maintain it   271 **moated grange** farmhouse surrounded by a moat
272 **dispatch** make arrangements   278 **brown . . . bastard** sweet Spanish wine (plays on
the sense of "illegitimate mixed-race children")   279 **stuff** nonsense   280 **'Twas . . . since**
the world is not as enjoyable since   **two usuries** i.e. money lending and prostitution
281 **merriest** most enjoyable (prostitution)   282 **fox** fox fur (with connotations of cunning)
283 **craft** deceit   284 **stands . . . facing** trims the outside of the garment/puts itself on show
to the world   286 **brother father** "friar" means "brother," so the duke is making fun of
Elbow's terms of address   290 **picklock** device for picking locks (here, those of chastity belts)
291 **sirrah** sir (contemptuous)   294 **maw** gullet/stomach

From their abominable and beastly touches
I drink, I eat, array myself, and live.
Canst thou believe thy living is a life,
So stinkingly depending? Go mend, go mend.

300 POMPEY   Indeed, it does stink in some sort, sir, but yet, sir, I
would prove—

DUKE   Nay, if the devil have given thee proofs for sin,
Thou wilt prove his. Take him to prison, officer:
Correction and instruction must both work

305 Ere this rude beast will profit.

ELBOW   He must before the deputy, sir, he has given him
warning. The deputy cannot abide a whoremaster. If he be a
whoremonger, and comes before him, he were as good go a
mile on his errand.

310 DUKE   That we were all, as some would seem to be,
Free from our faults, as faults from seeming free!

Enter Lucio

ELBOW   His neck will come to your waist — a cord, sir.

POMPEY   I spy comfort, I cry bail. Here's a gentleman and a
friend of mine.

315 LUCIO   How now, noble Pompey? What, at the wheels of
Caesar? Art thou led in triumph? What, is there none of
Pygmalion's images, newly made woman, to be had now, for
putting the hand in the pocket and extracting clutched?
What reply, ha? What sayest thou to this tune, matter and
320 method? Is't not drowned i'th'last rain, ha? What sayest

---

297 **array** dress   299 **So stinkingly depending** supported by such foulness   **mend** reform
your ways   300 **sort** way   302 **proofs** evidence   304 **Correction** punishment   305 **rude**
barbarous   306 **before** go before   308 **he . . . errand** i.e. he would be better doing anything
else than that   310 **That** if only   311 **Free . . . free** free from sin (as Angelo appears to be)
and sin free from hypocrisy   312 **come to resemble**   **cord** rope (Elbow imagines the noose
being like the cord that friars wore around the **waist**)   313 **cry** call out for   316 **led in**
triumph paraded in disgrace (in ancient Rome, following a triumph in war, prisoners were led
behind the chariots of the victors)   317 **Pygmalion** a sculptor and king of Cyprus, he fell in
love with an ivory statue he had made of his ideal woman   318 **putting . . . clutched** i.e. to be
had for money   **clutched** with a fist grasping money   320 **Is't . . . rain** i.e. lost (referring
either to the old way of life or to Pompey's **reply**)

thou, Trot? Is the world as it was, man? Which is the way? Is
it sad, and few words? Or how? The trick of it?

DUKE   Still thus, and thus, still worse!

LUCIO   How doth my dear morsel, thy mistress? Procures
325   she still, ha?

POMPEY   Troth, sir, she hath eaten up all her beef, and she is
herself in the tub.

LUCIO   Why, 'tis good: it is the right of it, it must be so. Ever
your fresh whore and your powdered bawd, an unshunned
330   consequence, it must be so. Art going to prison, Pompey?

POMPEY   Yes, faith, sir.

LUCIO   Why, 'tis not amiss, Pompey. Farewell: go, say I sent
thee thither. For debt, Pompey? Or how?

ELBOW   For being a bawd, for being a bawd.

335   LUCIO   Well, then, imprison him. If imprisonment be the
due of a bawd, why, 'tis his right. Bawd is he doubtless, and of
antiquity too, bawd-born. Farewell, good Pompey. Commend
me to the prison, Pompey: you will turn good husband now,
Pompey, you will keep the house.

340   POMPEY   I hope, sir, your good worship will be my bail.

LUCIO   No, indeed, will I not, Pompey, it is not the wear. I
will pray, Pompey, to increase your bondage. If you take it
not patiently, why, your mettle is the more. Adieu, trusty
Pompey.— Bless you, friar.

345   DUKE   And you.

LUCIO   Does Bridget paint still, Pompey, ha?

ELBOW   Come your ways, sir, come.

POMPEY   You will not bail me, then, sir?   *To Lucio*

---

321 **Trot** old hag, bawd   **way** response/fashion   322 **sad . . . words** i.e. dejected   **trick**
manner   323 **thus, and thus** more and more/the same (nonsense)   324 **morsel** mouthful,
tidbit   326 **Troth** in truth   **eaten . . . beef** exhausted her supply of prostitutes/eaten all the
supplies of salt beef   327 **tub** sweating-tub used to treat venereal disease/pickling tub for
curing beef   328 **right of it** the logical thing   329 **powdered** salted/heavily made-up
unshunned unavoidable   332 **amiss** wrong   336 **due** penalty   **of antiquity** of old
337 **bawd-born** son of a bawd/born to be a bawd   338 **husband** housekeeper   341 **wear**
fashion   342 **bondage** imprisonment   343 **mettle** spirit (plays on the idea of the metal
chains used to fetter prisoners)   346 **paint** wear makeup

LUCIO   Then, Pompey, nor now. What news abroad, friar?
350   What news?

ELBOW   Come your ways, sir, come.

LUCIO   Go to kennel, Pompey, go.

                        [*Exeunt Elbow, Pompey and Officers*]

What news, friar, of the duke?

DUKE   I know none. Can you tell me of any?

355   LUCIO   Some say he is with the Emperor of Russia. Other
            some, he is in Rome. But where is he, think you?

DUKE   I know not where: but wheresoever, I wish him well.

LUCIO   It was a mad fantastical trick of him to steal from
            the state, and usurp the beggary he was never born to. Lord
360   Angelo dukes it well in his absence: he puts transgression to't.

DUKE   He does well in't.

LUCIO   A little more lenity to lechery would do no harm in
            him: something too crabbed that way, friar.

DUKE   It is too general a vice, and severity must cure it.

365   LUCIO   Yes, in good sooth, the vice is of a great kindred; it is
            well allied, but it is impossible to extirp it quite, friar, till
            eating and drinking be put down. They say this Angelo was
            not made by man and woman after this downright way of
            creation. Is it true, think you?

370   DUKE   How should he be made, then?

LUCIO   Some report a sea-maid spawned him. Some, that
            he was begot between two stock-fishes. But it is certain that
            when he makes water his urine is congealed ice, that I know
            to be true: and he is a motion generative, that's infallible.

375   DUKE   You are pleasant, sir, and speak apace.

---

349 **abroad** in the world   352 **kennel** doghouse/gutter   355 **Other some** others
358 **fantastical trick** fanciful whim   **steal** steal away   359 **usurp the beggary** take on a
baseness   360 **puts transgression to't** i.e. punishes wrongdoers   362 **lenity** lenience
363 **crabbed** severe/harsh   364 **general** widespread   365 **sooth** truth   **great kindred** large
family   366 **allied** connected   **extirp** eliminate   367 **put down** stopped   368 **downright**
straightforward   371 **sea-maid** mermaid   372 **stock-fishes** dried cod (plays on sense of
"impotent penis")   373 **makes water** urinates   374 **motion generative** sexless puppet
infallible certain   375 **pleasant** humorous/facetious   **apace** rapidly/idly

LUCIO   Why, what a ruthless thing is this in him, for the
rebellion of a codpiece to take away the life of a man. Would
the duke that is absent have done this? Ere he would have
hanged a man for the getting a hundred bastards, he would
380   have paid for the nursing a thousand. He had some feeling of
the sport, he knew the service, and that instructed him to
mercy.

DUKE   I never heard the absent duke much detected for
women, he was not inclined that way.

385   LUCIO   O sir, you are deceived.

DUKE   'Tis not possible.

LUCIO   Who, not the duke? Yes, your beggar of fifty, and
his use was to put a ducat in her clack-dish; the duke had
crotchets in him. He would be drunk too, that let me
390   inform you.

DUKE   You do him wrong, surely.

LUCIO   Sir, I was an inward of his. A shy fellow was the
duke, and I believe I know the cause of his withdrawing.

DUKE   What, I prithee, might be the cause?

395   LUCIO   No, pardon. 'Tis a secret must be locked within the
teeth and the lips: but this I can let you understand, the
greater file of the subject held the duke to be wise.

DUKE   Wise? Why, no question but he was.

LUCIO   A very superficial, ignorant, unweighing fellow.

400   DUKE   Either this is the envy in you, folly, or mistaking: the
very stream of his life and the business he hath helmed must
upon a warranted need give him a better proclamation. Let
him be but testimonied in his own bringings-forth, and he
shall appear to the envious a scholar, a statesman and a

---

377 **codpiece** cloth appendage worn by men at the front of the breeches (euphemism for
"penis")   379 **getting** conception   380 **a** of a   **feeling** understanding   381 **sport** i.e. sex
service i.e. sexual business   383 **detected for women** accused of lechery   387 **beggar of
fifty** fifty-year-old beggar-woman   388 **use** habit/sexual practice   **ducat** gold coin   **clack-
dish** beggar's pot/vagina   389 **crotchets** fanciful notions   392 **inward** intimate friend
393 **withdrawing** sudden departure   397 **greater . . . subject** majority of his subjects
399 **unweighing** undiscriminating   400 **envy** malice   401 **helmed** steered   402 **warranted
need** justified necessity   **proclamation** reputation   403 **testimonied** judged   **bringings-
forth** achievements

405   soldier: therefore you speak unskilfully, or, if your knowledge
be more, it is much darkened in your malice.

LUCIO   Sir, I know him, and I love him.

DUKE   Love talks with better knowledge, and knowledge
with dearer love.

410 LUCIO   Come, sir, I know what I know.

DUKE   I can hardly believe that, since you know not what
you speak. But if ever the duke return — as our prayers are he
may — let me desire you to make your answer before him. If
it be honest you have spoke, you have courage to maintain it;

415   I am bound to call upon you — and, I pray you, your name?

LUCIO   Sir, my name is Lucio, well known to the duke.

DUKE   He shall know you better, sir, if I may live to report
you.

LUCIO   I fear you not.

420 DUKE   O, you hope the duke will return no more, or you
imagine me too unhurtful an opposite. But indeed I can do
you little harm. You'll forswear this again?

LUCIO   I'll be hanged first. Thou art deceived in me, friar. But
no more of this. Canst thou tell if Claudio die tomorrow or no?

425 DUKE   Why should he die, sir?

LUCIO   Why? For filling a bottle with a tundish. I would the
duke we talk of were returned again. This ungenitured agent
will unpeople the province with continency. Sparrows must
not build in his house-eaves, because they are lecherous. The

430   duke yet would have dark deeds darkly answered, he would
never bring them to light. Would he were returned! Marry,
this Claudio is condemned for untrussing. Farewell, good

---

405 **unskilfully** without justification/ignorantly   408 **Love . . . love** if you loved him you
would know him better, and if you knew him better you would love him more   413 **make
your answer** justify your comments   414 **maintain** defend   421 **unhurtful an opposite** weak
an adversary   422 **forswear** deny   **again** on another occasion   426 **filling . . . tundish** i.e.
having sex   **tundish** funnel with a long stem (i.e. penis)   427 **ungenitured** sexless/impotent
agent deputy, substitute   428 **unpeople** depopulate   **continency** sexual abstinence
Sparrows . . . lecherous sparrows were sacred to Venus and proverbially lascivious   430 **dark
deeds** secret sexual acts   **darkly answered** privately dealt with   432 **untrussing** undressing
(specifically, untying hose from doublet)

friar. I prithee, pray for me. The duke, I say to thee again,
would eat mutton on Fridays. He's now past it, yet and I say to
435   thee, he would mouth with a beggar, though she smelt brown
bread and garlic. Say that I said so. Farewell.   *Exit*

DUKE   No might nor greatness in mortality
Can censure 'scape. Back-wounding calumny
The whitest virtue strikes. What king so strong
440   Can tie the gall up in the sland'rous tongue?
But who comes here?

Enter Escalus, Provost and [Officers with] Bawd [Mistress Overdone]

ESCALUS   Go, away with her to prison.

MISTRESS OVERDONE   Good my lord, be good to me: your honour
is accounted a merciful man, good my lord.

445   ESCALUS   Double and treble admonition, and still forfeit in
the same kind? This would make mercy swear and play the
tyrant.

PROVOST   A bawd of eleven years' continuance, may it please
your honour.

450   MISTRESS OVERDONE   My lord, this is one Lucio's information
against me. Mistress Kate Keepdown was with child by him
in the duke's time, he promised her marriage. His child is a
year and a quarter old come Philip and Jacob. I have kept it
myself; and see how he goes about to abuse me!

455   ESCALUS   That fellow is a fellow of much licence. Let him be
called before us. Away with her to prison. Go to, no more
words.   [*Exeunt Officers with Mistress Overdone*]
Provost, my brother Angelo will not be altered: Claudio must
die tomorrow. Let him be furnished with divines, and have

---

434 mutton on Fridays i.e. break the ecclesiastical laws that forbade the eating of meat on
Fridays (**mutton** puns on the sense of "prostitute")   **435 mouth with** kiss   **brown bread**
coarse rye bread   **438 censure 'scape** escape condemnation   **440 gall** bile   **445 Double . . .
kind?** (You have been) warned two or three times and still continue to do wrong?
446 swear . . . tyrant become so exasperated that it would become pitiless   **450 information**
official legal complaint   **451 Keepdown** the name may imply sexual appetite and "lying
down"   **452 duke's time** under the rule of the duke   **453 Philip and Jacob** May 1, the day of
Saint Philip and Saint James   **455 licence** immorality/lechery   **458 brother** colleague
459 divines clergymen

460   all charitable preparation. If my brother wrought by my pity,
       it should not be so with him.

PROVOST   So please you, this friar hath been with him, and
       advised him for th'entertainment of death.

ESCALUS   Good even, good father.

465 DUKE   Bliss and goodness on you!

ESCALUS   Of whence are you?

DUKE   Not of this country, though my chance is now
       To use it for my time. I am a brother
       Of gracious order, late come from the See

470   In special business from his holiness.

ESCALUS   What news abroad i'th'world?

DUKE   None, but that there is so great a fever on goodness
       that the dissolution of it must cure it. Novelty is only in
       request, and it is as dangerous to be aged in any kind of

475   course as it is virtuous to be constant in any undertaking.
       There is scarce truth enough alive to make societies secure,
       but security enough to make fellowships accurst. Much
       upon this riddle runs the wisdom of the world. This news is
       old enough, yet it is every day's news. I pray you, sir, of what

480   disposition was the duke?

ESCALUS   One that, above all other strifes, contended especially
       to know himself.

DUKE   What pleasure was he given to?

ESCALUS   Rather rejoicing to see another merry than merry

485   at anything which professed to make him rejoice. A
       gentleman of all temperance. But leave we him to his events,
       with a prayer they may prove prosperous, and let me desire

---

460 **wrought . . . pity** acted with the same amount of pity I feel   463 **entertainment** reception
466 **whence are you** where are you from   467 **chance** situation   468 **my time** the time
being   469 **See** Holy See, Rome   471 **abroad** out   472 **so . . . it** (goodness) is so sick with
worldly ills that it can only cure itself by dying   473 **in request** (exists only when it is) in
demand/fashionable   474 **aged** consistent   475 **course** course of action/mode of behavior
476 **societies** associations between people   477 **security** overconfidence (plays on sense of
"financial pledge guaranteeing a loan") · **fellowships** partnerships (plays on sense of "trading
corporations")   481 **strifes** objectives/endeavors   483 **pleasure** enjoyments   486 **events**
activities

to know how you find Claudio prepared. I am made to understand that you have lent him visitation.

490 **DUKE**   He professes to have received no sinister measure from his judge, but most willingly humbles himself to the determination of justice: yet had he framed to himself, by the instruction of his frailty, many deceiving promises of life, which I by my good leisure have discredited to him, and now
500 is he resolved to die.

ESCALUS   You have paid the heavens your function, and the prisoner the very debt of your calling. I have laboured for the poor gentleman to the extremest shore of my modesty, but my brother justice have I found so severe that he hath forced
505 me to tell him he is indeed Justice.

DUKE   If his own life answer the straitness of his proceeding, it shall become him well: wherein if he chance to fail, he hath sentenced himself.

ESCALUS   I am going to visit the prisoner. Fare you well.

510 **DUKE**   Peace be with you.   [*Exeunt Escalus and Provost*]
He who the sword of heaven will bear
Should be as holy as severe:
Pattern in himself to know,
Grace to stand, and virtue go,
515 More nor less to others paying
Than by self-offences weighing.
Shame to him whose cruel striking
Kills for faults of his own liking.
Twice treble shame on Angelo,
520 To weed my vice and let his grow!
O, what may man within him hide,

---

489 **lent him visitation** paid him a visit   490 **sinister measure** unfair treatment
492 **determination** resolution, decision   **framed to** devised for   493 **instruction** prompting
494 **good leisure** own time   **discredited** shown to be false   501 **You . . . calling** you have
fulfilled your divine duties to both God and the prisoner   503 **extremest . . . modesty** limits of
my abilities   505 **indeed Justice** Justice itself   506 **straitness** severity   511 **sword of
heaven** emblem of religious/legal authority   513 **Pattern . . . know** be himself a model of
virtue   514 **Grace to stand** support himself with grace   **virtue go** conduct himself with
virtue   515 **More . . . weighing** administering no more or less justice to himself than he
would to others   520 **weed** weed out

Though angel on the outward side!
How may likeness made in crimes,
Making practice on the times,
525   To draw with idle spiders' strings
Most pond'rous and substantial things!
Craft against vice I must apply.
With Angelo tonight shall lie
His old betrothèd but despised,
530   So disguise shall, by th'disguised,
Pay with falsehood false exacting,
And perform an old contracting.   *Exit*

Act 4 Scene 1   *running scene 9*

Enter Mariana and [a] Boy, singing

BOY   Take, O, take those lips away,
That so sweetly were forsworn,
And those eyes, the break of day,
Lights that do mislead the morn;
5   But my kisses bring again, bring again,
Seals of love, but sealed in vain, sealed in vain.

Enter Duke [disguised as before]

MARIANA   Break off thy song, and haste thee quick away:
Here comes a man of comfort, whose advice
Hath often stilled my brawling discontent.   *[Exit Boy]*
10   I cry you mercy, sir, and well could wish
You had not found me here so musical.
Let me excuse me, and believe me so,
My mirth it much displeased, but pleased my woe.

---

523 **likeness . . . crimes** seemingly virtuous behavior founded on sin   524 **Making practice**
practice deception   525 **draw . . . things** pretend to catch big things, but with merely
insubstantial means   527 **Craft** cunning, skill   529 **old betrothèd** ex-fiancée (Mariana)
despised scorned   530 **disguise** deception   **th'disguised** the disguised Mariana
531 **Pay . . . exacting** repay with deception the wrongful demands (made on Isabella)
532 **contracting** marriage contract   **4.1** *Location: outside Vienna*   2 **forsworn** perjured,
false   3 **the . . . day** like the dawn   9 **stilled** quieted   **brawling** clamorous   10 **cry you
mercy** beg your pardon   13 **My . . . woe** my music does not mean I am merry but it soothed
my grief

DUKE 'Tis good; though music oft hath such a charm
15 To make bad good, and good provoke to harm.
I pray you tell me, hath anybody inquired for me here today?
Much upon this time have I promised here to meet.

MARIANA You have not been inquired after: I have sat here
all day.

Enter Isabella

20 DUKE I do constantly believe you. The time is come even
now. I shall crave your forbearance a little, maybe I will call
upon you anon for some advantage to yourself.

MARIANA I am always bound to you.   *Exit*

DUKE Very well met, and well come.
25 What is the news from this good deputy?

ISABELLA He hath a garden circummured with brick,
Whose western side is with a vineyard backed,
And to that vineyard is a planchèd gate
That makes his opening with this bigger key.   *Shows keys*
30 This other doth command a little door,
Which from the vineyard to the garden leads.
There have I made my promise, upon the
Heavy middle of the night to call upon him.

DUKE But shall you on your knowledge find this way?

35 ISABELLA I have ta'en a due and wary note upon't:
With whispering and most guilty diligence,
In action all of precept, he did show me
The way twice o'er.

DUKE Are there no other tokens
40 Between you 'greed concerning her observance?

ISABELLA No, none, but only a repair i'th'dark,
And that I have possessed him my most stay

---

14 **charm** magical ability   17 **Much upon** at about this   20 **constantly** entirely
21 **forbearance** patience/absence   22 **anon** immediately afterward/in a while   24 **well met**
perfect timing   **well come** welcome   26 **circummured** walled around   28 **planchèd** made
of planks   29 **makes his opening** opens   30 **command** unlock   33 **Heavy** dark/
sleepy   34 **on your knowledge** with the information you have   35 **due** careful/adequate
wary cautious   37 **action ... precept** verbal directions   39 **tokens** signals   40 **'greed**
agreed   **her observance** particulars she must adhere to   41 **repair** visit   42 **possessed**
informed   **most** longest

Can be but brief, for I have made him know
I have a servant comes with me along,
45   That stays upon me, whose persuasion is
I come about my brother.

DUKE   'Tis well borne up.
I have not yet made known to Mariana
A word of this.— What ho, within! Come forth!

Enter Mariana

50   I pray you be acquainted with this maid,
She comes to do you good.

ISABELLA   I do desire the like.

DUKE   Do you persuade yourself that I respect you?

MARIANA   Good friar, I know you do, and have found it.

55   DUKE   Take, then, this your companion by the hand,
Who hath a story ready for your ear.
I shall attend your leisure, but make haste,
The vaporous night approaches.

MARIANA   Will't please you walk aside?

Exit [Mariana with Isabella]

60   DUKE   O place and greatness! Millions of false eyes
Are stuck upon thee: volumes of report
Run with these false and most contrarious quests
Upon thy doings, thousand escapes of wit
Make thee the father of their idle dream
65   And rack thee in their fancies.

Enter Mariana and Isabella

Welcome, how agreed?

ISABELLA   She'll take the enterprise upon her, father,
If you advise it.

DUKE   It is not my consent,
70   But my entreaty too.

---

45 stays upon attends   persuasion belief   47 borne up sustained, managed   52 like same
54 have found it have experience of it   57 attend your leisure wait for you until you are ready
60 place status, position   false treacherous   61 stuck fixed   report rumor   62 quests . . .
doings inquiries into your business   63 escapes outbursts   64 father . . . dream source of
their delusion   65 rack torment/distort   fancies imaginations   69 It . . . too I not only
agree to it, but beg you to do it

ISABELLA   Little have you to say

       When you depart from him, but, soft and low,

       'Remember now my brother.'

MARIANA   Fear me not.

75   DUKE   Nor, gentle daughter, fear you not at all.

       He is your husband on a pre-contract:

       To bring you thus together 'tis no sin,

       Sith that the justice of your title to him

       Doth flourish the deceit. Come, let us go:

80   Our corn's to reap, for yet our tithe's to sow.   *Exeunt*

Act 4 Scene 2   *running scene 10*

Enter Provost and Clown [Pompey]

PROVOST   Come hither, sirrah. Can you cut off a man's head?

POMPEY   If the man be a bachelor, sir, I can. But if he be a
       married man, he's his wife's head, and I can never cut off a
       woman's head.

5   PROVOST   Come, sir, leave me your snatches, and yield me a
       direct answer. Tomorrow morning are to die Claudio and
       Barnardine. Here is in our prison a common executioner, who
       in his office lacks a helper: if you will take it on you to assist
       him, it shall redeem you from your gyves: if not, you shall have
10   your full time of imprisonment and your deliverance with an
       unpitied whipping, for you have been a notorious bawd.

POMPEY   Sir, I have been an unlawful bawd time out of mind,
       but yet I will be content to be a lawful hangman. I would be
       glad to receive some instruction from my fellow partner.

---

71 **Little . . . say** say little   76 **pre-contract** betrothal, a binding contract   78 **Sith** since
title claim   79 **flourish** adorn, render attractive   80 **Our . . . sow** we have yet to reap the
harvest for we have not sown the seed   **tithe** a tenth of the crop, due to the Church (some
editors emend to "tilth," plowed field)   **4.2**   *Location: Vienna*   3 **head** master (the
sense then shifts to pun on "maidenhead"—i.e. virginity)   5 **leave . . . snatches** leave out
your quibbles   7 **common** public   9 **redeem** release   **gyves** shackles, ankle fetters
10 **deliverance** release   11 **unpitied** relentless, merciless   12 **time . . . mind** for longer than I
can remember

15   PROVOST   What, ho, Abhorson! Where's Abhorson there?

Enter Abhorson

    ABHORSON   Do you call, sir?

    PROVOST   Sirrah, here's a fellow will help you tomorrow in
your execution. If you think it meet, compound with him by
the year, and let him abide here with you. If not, use him for
20   the present and dismiss him. He cannot plead his estimation
with you: he hath been a bawd.

    ABHORSON   A bawd, sir? Fie upon him, he will discredit our
mystery.

    PROVOST   Go to, sir, you weigh equally: a feather will turn the
25   scale.   *Exit*

    POMPEY   Pray, sir, by your good favour — for surely, sir, a
good favour you have, but that you have a hanging look —
do you call, sir, your occupation a mystery?

    ABHORSON   Ay, sir, a mystery.

30   POMPEY   Painting, sir, I have heard say, is a mystery; and
your whores, sir, being members of my occupation, using
painting, do prove my occupation a mystery. But what
mystery there should be in hanging, if I should be hanged, I
cannot imagine.

35   ABHORSON   Sir, it is a mystery.

    POMPEY   Proof?

    ABHORSON   Every true man's apparel fits your thief—

    POMPEY   If it be too little for your thief, your true man thinks
it big enough. If it be too big for your thief, your thief thinks
40   it little enough. So every true man's apparel fits your thief.

Enter Provost

    PROVOST   Are you agreed?

---

15 **Abhorson** a conflation of "abhor" and "whoreson" (son of a whore), with connotations of
"abortion" (i.e. monstrosity)   18 **meet** fitting   **compound . . . year** agree on an annual sum
19 **abide** remain   20 **plead his estimation** argue he is superior to the job   23 **mystery** craft,
profession   24 **weigh equally** are worth the same   26 **favour** permission (sense then shifts to
"face")   27 **hanging look** downcast expression/the look of a hangman or of someone
destined for hanging   28 **mystery** Pompey responds to the sense of "art, skill"   30 **Painting**
art/cosmetics   37 **true** honest   39 **big** large/valuable   40 **little** small/worthless

POMPEY   Sir, I will serve him, for I do find your hangman is a
more penitent trade than your bawd: he doth oftener ask
forgiveness.

45   PROVOST   You, sirrah, provide your block and your axe
tomorrow, four o'clock.

ABHORSON   Come on, bawd, I will instruct thee in my trade.
Follow.

POMPEY   I do desire to learn, sir, and I hope, if you have
50   occasion to use me for your own turn, you shall find me yare.
For truly, sir, for your kindness I owe you a good turn.

[Exeunt Pompey and Abhorson]

PROVOST   Call hither Barnardine and Claudio.
The one has my pity; not a jot the other,
Being a murderer, though he were my brother.

Enter Claudio

55   Look, here's the warrant, Claudio, for thy death.   *Shows warrant*
'Tis now dead midnight, and by eight tomorrow
Thou must be made immortal. Where's Barnardine?

CLAUDIO   As fast locked up in sleep as guiltless labour
When it lies starkly in the traveller's bones.

60   He will not wake.

PROVOST   Who can do good on him?
Well, go, prepare yourself. But hark, what noise?   *Knocking within*
Heaven give your spirits comfort.— By and by.   *[Exit Claudio]*
I hope it is some pardon or reprieve

65   For the most gentle Claudio.

Enter Duke [disguised as before]

Welcome father.

DUKE   The best and wholesom'st spirits of the night
Envelop you, good provost. Who called here of late?

PROVOST   None, since the curfew rung.

---

43 **penitent** repentant   **he . . . forgiveness** the executioner would ask the condemned person
for forgiveness   50 **turn** purpose/hanging   **yare** quick, ready   51 **good turn** favor/skillful
execution (perhaps, given Pompey is a bawd, with play on the sexual sense)   54 **though** even if
58 **guiltless labour** innocent toil   59 **starkly** stiffly   **traveller's** laborer's ("travailer's")   61 **do
good on** improve   69 **curfew** in London, the curfew bell was rung at dusk in the winter and
9 p.m. in the summer to call all persons in until dawn the next day

70	DUKE	Not Isabel?
	PROVOST	No.
	DUKE	They will, then, ere't be long.
	PROVOST	What comfort is for Claudio?
	DUKE	There's some in hope.
75	PROVOST	It is a bitter deputy.
	DUKE	Not so, not so: his life is paralleled

Even with the stroke and line of his great justice.
He doth with holy abstinence subdue
That in himself which he spurs on his power
80 To qualify in others. Were he mealed with that
Which he corrects, then were he tyrannous,
But this being so, he's just. Now are they come.

                                        [*Exit Provost*]

This is a gentle provost: seldom when
The steelèd jailer is the friend of men.   *Knocking within*
85 How now? What noise? That spirit's possessed with haste
That wounds th'unsisting postern with these strokes.

[*Enter Provost*]

	PROVOST	There he must stay until the officer

Arise to let him in. He is called up.

	DUKE	Have you no countermand for Claudio yet,
90		But he must die tomorrow?
	PROVOST	None, sir, none.
	DUKE	As near the dawning, Provost, as it is,
		You shall hear more ere morning.
	PROVOST	Happily

95 You something know, yet I believe there comes
No countermand, no such example have we:
Besides, upon the very siege of justice

---

76 **paralleled** reflected/modeled on   77 **Even** exactly   **stroke and line** linear course/written
authority   80 **qualify** moderate/control   **mealed** stained   81 **corrects** punishes   82 **this**
i.e. his virtuous nature   83 **gentle** honorable   **seldom when** it is seldom that   84 **steelèd**
hardened   85 **spirit's** i.e. the messenger   86 **unsisting** unyielding   **postern** back or side
gate   88 **He . . . up** he (the officer) has arisen to attend the call   89 **countermand** reprieve
94 **Happily** perhaps   96 **example** precedent   97 **siege** seat

Lord Angelo hath to the public ear
Professed the contrary.

Enter a Messenger

100   This is his lordship's man.

DUKE   And here comes Claudio's pardon.   *Aside?*

MESSENGER   My lord hath sent you this note, and   *Gives a paper*
by me this further charge, that you swerve not from the
smallest article of it, neither in time, matter, or other
105   circumstance. Good morrow, for, as I take it, it is almost day.

PROVOST   I shall obey him.   [*Exit Messenger*]

DUKE   This is his pardon, purchased by such sin   *Aside*
For which the pardoner himself is in.
Hence hath offence his quick celerity,
110   When it is borne in high authority.
When vice makes mercy, mercy's so extended,
That for the fault's love is th'offender friended.—
Now, sir, what news?

PROVOST   I told you. Lord Angelo, belike thinking me remiss
115   in mine office, awakens me with this unwonted putting-on,
methinks strangely, for he hath not used it before.

DUKE   Pray you let's hear.

PROVOST   'Whatsoever you may hear to the   *Reads the letter*
contrary, let Claudio be executed by four of the clock, and
120   in the afternoon Barnardine. For my better satisfaction, let
me have Claudio's head sent me by five. Let this be duly
performed with a thought that more depends on it than we
must yet deliver. Thus fail not to do your office, as you will
answer it at your peril.' What say you to this, sir?

125   DUKE   What is that Barnardine who is to be executed in
th'afternoon?

---

107 purchased . . . in bought by the same sin as Angelo has committed   109 Hence . . .
authority sin grows rapidly when it is supported by (borne in) those in power   111 extended
stretched/widened   112 fault's love love of the sin   friended befriended, assisted
114 belike perhaps   remiss negligent, careless   115 unwonted unusual   putting-on
prompting   120 satisfaction assurance   121 duly dutifully/fully   122 a thought the
knowledge   123 deliver communicate   124 answer be accountable   your peril risk of
punishment   125 What who

PROVOST   A Bohemian born, but here nursed up and bred, one that is a prisoner nine years old.

130 DUKE   How came it that the absent duke had not either delivered him to his liberty or executed him? I have heard it was ever his manner to do so.

PROVOST   His friends still wrought reprieves for him: and indeed, his fact, till now in the government of Lord Angelo, came not to an undoubtful proof.

135 DUKE   It is now apparent?

PROVOST   Most manifest, and not denied by himself.

DUKE   Hath he borne himself penitently in prison? How seems he to be touched?

PROVOST   A man that apprehends death no more dreadfully
140 but as a drunken sleep, careless, reckless, and fearless of what's past, present, or to come: insensible of mortality and desperately mortal.

DUKE   He wants advice.

PROVOST   He will hear none. He hath evermore had the liberty
145 of the prison. Give him leave to escape hence, he would not. Drunk many times a day, if not many days entirely drunk. We have very oft awaked him, as if to carry him to execution, and showed him a seeming warrant for it, it hath not moved him at all.

150 DUKE   More of him anon. There is written in your brow, Provost, honesty and constancy. If I read it not truly, my ancient skill beguiles me, but in the boldness of my cunning, I will lay myself in hazard. Claudio, whom here you have warrant to execute, is no greater forfeit to the law than
155 Angelo who hath sentenced him. To make you understand this in a manifested effect, I crave but four days' respite, for

---

128 **nine years old** for the last nine years   132 **wrought** obtained   133 **fact** crime
134 **undoubtful** absolute   138 **touched** affected (by the thought of his impending execution)
139 **apprehends** conceives of/fears   **dreadfully** fearfully   141 **insensible . . . mortal**
unmoved by death and yet irredeemably condemned to die   143 **wants** lacks/needs   **advice**
guidance/spiritual counsel   144 **evermore . . . prison** always had the freedom to go anywhere
within the prison   148 **seeming** supposed   152 **beguiles** deceives   **boldness . . . cunning**
confidence of my skill   153 **lay . . . hazard** put myself at risk   156 **manifested effect** visible
way

the which you are to do me both a present and a dangerous courtesy.

PROVOST   Pray, sir, in what?

160   DUKE   In the delaying death.

PROVOST   Alack, how may I do it, having the hour limited and an express command, under penalty, to deliver his head in the view of Angelo? I may make my case as Claudio's, to cross this in the smallest.

165   DUKE   By the vow of mine order, I warrant you, if my instructions may be your guide, let this Barnardine be this morning executed, and his head borne to Angelo.

PROVOST   Angelo hath seen them both and will discover the favour.

170   DUKE   O, death's a great disguiser, and you may add to it. Shave the head and tie the beard and say it was the desire of the penitent to be so bared before his death: you know the course is common. If anything fall to you upon this, more than thanks and good fortune, by the saint whom I profess, I

175   will plead against it with my life.

PROVOST   Pardon me, good father, it is against my oath.

DUKE   Were you sworn to the duke or to the deputy?

PROVOST   To him and to his substitutes.

DUKE   You will think you have made no offence, if the

180   duke avouch the justice of your dealing?

PROVOST   But what likelihood is in that?

DUKE   Not a resemblance, but a certainty. Yet since I see you fearful that neither my coat, integrity, nor persuasion can with ease attempt you, I will go further than I meant, to

185   pluck all fears out of you. Look you, sir, here is the hand and seal of the duke: you know the character, I   *Shows a letter* doubt not, and the signet is not strange to you.

---

157 **present** immediate   158 **courtesy** service   161 **limited** specified   163 **make . . . Claudio's** i.e. be subject to the death penalty   164 **cross** thwart, obstruct   165 **warrant** guarantee (your safety)   168 **discover the favour** recognize the face   171 **tie** knot/tie together (to control any straggly hair)   172 **bared** shaved, trimmed   173 **course** practice   **fall . . . this** happens to you as a result of this   180 **avouch** confirms   182 **resemblance** possibility   183 **coat** friar's habit   184 **attempt** persuade   185 **hand** signature/handwriting   186 **character** handwriting   187 **signet** seal of authority   **strange** unfamiliar

PROVOST   I know them both.

DUKE   The contents of this is the return of the duke; you
190   shall anon over-read it at your pleasure, where you shall find
within these two days he will be here. This is a thing that
Angelo knows not, for he this very day receives letters of
strange tenor, perchance of the duke's death, perchance
entering into some monastery, but by chance nothing of
195   what is writ. Look, th'unfolding star calls up the shepherd.
Put not yourself into amazement how these things should
be; all difficulties are but easy when they are known. Call
your executioner, and off with Barnardine's head. I will give
him a present shrift and advise him for a better place. Yet you
200   are amazed, but this shall absolutely resolve you. Come
away. It is almost clear dawn.   *Exeunt*

Act 4 Scene 3   *running scene 10 continues*

Enter Clown [Pompey]

POMPEY   I am as well acquainted here as I was in our house of
profession: one would think it were Mistress Overdone's own
house, for here be many of her old customers. First, here's
young Master Rash. He's in for a commodity of brown paper
5   and old ginger, ninescore and seventeen pounds, of which
he made five marks ready money. Marry, then ginger was not
much in request, for the old women were all dead. Then is
there here one Master Caper, at the suit of Master Three-
pile the mercer, for some four suits of peach-coloured satin,
10   which now peaches him a beggar. Then have we here young

193 **tenor** substance   194 **nothing . . . writ** none of the above   195 **unfolding star** i.e.
Morning Star, when the **shepherd** releases his sheep from the fold   199 **present shrift**
immediate confession   **better place** i.e. heaven   Yet still   200 **this** i.e. the letter
absolutely resolve you explain everything to you   **4.3** 1 **acquainted** known   **house of
profession** i.e. the brothel   4 **Rash** impetuous, capricious   **commodity** supply   **brown
paper** coarse, poor-quality wrapping paper   5 **old** stale   **ninescore . . . money** which he
believed to be worth £197; only making £3.33 in actual cash, he is now in prison for debt
7 **old women** proverbially fond of ginger   8 **Caper** leaping or skipping while dancing   **suit**
lawsuit (sense then shifts to "clothing")   **Three-pile** luxuriously thick material, usually velvet
9 **mercer** a dealer in fabrics   10 **peaches** impeaches, denounces

Dizzy and young Master Deep-vow and Master Copperspur
and Master Starve-lackey the rapier and dagger man, and
young Drop-heir that killed lusty Pudding, and Master
Forthright the tilter, and brave Master Shoe-tie the great
15   traveller, and wild Half-can that stabbed Pots, and I think
forty more, all great doers in our trade, and are now 'for the
Lord's sake'.

Enter Abhorson

ABHORSON   Sirrah, bring Barnardine hither.

POMPEY   Master Barnardine! You must rise and be hanged.
20   Master Barnardine!

ABHORSON   What ho, Barnardine!

BARNARDINE   A pox o'your throats! Who makes that   *Within*
noise there? What are you?

POMPEY   Your friends, sir, the hangman. You must be so
25   good, sir, to rise and be put to death.

BARNARDINE   Away, you rogue, away! I am sleepy.   *Within*

ABHORSON   Tell him he must awake, and that quickly too.

POMPEY   Pray, Master Barnardine, awake till you are executed,
and sleep afterwards.

30   ABHORSON   Go in to him and fetch him out.

POMPEY   He is coming, sir, he is coming: I hear his straw
rustle.

Enter Barnardine

ABHORSON   Is the axe upon the block, sirrah?

POMPEY   Very ready, sir.

---

11 **Dizzy** silly, vacuous **Deep-vow** perhaps a lover who falls passionately, but frequently, in
love **Copperspur** perhaps a man who has spurs made of copper in the hope they may pass
for gold 12 **Starve-lackey** mean person who starves his servants **rapier** fencing was done
with a rapier (sword) and dagger 13 **Drop-heir** perhaps someone who kills heirs, or marries
them only to drop them; or "dropsied" (i.e. pretentious); or one with "hair" that is dropping
out, a symptom of syphilis **lusty Pudding** perhaps a rich, fat heir (a **pudding** was a sausage)
14 **Forthright** moving forward, charging **tilter** jouster **brave** splendidly dressed **Shoe-tie**
elaborate shoe-lace or bow 15 **Half-can . . . Pots** probably refers to a drunken brawl in which
Half-can, someone "half-cut" (drunk), or someone who drank smaller measures of liquor,
stabbed Pots (named after a drinking vessel) 16 **doers . . . trade** frequenters of brothels (to
"do" meant to have sex with) **"for . . . sake"** "meat for the Lord's sake" was the frequent cry
of prisoners asking for food 19 **rise** awake/ascend the scaffold 22 **pox** plague 25 **to** as to
31 **straw** floors of prisons were strewn with straw

35 BARNARDINE   How now, Abhorson? What's the news with you?

    ABHORSON   Truly, sir, I would desire you to clap into your
    prayers, for, look you, the warrant's come.

    BARNARDINE   You rogue, I have been drinking all night, I am not
    fitted for't.

40 POMPEY   O, the better, sir, for he that drinks all night, and is
    hanged betimes in the morning, may sleep the sounder all
    the next day.

    Enter Duke [disguised as before]

    ABHORSON   Look you, sir, here comes your ghostly father. Do we
    jest now, think you?

45 DUKE   Sir, induced by my charity, and hearing how hastily
    you are to depart, I am come to advise you, comfort you and
    pray with you.

    BARNARDINE   Friar, not I. I have been drinking hard all night,
    and I will have more time to prepare me, or they shall beat
50 out my brains with billets. I will not consent to die this day,
    that's certain.

    DUKE   O, sir, you must, and therefore I beseech you
    Look forward on the journey you shall go.

    BARNARDINE   I swear I will not die today for any man's
55 persuasion.

    DUKE   But hear you—

    BARNARDINE   Not a word. If you have anything to say to me,
    come to my ward, for thence will not I today.   *Exit*

    Enter Provost

    DUKE   Unfit to live or die. O, gravel heart!
60 After him, fellows, bring him to the block.

                                    [Exeunt Abhorson and Pompey]

    PROVOST   Now, sir, how do you find the prisoner?

    DUKE   A creature unprepared, unmeet for death,
    And to transport him in the mind he is
    Were damnable.

---

36 **clap into** get on with   39 **fitted** in a suitable condition   41 **betimes** early   43 **ghostly**
father holy confessor   50 **billets** wooden sticks   56 **hear you** listen   58 **ward** cell   **thence**
from there   59 **gravel** stony   62 **unmeet** unfit   63 **transport him** i.e. put him to death

65	PROVOST	Here in the prison, father,

There died this morning of a cruel fever
One Ragozine, a most notorious pirate,
A man of Claudio's years, his beard and head
Just of his colour. What if we do omit
70   This reprobate till he were well inclined,
And satisfy the deputy with the visage
Of Ragozine, more like to Claudio?

DUKE   O, 'tis an accident that heaven provides!
Dispatch it presently, the hour draws on
75   Prefixed by Angelo. See this be done,
And sent according to command, whiles I
Persuade this rude wretch willingly to die.

PROVOST   This shall be done, good father, presently.
But Barnardine must die this afternoon.
80   And how shall we continue Claudio,
To save me from the danger that might come
If he were known alive?

DUKE   Let this be done:
Put them in secret holds, both Barnardine and Claudio.
85   Ere twice the sun hath made his journal greeting
To yonder generation, you shall find
Your safety manifested.

PROVOST   I am your free dependant.

DUKE   Quick, dispatch, and send the head to Angelo.

Exit [*Provost*]

90   Now will I write letters to Angelo —
The provost, he shall bear them — whose contents
Shall witness to him I am near at home,
And that by great injunctions I am bound
To enter publicly. Him I'll desire

---

67 **Ragozine** possibly a native of Ragusa, a successful Adriatic port, now Dubrovnik
68 **years** age   **head** hair   69 **omit** disregard   70 **reprobate** villain   71 **visage** head/face
73 **accident** event   74 **Dispatch it** carry it out   75 **Prefixed** determined   77 **rude** vulgar,
uncivilized   80 **continue** keep alive   84 **holds** cells   85 **journal greeting** daily appearance
86 **yonder generation** those outside of the prison   87 **manifested** apparent   88 **free
dependant** willing servant/entirely under your protection   93 **injunctions** commands
bound required

95 To meet me at the consecrated fount,
  A league below the city, and from thence,
  By cold gradation and well-balanced form,
  We shall proceed with Angelo.

Enter Provost [with Ragozine's head]

PROVOST Here is the head. I'll carry it myself.
100 DUKE Convenient is it. Make a swift return,
  For I would commune with you of such things
  That want no ear but yours.

PROVOST I'll make all speed.   *Exit*
ISABELLA Peace, ho, be here!   *Within*
105 DUKE The tongue of Isabel. She's come to know
  If yet her brother's pardon be come hither.
  But I will keep her ignorant of her good,
  To make her heavenly comforts of despair,
  When it is least expected.

Enter Isabella

110 ISABELLA Ho, by your leave!
 DUKE Good morning to you, fair and gracious daughter.
 ISABELLA The better, given me by so holy a man.
  Hath yet the deputy sent my brother's pardon?
 DUKE He hath released him, Isabel — from the world.
115 His head is off and sent to Angelo.
 ISABELLA Nay, but it is not so.
 DUKE It is no other.
  Show your wisdom, daughter, in your close patience.
 ISABELLA O, I will to him and pluck out his eyes!
120 DUKE You shall not be admitted to his sight.
 ISABELLA Unhappy Claudio, wretched Isabel,
  Injurious world, most damnèd Angelo!
 DUKE This nor hurts him nor profits you a jot.
  Forbear it therefore, give your cause to heaven.
125 Mark what I say, which you shall find

---

95 **consecrated fount** holy spring 96 **league** three miles **below** outside 97 **cold gradation** calm advancement **well-balanced form** careful observance of the proper procedures 101 **commune** discuss 108 **of** out of 118 **close** controlled, silent
124 **Forbear it** restrain yourself

By every syllable a faithful verity.
The duke comes home tomorrow — nay, dry your eyes —
One of our convent, and his confessor,
Gives me this instance. Already he hath carried
130 Notice to Escalus and Angelo,
Who do prepare to meet him at the gates,
There to give up their power. If you can, pace your wisdom
In that good path that I would wish it go,
And you shall have your bosom on this wretch,
135 Grace of the duke, revenges to your heart,
And general honour.

ISABELLA   I am directed by you.

DUKE   This letter, then, to Friar Peter give,   *Gives a letter*
'Tis that he sent me of the duke's return.
140 Say, by this token I desire his company
At Mariana's house tonight. Her cause and yours
I'll perfect him withal, and he shall bring you
Before the duke, and to the head of Angelo
Accuse him home and home. For my poor self,
145 I am combinèd by a sacred vow,
And shall be absent. Wend you with this letter:
Command these fretting waters from your eyes
With a light heart; trust not my holy order
If I pervert your course. Who's here?

Enter Lucio

150 LUCIO   Good even. Friar, where's the provost?

DUKE   Not within, sir.

LUCIO   O, pretty Isabella, I am pale at mine heart to see
thine eyes so red: thou must be patient. I am fain to dine and
sup with water and bran: I dare not for my head fill my belly.

---

126 **verity** truth   128 **confessor** either Friar Thomas (mentioned in Act 1) or Friar Peter
129 **instance** information   132 **pace** control, maneuver   133 **good path** right direction
134 **bosom** on dearest wish inflicted on   135 **Grace** by virtue   **heart** heart's content
142 **perfect him withal** tell him about   143 **to . . . of** face to face with   144 **home and home**
thoroughly   145 **combinèd** bound   146 **Wend you** direct yourself, go   147 **waters** i.e. tears
149 **pervert** turn aside   153 **fain** obliged   154 **bran** coarse brown bread   **for my head** for
fear of losing my head

155   One fruitful meal would set me to't. But they say the duke
    will be here tomorrow. By my troth, Isabel, I loved thy
    brother. If the old fantastical duke of dark corners had been
    at home, he had lived.   *[Exit Isabella]*

DUKE   Sir, the duke is marvellous little beholding to your
160   reports, but the best is, he lives not in them.

LUCIO   Friar, thou knowest not the duke so well as I do. He's
    a better woodman than thou tak'st him for.

DUKE   Well, you'll answer this one day. Fare ye   *Starts to go*
    well.

165 **LUCIO**   Nay, tarry, I'll go along with thee. I can tell thee
    pretty tales of the duke.

DUKE   You have told me too many of him already, sir, if
    they be true. If not true, none were enough.

LUCIO   I was once before him for getting a wench with child.

170 **DUKE**   Did you such a thing?

LUCIO   Yes, marry, did I, but I was fain to forswear it. They
    would else have married me to the rotten medlar.

DUKE   Sir, your company is fairer than honest. Rest you
    well.

175 **LUCIO**   By my troth, I'll go with thee to the lane's end. If
    bawdy talk offend you, we'll have very little of it. Nay, friar, I
    am a kind of burr, I shall stick.   *Exeunt*

Act 4 Scene 4   *running scene 11*

Enter Angelo and Escalus

ESCALUS   Every letter he hath writ hath disvouched other.

ANGELO   In most uneven and distracted manner. His actions

---

155 fruitful fulfilling (with sexual connotations)   **set me to't** set me to work sexually/provide
the strength for sex   **157 fantastical** whimsical, capricious   **dark corners** i.e. secretive/given
to lurking in dark corners (plays on the sense of "vaginas")   **159 beholding** beholden,
indebted   **160 he . . . them** he is nothing like you say/his reputation does not depend on
you   **162 woodman** hunter (of women)   **166 pretty** fine/clever   **171 fain to forswear** eager
to deny   **172 medlar** type of fruit/whore (slang term for the vagina)   **173 fairer** more
(falsely) attractive, entertaining   **177 burr** prickly seed-head that sticks easily to clothing
4.4   **1 disvouched** contradicted   **2 uneven** erratic

show much like to madness. Pray heaven his wisdom be not
tainted. And why meet him at the gates and redeliver our
5   authorities there?

ESCALUS   I guess not.

ANGELO   And why should we proclaim it in an hour before
his entering, that if any crave redress of injustice, they
should exhibit their petitions in the street?

10   ESCALUS   He shows his reason for that: to have a dispatch of
complaints and to deliver us from devices hereafter, which
shall then have no power to stand against us.

ANGELO   Well, I beseech you, let it be proclaimed betimes
i'th'morn. I'll call you at your house. Give notice to such
15   men of sort and suit as are to meet him.

ESCALUS   I shall, sir. Fare you well.

ANGELO   Good night.   *Exit* [*Escalus*]
This deed unshapes me quite, makes me unpregnant
And dull to all proceedings. A deflowered maid,
20   And by an eminent body that enforced
The law against it! But that her tender shame
Will not proclaim against her maiden loss,
How might she tongue me? Yet reason dares her no,
For my authority bears of a credent bulk
25   That no particular scandal once can touch
But it confounds the breather. He should have lived,
Save that his riotous youth with dangerous sense
Might in the times to come have ta'en revenge
By so receiving a dishonoured life
30   With ransom of such shame. Would yet he had lived!

---

3 **wisdom . . . tainted** wits are not infected   4 **redeliver** hand back, restore (legal term)
9 **exhibit their petitions** utter their complaints/requests   10 **dispatch** swift settlement
11 **devices** plots, contrivances   13 **betimes** early   15 **sort and suit** social rank and personal
retinue   18 **unshapes** confounds, deforms   **unpregnant** unreceptive, unprepared   19 **dull**
sluggish, unresponsive   20 **eminent body** respected public figure   21 **it** i.e. extramarital sex
But were it not   **tender** vulnerable, raw, pitiable   22 **proclaim** publicly complain of   **maiden**
loss loss of virginity   23 **tongue** reproach, denounce   **dares her no** frightens her not to
24 **bears . . . bulk** carries such weighty credibility   26 **confounds the breather** discredits the
person who utters the complaint   27 **riotous** unrestrained   **sense** passion/awareness (of
Angelo's actions)   29 **By** as a result of

> Alack, when once our grace we have forgot,
> Nothing goes right: we would, and we would not.   *Exit*

Act 4 Scene 5

Enter Duke [in his own habit] and Friar Peter

DUKE   These letters at fit time deliver me.   *Gives letters*
    The provost knows our purpose and our plot.
    The matter being afoot, keep your instruction
    And hold you ever to our special drift,
5 Though sometimes you do blench from this to that,
    As cause doth minister. Go call at Flavius' house,
    And tell him where I stay. Give the like notice
    To Valentius, Rowland, and to Crassus,
    And bid them bring the trumpets to the gate.
10 But send me Flavius first.
FRIAR PETER   It shall be speeded well.   *[Exit]*
Enter Varrius
DUKE   I thank thee, Varrius, thou hast made good haste.
    Come, we will walk. There's other of our friends
    Will greet us here anon, my gentle Varrius.   *Exeunt*

Act 4 Scene 6

Enter Isabella and Mariana

ISABELLA   To speak so indirectly I am loath.
    I would say the truth, but to accuse him so,
    That is your part. Yet I am advised to do it,
    He says, to veil full purpose.
5 MARIANA   Be ruled by him.

4.5 *Location: outside Vienna*   1 me for me   **3 keep your instruction** stick to your task
4 hold you ever stand firm   **special drift** particular aim   **5 blench** swerve   **6 cause doth
minister** circumstances require   **9 trumpets** trumpeters   **11 speeded** done swiftly,
accomplished   **14 gentle** honorable   **4.6 *Location: Vienna*   1 indirectly** dishonestly
2 him Angelo   **so** in that manner (truthfully)   **4 He** i.e. the duke/friar

ISABELLA	Besides, he tells me that if peradventure
	He speak against me on the adverse side,
	I should not think it strange, for 'tis a physic
	That's bitter to sweet end.

Enter [Friar] Peter

10 | MARIANA | I would Friar Peter— |
ISABELLA	O, peace, the friar is come.
FRIAR PETER	Come, I have found you out a stand most fit,
	Where you may have such vantage on the duke
	He shall not pass you. Twice have the trumpets sounded.
15		The generous and gravest citizens
	Have hent the gates, and very near upon
	The duke is entering: therefore hence, away! *Exeunt*

Act 5 Scene 1   *running scene 14*

Enter Duke [in his own habit], Varrius, Lords, Angelo, Escalus, Lucio, [and] Citizens, at several doors

DUKE	My very worthy cousin, fairly met! — *To Angelo*
	Our old and faithful friend, we are glad to see you. *To Escalus*
ANGELO *and* ESCALUS	Happy return be to your royal grace!
DUKE	Many and hearty thankings to you both.
5		We have made inquiry of you, and we hear
	Such goodness of your justice that our soul
	Cannot but yield you forth to public thanks,
	Forerunning more requital.
ANGELO	You make my bonds still greater.
10	DUKE	O, your desert speaks loud, and I should wrong it
	To lock it in the wards of covert bosom,
	When it deserves with characters of brass

6 **peradventure** by any chance   8 **physic** medicine   9 **bitter . . . end** unpleasant to taste but good for the health   10 **would** wish   12 **stand** place to stand   13 **vantage on** advantageous position (from which to intercept)   16 **hent** arrived, taken up positions at   **near upon** shortly
5.1   1 **cousin** a friendly form of address   7 **yield . . . thanks** thank you publicly
8 **Forerunning more requital** preceding further gratitude/reward   9 **bonds** obligations
11 **wards . . . bosom** secret confines of my heart   12 **characters** letters

A forted residence 'gainst the tooth of time
And razure of oblivion. Give me your hand,
15   And let the subject see, to make them know
That outward courtesies would fain proclaim
Favours that keep within. Come, Escalus,
You must walk by us on our other hand,
And good supporters are you.

Enter [Friar] Peter and Isabella

20   FRIAR PETER   Now is your time. Speak loud and kneel before him.

ISABELLA   Justice, O royal duke! Vail your regard   *Kneels*
Upon a wronged — I would fain have said, a maid.
O worthy prince, dishonour not your eye
By throwing it on any other object
25   Till you have heard me in my true complaint
And given me justice, justice, justice, justice!

DUKE   Relate your wrongs: in what, by whom? Be brief.
Here is Lord Angelo shall give you justice,
Reveal yourself to him.

30   ISABELLA   O worthy duke,
You bid me seek redemption of the devil.
Hear me yourself, for that which I must speak
Must either punish me, not being believed,
Or wring redress from you. Hear me, O, hear me here!

35   ANGELO   My lord, her wits, I fear me, are not firm.
She hath been a suitor to me for her brother
Cut off by course of justice—

ISABELLA   By course of justice!

ANGELO   And she will speak most bitterly and strange.

40   ISABELLA   Most strange, but yet most truly will I speak.
That Angelo's forsworn, is it not strange?
That Angelo's a murderer, is't not strange?
That Angelo is an adulterous thief,

---

13 **forted** fortified   **tooth** i.e. ravages   14 **razure** obliteration   15 **subject** duke's citizens
16 **fain** gladly   17 **Favours** high regard   **keep within** live inside (my heart)   21 **Vail your**
regard cast your gaze downward   22 **fain** much more willingly   29 **Reveal** explain
34 **wring** bring about   36 **suitor** petitioner, supplicant   37 **Cut off** (whose life was) cut short
39 **strange** oddly (Isabella shifts the sense to "unprecedentedly")   41 **forsworn** perjured, false

An hypocrite, a virgin-violator,

45   Is it not strange and strange?

DUKE   Nay, it is ten times strange.

ISABELLA   It is not truer he is Angelo

Than this is all as true as it is strange;

Nay, it is ten times true, for truth is truth

50   To th' end of reck'ning.

DUKE   Away with her. Poor soul,

She speaks this in th'infirmity of sense.

ISABELLA   O prince, I conjure thee, as thou believ'st

There is another comfort than this world,

55   That thou neglect me not with that opinion

That I am touched with madness. Make not impossible

That which but seems unlike. 'Tis not impossible

But one, the wicked'st caitiff on the ground,

May seem as shy, as grave, as just, as absolute

60   As Angelo: even so may Angelo,

In all his dressings, caracts, titles, forms,

Be an arch-villain. Believe it, royal prince:

If he be less, he's nothing, but he's more,

Had I more name for badness.

65   DUKE   By mine honesty,

If she be mad — as I believe no other —

Her madness hath the oddest frame of sense,

Such a dependency of thing on thing,

As e'er I heard in madness.

70 ISABELLA   O gracious duke,

Harp not on that, nor do not banish reason

For inequality, but let your reason serve

---

47 **truer** more certain   50 **To . . . reck'ning** to the end of time/no matter how far we examine the matter   52 **in . . . sense** from a diseased mind   53 **conjure** entreat   54 **comfort** godly realm/source of divine comfort   55 **with that opinion** in the belief that   56 **touched** tainted/affected   **Make . . . unlike** do not assume it is impossible because it seems unlikely   58 **caitiff** wretch   **ground** face of the earth   59 **shy** cautious, reserved   **grave** wise, dignified, revered   **absolute** perfect, complete   61 **dressings** finery, official robes   **caracts** badges (of office)   **forms** formal procedures   64 **more name** a greater vocabulary/more terms   67 **frame of sense** lucidity, rational structure   68 **dependency . . . thing** coherent relationship of ideas   71 **Harp** dwell   **banish . . . inequality** assume I am mad because I am socially inferior or because my words contradict Angelo's reputation

To make the truth appear where it seems hid,
And hide the false seems true.

75   DUKE   Many that are not mad
Have, sure, more lack of reason. What would you say?

ISABELLA   I am the sister of one Claudio,
Condemned upon the act of fornication
To lose his head, condemned by Angelo.

80   I, in probation of a sisterhood,
Was sent to by my brother, one Lucio
As then the messenger—

LUCIO   That's I, an't like your grace.
I came to her from Claudio, and desired her

85   To try her gracious fortune with Lord Angelo
For her poor brother's pardon.

ISABELLA   That's he indeed.

DUKE   You were not bid to speak.

LUCIO   No, my good lord,

90   Nor wished to hold my peace.

DUKE   I wish you now, then.
Pray you take note of it. And when you have
A business for yourself, pray heaven you then
Be perfect.

95   LUCIO   I warrant your honour.

DUKE   The warrant's for yourself: take heed to't.

ISABELLA   This gentleman told somewhat of my tale—

LUCIO   Right.

DUKE   It may be right, but you are i'the wrong

100   To speak before your time.— Proceed.

ISABELLA   I went
To this pernicious caitiff deputy—

DUKE   That's somewhat madly spoken.

---

74 hide . . . true (let the truth) eclipse the falsehood that merely seems plausible/(let your
reason) ignore the falsehood that seems to be true   78 act legal act prohibiting premarital
sex/deed   80 probation . . . sisterhood i.e. a novice   82 As then at that time   90 wished
was I asked   93 business for yourself matter concerning yourself   94 perfect fully
prepared/accurate   95 warrant assure (the duke shifts the sense to "document authorizing
arrest")   97 somewhat some part   102 pernicious destructive

ISABELLA   Pardon it,

105   The phrase is to the matter.

DUKE   Mended again. The matter: proceed.

ISABELLA   In brief, to set the needless process by —

How I persuaded, how I prayed and kneeled,

How he refelled me, and how I replied,

110   For this was of much length — the vile conclusion

I now begin with grief and shame to utter.

He would not, but by gift of my chaste body

To his concupiscible intemperate lust

Release my brother. And after much debatement

115   My sisterly remorse confutes mine honour,

And I did yield to him. But the next morn betimes,

His purpose surfeiting, he sends a warrant

For my poor brother's head.

DUKE   This is most likely.

120   ISABELLA   O, that it were as like as it is true!

DUKE   By heaven, fond wretch, thou know'st not what

thou speak'st,

Or else thou art suborned against his honour

In hateful practice. First, his integrity

125   Stands without blemish. Next, it imports no reason

That with such vehemency he should pursue

Faults proper to himself. If he had so offended,

He would have weighed thy brother by himself,

And not have cut him off. Someone hath set you on.

130   Confess the truth, and say by whose advice

Thou cam'st here to complain.

---

105 to the matter relevant   106 Mended set right   107 to . . . by leaving out unnecessary
details   108 persuaded entreated, urged   109 refelled refused   113 concupiscible hotly
desirous   114 debatement argument, deliberation   115 remorse pity   confutes overcomes
116 the . . . betimes early the next morning   117 surfeiting being overindulged   119 likely
probable (ironic)   120 that . . . true i.e. as then the duke might believe her   121 fond foolish
123 suborned bribed to make false accusations   124 practice conspiracy   125 imports no
reason makes no sense   126 pursue . . . himself seek to punish a crime he had also
committed   128 weighed judged   129 cut him off had him executed   set you on put you
up to this

ISABELLA   And is this all?
Then, O you blessèd ministers above,
Keep me in patience, and with ripened time
135   Unfold the evil which is here wrapt up
In countenance! Heaven shield your grace from woe,
As I, thus wronged, hence unbelievèd go!   *She starts to go*

DUKE   I know you'd fain be gone. An officer!
To prison with her. Shall we thus permit   *Isabella is arrested*
140   A blasting and a scandalous breath to fall
On him so near us? This needs must be a practice.
Who knew of your intent and coming hither?

ISABELLA   One that I would were here, Friar Lodowick.

DUKE   A ghostly father, belike. Who knows that Lodowick?

145   LUCIO   My lord, I know him, 'tis a meddling friar,
I do not like the man. Had he been lay, my lord,
For certain words he spake against your grace
In your retirement, I had swinged him soundly.

DUKE   Words against me? This' a good friar, belike.
150   And to set on this wretched woman here
Against our substitute! Let this friar be found.

LUCIO   But yesternight, my lord, she and that friar,
I saw them at the prison: a saucy friar,
A very scurvy fellow.

155   FRIAR PETER   Blessèd be your royal grace.
I have stood by, my lord, and I have heard
Your royal ear abused. First, hath this woman
Most wrongfully accused your substitute,
Who is as free from touch or soil with her
160   As she from one ungot.

DUKE   We did believe no less.
Know you that Friar Lodowick that she speaks of?

---

133 ministers angels   135 Unfold reveal   136 countenance social standing/outward show
140 blasting destructive, withering   141 practice plot   143 Lodowick the duke's assumed
name as a friar   144 ghostly holy (plays on the sense of "insubstantial")   146 lay not a
clergyman   148 retirement absence   had swinged would have beaten   149 This' this is
153 saucy insolent   154 scurvy contemptible   157 abused deceived   159 touch or soil
moral blemish/sexual stain   160 ungot not yet conceived

FRIAR PETER   I know him for a man divine and holy,
Not scurvy, nor a temporary meddler,
165   As he's reported by this gentleman.
And on my trust a man that never yet
Did, as he vouches, misreport your grace.

LUCIO   My lord, most villainously, believe it.

FRIAR PETER   Well, he in time may come to clear himself,
170   But at this instant he is sick, my lord,
Of a strange fever. Upon his mere request,
Being come to knowledge that there was complaint
Intended 'gainst Lord Angelo, came I hither,
To speak, as from his mouth, what he doth know
175   Is true and false, and what he with his oath
And all probation will make up full clear,
Whensoever he's convented. First, for this woman,
To justify this worthy nobleman
So vulgarly and personally accused,
180   Her shall you hear disprovèd to her eyes,
Till she herself confess it.

DUKE   Good friar, let's hear it.   [Exit Isabella, guarded]
Do you not smile at this, Lord Angelo?
O heaven, the vanity of wretched fools!
185   Give us some seats. Come, cousin Angelo,
In this I'll be impartial: be you judge
Of your own cause.

Enter Mariana [veiled]   Seats brought in for Duke and Angelo
Is this the witness, friar?
First, let her show her face, and after speak.

MARIANA   Pardon, my lord, I will not show my face   Kneels?
190   Until my husband bid me.

DUKE   What, are you married?

MARIANA   No, my lord.

---

164 **temporary meddler** one who interferes in secular matters   167 **vouches** testifies, asserts
misreport slander   168 **most villainously** he did, and most villainously too   171 **strange**
unknown/severe   **mere** sole/personal   176 **probation** proof   **make . . . clear** make
absolutely clear   177 **convented** summoned to appear   178 **justify** exonerate   179 **vulgarly**
publicly   180 **to her eyes** to her face   184 **vanity** futile actions/foolishness

	DUKE	Are you a maid?
	MARIANA	No, my lord.
195	DUKE	A widow, then?
	MARIANA	Neither, my lord.
	DUKE	Why, you are nothing then: neither maid, widow, nor wife?
	LUCIO	My lord, she may be a punk, for many of them are
200		neither maid, widow, nor wife.
	DUKE	Silence that fellow. I would he had some cause
		To prattle for himself.
	LUCIO	Well, my lord.
	MARIANA	My lord, I do confess I ne'er was married,
205		And I confess besides I am no maid.
		I have known my husband, yet my husband
		Knows not that ever he knew me.
	LUCIO	He was drunk then, my lord, it can be no better.
	DUKE	For the benefit of silence, would thou wert so too.
210	LUCIO	Well, my lord.
	DUKE	This is no witness for Lord Angelo.
	MARIANA	Now I come to't, my lord.
		She that accuses him of fornication,
		In self-same manner doth accuse my husband,
215		And charges him, my lord, with such a time
		When I'll depose I had him in mine arms
		With all th'effect of love.
	ANGELO	Charges she more than me?
	MARIANA	Not that I know.
220	DUKE	No? You say your husband.
	MARIANA	Why, just, my lord, and that is Angelo,
		Who thinks he knows that he ne'er knew my body,
		But knows he thinks that he knows Isabel's.

---

199 **punk** prostitute   201 **cause . . . himself** reason to speak/charge of his own to defend himself against   206 **known** had sex with   209 **For . . . too** if it kept you quiet I wish you were also drunk   215 **charges** accuses, indicts   **with** at   216 **depose** testify   217 **th'effect** the manifestations/fulfillment   218 **Charges she more** is she accusing other men   221 **just** exactly

ANGELO   This is a strange abuse. Let's see thy face.

225 MARIANA   My husband bids me, now I will unmask.   *Unveils*
This is that face, thou cruel Angelo,
Which once thou swor'st was worth the looking on:
This is the hand which, with a vowed contract,
Was fast belocked in thine: this is the body

230   That took away the match from Isabel,
And did supply thee at thy garden-house
In her imagined person.

DUKE   Know you this woman?

LUCIO   Carnally, she says.

235 DUKE   Sirrah, no more!

LUCIO   Enough, my lord.

ANGELO   My lord, I must confess I know this woman,
And five years since there was some speech of marriage
Betwixt myself and her, which was broke off,

240   Partly for that her promised proportions
Came short of composition, but in chief
For that her reputation was disvalued
In levity. Since which time of five years
I never spake with her, saw her, nor heard from her,

245   Upon my faith and honour.

MARIANA   Noble prince,   *Kneels?*
As there comes light from heaven and words from breath,
As there is sense in truth and truth in virtue,
I am affianced this man's wife as strongly

250   As words could make up vows. And, my good lord,
But Tuesday night last gone in's garden-house
He knew me as a wife. As this is true,
Let me in safety raise me from my knees,
Or else forever be confixèd here,

255   A marble monument!

---

224 abuse deception   229 fast belocked locked firmly   230 match assignation
231 supply satisfy   garden-house summer house   232 In . . . person disguised as Isabella
240 proportions dowry   241 composition the agreed amount   in chief principally
242 For that because   disvalued in levity discredited on grounds of (sexual) immorality
254 confixèd fixed firmly

ANGELO   I did but smile till now.
 Now, good my lord, give me the scope of justice,
 My patience here is touched. I do perceive
 These poor informal women are no more
260 But instruments of some more mightier member
 That sets them on. Let me have way, my lord,
 To find this practice out.

DUKE   Ay, with my heart
 And punish them to your height of pleasure.
265 Thou foolish friar, and thou pernicious woman,
 Compact with her that's gone, think'st thou thy oaths,
 Though they would swear down each particular saint,
 Were testimonies against his worth and credit
 That's sealed in approbation? You, Lord Escalus,
270 Sit with my cousin, lend him your kind pains
 To find out this abuse, whence 'tis derived.
 There is another friar that set them on,
 Let him be sent for.   *Duke gets up and Escalus takes his seat*

FRIAR PETER   Would he were here, my lord, for he indeed
275 Hath set the women on to this complaint.
 Your provost knows the place where he abides,
 And he may fetch him.

DUKE   Go do it instantly.   [*Exit Provost*]
 And you, my noble and well-warranted cousin,
280 Whom it concerns to hear this matter forth,
 Do with your injuries as seems you best
 In any chastisement. I for a while
 Will leave you, but stir not you till you have
 Well determined upon these slanderers.

---

256 **smile** i.e. regard such accusations as foolish/amusing   257 **scope** full extent
258 **touched** affected/hurt   259 **informal** demented   260 **mightier member** more powerful
person   261 **way** opportunity, scope   266 **Compact** in collusion   267 **swear down** invoke
particular individual   269 **sealed in approbation** confirmed and approved   270 **pains**
efforts   279 **well-warranted** eminently approved of   280 **forth** fully, to the end
282 **chastisement** form of punishment   283 **stir not you** do not move   284 **determined**
made a judgment on

285 ESCALUS   My lord, we'll do it throughly.   *Exit [Duke]*

Signior Lucio, did not you say you knew that Friar Lodowick
to be a dishonest person?

LUCIO   *Cucullus non facit monachum*: honest in nothing but
in his clothes, and one that hath spoke most villainous

290 speeches of the duke.

ESCALUS   We shall entreat you to abide here till he come and
enforce them against him. We shall find this friar a notable
fellow.

LUCIO   As any in Vienna, on my word.

295 ESCALUS   Call that same Isabel here once again, I would speak
with her.   *Exit an Attendant*

Pray you, my lord, give me leave to question, you   *To Angelo*
shall see how I'll handle her.

LUCIO   Not better than he, by her own report.

300 ESCALUS   Say you?

LUCIO   Marry, sir, I think, if you handled her privately, she
would sooner confess, perchance publicly she'll be ashamed.

Enter Duke [in his friar's disguise], Provost, Isabella [and Officers]

ESCALUS   I will go darkly to work with her.

LUCIO   That's the way, for women are light at midnight.

305 ESCALUS   Come on, mistress, here's a gentlewoman denies all
that you have said.

LUCIO   My lord, here comes the rascal I spoke of, here with
the provost.

ESCALUS   In very good time. Speak not you to him till we call

310 upon you.

LUCIO   Mum.

ESCALUS   Come, sir, did you set these women on to slander
Lord Angelo? They have confessed you did.

---

285 **throughly** thoroughly   288 *Cucullus . . . monachum* "a hood does not make a monk"
(Latin)   292 **enforce . . . him** lay your charges against him   **notable** notorious   298 **handle**
deal with (Lucio then plays on the sense of "fondle")   300 **Say you?** What did you say?
301 **privately** alone/in her private parts   302 **perchance . . . ashamed** perhaps she will be too
ashamed to admit her deceit/be made love to in public   303 **go . . . her** question her in a
cryptic or cunning manner (perhaps with unwitting play on "have sex with her in the
dark/sinfully")   304 **light** bright/promiscuous   311 **Mum** (I shall be) silent

DUKE		'Tis false.
315	ESCALUS	How? Know you where you are?

DUKE   Respect to your great place, and let the devil
Be sometime honoured for his burning throne.
Where is the duke? 'Tis he should hear me speak.

ESCALUS   The duke's in us, and we will hear you speak:
320   Look you speak justly.

DUKE   Boldly, at least. But, O, poor souls,
Come you to seek the lamb here of the fox?
Good night to your redress! Is the duke gone?
Then is your cause gone too. The duke's unjust,
325   Thus to retort your manifest appeal,
And put your trial in the villain's mouth
Which here you come to accuse.

LUCIO   This is the rascal, this is he I spoke of.

ESCALUS   Why, thou unreverend and unhallowed friar,
330   Is't not enough thou hast suborned these women
To accuse this worthy man, but, in foul mouth
And in the witness of his proper ear,
To call him villain, and then to glance from him
To th'duke himself, to tax him with injustice?
335   Take him hence, to th'rack with him! We'll touse you
Joint by joint, but we will know his purpose.
What? Unjust?

DUKE   Be not so hot. The duke dare
No more stretch this finger of mine than he
340   Dare rack his own. His subject am I not,
Nor here provincial. My business in this state
Made me a looker-on here in Vienna,
Where I have seen corruption boil and bubble

---

315 How? What?   316 Respect let respect be shown/I am respectful   317 honoured . . .
throne respected, if not for anything else, for the fact that he is the king of hell   319 in us is
represented by us   320 Look make sure   323 Good . . . redress! Farewell to any hope of
justice!   325 retort reject   manifest evidently truthful   329 unreverend disrespectful/
irreligious   unhallowed unholy   331 mouth language   332 proper ear own hearing
333 glance move rapidly/turn   334 tax charge, blame   335 th'rack torture instrument that
stretched the limbs   touse pull violently   338 hot rash, hasty   339 stretch upon the rack
341 here provincial of this province (hence not subject to its laws)

Till it o'errun the stew: laws for all faults,
345 But faults so countenanced that the strong statutes
Stand like the forfeits in a barber's shop,
As much in mock as mark.

ESCALUS   Slander to th'state! Away with him to prison!

ANGELO   What can you vouch against him, Signior Lucio?
350 Is this the man that you did tell us of?

LUCIO   'Tis he, my lord. Come hither, goodman baldpate.
Do you know me?

DUKE   I remember you, sir, by the sound of your voice. I
met you at the prison, in the absence of the duke.

355 **LUCIO**   O, did you so? And do you remember what you said
of the duke?

DUKE   Most notedly, sir.

LUCIO   Do you so, sir? And was the duke a fleshmonger, a
fool, and a coward, as you then reported him to be?

360 **DUKE**   You must, sir, change persons with me, ere you
make that my report: you indeed spoke so of him, and much
more, much worse.

LUCIO   O thou damnable fellow, did not I pluck thee by the
nose for thy speeches?

365 **DUKE**   I protest I love the duke as I love myself.

ANGELO   Hark, how the villain would close now, after his
treasonable abuses.

ESCALUS   Such a fellow is not to be talked withal. Away with
him to prison. Where is the provost? Away with him to prison.
370 Lay bolts enough upon him. Let him speak   *Provost lays*
no more. Away with those giglots too, and   *hands on the*
with the other confederate companion!   *Duke*

DUKE   Stay, sir, stay awhile.   *To Provost*

ANGELO   What, resists he? Help him, Lucio.

---

344 **stew** cauldron/brothel   345 **countenanced** endorsed (by those in authority)
346 **forfeits . . . shop** Elizabethan barbers displayed lists of penalties for misbehavior in their
shops   347 **in . . . mark** in jest as a serious warning   351 **goodman** form of address to one
below the rank of gentleman   **baldpate** monks were required to shave parts of their heads
357 **notedly** particularly   358 **fleshmonger** fornicator/pimp   361 **make . . . report** attribute
those remarks to me   366 **close** compromise/conclude   370 **bolts** leg-irons, fetters
371 **giglots** harlots   372 **confederate companion** accomplice (Friar Peter)

375 LUCIO   Come, sir, come, sir, come, sir. Foh, sir! Why, you bald-
           pated, lying rascal, you must be hooded, must you? Show your
           knave's visage, with a pox to you: show your   *Lucio pulls off*
           sheep-biting face, and be hanged an hour!   *the friar's hood*
           Will't not off?   *and discovers*
380 DUKE   Thou art the first knave that e'er   *the Duke; all rise*
           mad'st a duke.—
           First, provost, let me bail these gentle three.—
           Sneak not away, sir, for the friar and you   *To Lucio*
           Must have a word anon.— Lay hold on him.   *Lucio is arrested*
    LUCIO   This may prove worse than hanging.   *Aside?*
385 DUKE   What you have spoke I pardon. Sit you   *To Escalus*
           down,
           We'll borrow place of him.—
           Sir, by your leave.   *To Angelo, whose seat he takes*
           Hast thou or word or wit or impudence
           That yet can do thee office? If thou hast,
390   Rely upon it till my tale be heard,
           And hold no longer out.
    ANGELO   O, my dread lord,
           I should be guiltier than my guiltiness,
           To think I can be undiscernible,
395   When I perceive your grace, like power divine,
           Hath looked upon my passes. Then, good prince,
           No longer session hold upon my shame,
           But let my trial be mine own confession:
           Immediate sentence then and sequent death
400   Is all the grace I beg.
    DUKE   Come hither, Mariana.—
           Say: wast thou e'er contracted to this woman?   *To Angelo*

---

378 **sheep-biting** whoremongering/thieving (said of a dog that would attack sheep)   **hanged**
the fate of dogs caught attacking sheep   **an hour** in an hour/for an hour or so   380 **mad'st**
created   381 **bail** free   **gentle three** i.e. Isabella, Mariana, and Friar Peter   386 **place** i.e. the
position where Angelo is presiding   388 **or** either   389 **do thee office** be of service to you
391 **hold . . . out** give in (to the truth)   392 **dread** revered   394 **undiscernible** undetected
396 **passes** actions/trespasses   397 **session** trial   399 **sequent** subsequent

ANGELO   I was, my lord.

DUKE   Go take her hence, and marry her instantly.—

405   Do you the office, friar, which consummate,
Return him here again.— Go with him, provost.

Exeunt [Angelo, Mariana, Friar Peter and Provost]

ESCALUS   My lord, I am more amazed at his dishonour
Than at the strangeness of it.

DUKE   Come hither, Isabel.

410   Your friar is now your prince. As I was then
Advertising and holy to your business,
Not changing heart with habit, I am still
Attorneyed at your service.

ISABELLA   O give me pardon

415   That I, your vassal, have employed and pained
Your unknown sovereignty.

DUKE   You are pardoned, Isabel:
And now, dear maid, be you as free to us.
Your brother's death, I know, sits at your heart,

420   And you may marvel why I obscured myself,
Labouring to save his life, and would not rather
Make rash remonstrance of my hidden power
Than let him so be lost. O most kind maid,
It was the swift celerity of his death,

425   Which I did think with slower foot came on,
That brained my purpose. But, peace be with him.
That life is better life, past fearing death,
Than that which lives to fear. Make it your comfort,
So happy is your brother.

430   ISABELLA   I do, my lord.

Enter Angelo, Mariana, [Friar] Peter [and] Provost

---

405 Do . . . office undertake the task   consummate being completed   408 at . . . it at the
fact that he behaved like this than at the extraordinary nature of the situation
411 Advertising attentive   holy devoted   412 changing . . . habit having changed my feelings
with my appearance   413 Attorneyed serving as your agent   415 vassal servant, subject
pained put to effort   418 free generous   420 obscured disguised   422 rash remonstrance
sudden revelation   423 so be lost i.e. executed   kind fond, sisterly   424 celerity speed
426 brained destroyed, dashed the brains from   429 So thus

DUKE   For this new-married man approaching here,
              Whose salt imagination yet hath wronged
              Your well defended honour, you must pardon
              For Mariana's sake. But as he adjudged your brother,
435   Being criminal, in double violation
              Of sacred chastity and of promise-breach
              Thereon dependent for your brother's life,
              The very mercy of the law cries out
              Most audible, even from his proper tongue,
440   'An Angelo for Claudio, death for death!'
              Haste still pays haste, and leisure answers leisure,
              Like doth quit like, and measure still for measure.
              Then, Angelo, thy fault's thus manifested,
              Which, though thou wouldst deny, denies thee vantage.
445   We do condemn thee to the very block
              Where Claudio stooped to death, and with like haste.
              Away with him!

MARIANA   O my most gracious lord,
              I hope you will not mock me with a husband.
450 DUKE   It is your husband mocked you with a husband.
              Consenting to the safeguard of your honour,
              I thought your marriage fit, else imputation,
              For that he knew you, might reproach your life
              And choke your good to come. For his possessions,
455   Although by confiscation they are ours,
              We do instate and widow you withal,
              To buy you a better husband.

MARIANA   O my dear lord,
              I crave no other, nor no better man.
460 DUKE   Never crave him, we are definitive.

---

432 salt lecherous   434 adjudged condemned   436 promise-breach Thereon dependent
i.e. the breaking of the promise to save Claudio, made in return for Isabella giving up her
chastity   439 proper own   441 still always   442 quit repay   measure retribution/
judgment/due proportion   444 though . . . vantage even were you to deny it you would not
benefit   445 very block same executioner's block   449 mock deceive/tantalize/taunt
452 else . . . you otherwise accusations regarding your sexual relations with him   454 For as
for   456 instate endow   widow you withal grant you a widow's settlement with them
460 definitive determined

MARIANA	Gentle my liege—	*Kneels*
DUKE	You do but lose your labour.	

     Away with him to death.— Now, sir, to you.   *To Lucio*

MARIANA   O my good lord! Sweet Isabel, take my part,

465   Lend me your knees, and all my life to come

    I'll lend you all my life to do you service.

DUKE   Against all sense you do importune her.

    Should she kneel down in mercy of this fact,

    Her brother's ghost his pavèd bed would break,

470   And take her hence in horror.

MARIANA   Isabel,

    Sweet Isabel, do yet but kneel by me,

    Hold up your hands, say nothing, I'll speak all.

    They say best men are moulded out of faults,

475   And for the most become much more the better

    For being a little bad: so may my husband.

    O Isabel, will you not lend a knee?

DUKE   He dies for Claudio's death.

ISABELLA   Most bounteous sir,

480   Look, if it please you, on this man condemned,   *Kneels*

    As if my brother lived. I partly think

    A due sincerity governed his deeds,

    Till he did look on me: since it is so,

    Let him not die. My brother had but justice,

485   In that he did the thing for which he died.

    For Angelo,

    His act did not o'ertake his bad intent,

    And must be buried but as an intent

    That perished by the way. Thoughts are no subjects,

490   Intents but merely thoughts.

MARIANA   Merely, my lord.

---

462 **lose your labour** waste your efforts   467 **Against all sense** totally unreasonably
importune entreat   468 **of this fact** for this crime   469 **pavèd bed** grave covered with a
stone slab   475 **most** most part   484 **but** only   487 **His . . . intent** despite his bad intentions
he did not fulfill them   489 **subjects** actual things/people subject to the ruling power

DUKE	Your suit's unprofitable. Stand up, I say.	*They stand*

I have bethought me of another fault.
Provost, how came it Claudio was beheaded
495　At an unusual hour?

PROVOST　　It was commanded so.

DUKE　　Had you a special warrant for the deed?

PROVOST　　No, my good lord, it was by private message.

DUKE　　For which I do discharge you of your office.
500　Give up your keys.

PROVOST　　Pardon me, noble lord,
I thought it was a fault, but knew it not,
Yet did repent me after more advice,
For testimony whereof, one in the prison,
505　That should by private order else have died,
I have reserved alive.

DUKE　　What's he?

PROVOST　　His name is Barnardine.

DUKE　　I would thou hadst done so by Claudio.
510　Go fetch him hither, let me look upon him.　　[*Exit Provost*]

ESCALUS　　I am sorry, one so learnèd and so wise
As you, Lord Angelo, have still appeared,
Should slip so grossly, both in the heat of blood
And lack of tempered judgement afterward.

515　ANGELO　　I am sorry that such sorrow I procure,
And so deep sticks it in my penitent heart
That I crave death more willingly than mercy,
'Tis my deserving, and I do entreat it.

Enter Provost, Barnardine, Claudio [muffled, and] Julietta

DUKE　　Which is that Barnardine?

520　PROVOST　　This, my lord.

DUKE　　There was a friar told me of this man.
Sirrah, thou art said to have a stubborn soul
That apprehends no further than this world,

---

492 **unprofitable** pointless/unsuccessful　502 **knew it not** was not sure　503 **advice**
consideration　506 **reserved** preserved　512 **still** always　513 **blood** sexual desire
514 **tempered** self-controlled　515 **procure** bring about　523 **apprehends** comprehends

And squar'st thy life according. Thou'rt condemned,
525　But, for those earthly faults, I quit them all,
And pray thee take this mercy to provide
For better times to come. Friar, advise him,
I leave him to your hand. What muffled fellow's that?

PROVOST　　This is another prisoner that I saved,
530　Who should have died when Claudio lost his head,
As like almost to Claudio as himself.　　　*Unmuffles Claudio*

DUKE　　　If he be like your brother, for his sake　　*To Isabella*
Is he pardoned. And, for your lovely sake,
Give me your hand and say you will be mine,
535　He is my brother too. But fitter time for that.
By this Lord Angelo perceives he's safe,
Methinks I see a quickening in his eye.
Well, Angelo, your evil quits you well:
Look that you love your wife, her worth worth yours.
540　I find an apt remission in myself.
And yet here's one in place I cannot pardon.
You, sirrah, that knew me for a fool, a coward,　　*To Lucio*
One all of luxury, an ass, a madman —
Wherein have I so deserved of you,
545　That you extol me thus?

LUCIO　　　'Faith, my lord. I spoke it but according to the trick.
If you will hang me for it, you may, but I had rather it would
please you I might be whipped.

DUKE　　　Whipped first, sir, and hanged after.
550　Proclaim it, provost, round about the city:
If any woman wronged by this lewd fellow —
As I have heard him swear himself there's one
Whom he begot with child — let her appear,
And he shall marry her. The nuptial finished,
555　Let him be whipped and hanged.

---

524 **squar'st** measures/shapes　　525 **quit** acquit, pardon　　528 **muffled** concealed (with a hood or clothing)　　537 **quickening** fresh animation　　538 **quits** repays/leaves　　539 **Look** make sure　**her . . . yours** her worth is equal to yours/let your worth be deserving of hers　540 **apt remission** ready forgiveness　　541 **in place** present　　543 **luxury** lust　　545 **extol** praise　　546 **trick** custom/whim/prank/foolishness

LUCIO   I beseech your highness, do not marry me to a
whore. Your highness said even now, I made you a duke. Good
my lord, do not recompense me in making me a cuckold.

DUKE   Upon mine honour, thou shalt marry her.
560   Thy slanders I forgive, and therewithal
Remit thy other forfeits. Take him to prison,
And see our pleasure herein executed.

LUCIO   Marrying a punk, my lord, is pressing to death,
whipping, and hanging.

565   DUKE   Slandering a prince deserves it.

[*Exeunt Officers with Lucio*]

She, Claudio, that you wronged, look you restore.
Joy to you, Mariana. Love her, Angelo:
I have confessed her and I know her virtue.
Thanks, good friend Escalus, for thy much goodness,
570   There's more behind that is more gratulate.
Thanks, provost, for thy care and secrecy,
We shall employ thee in a worthier place.
Forgive him, Angelo, that brought you home
The head of Ragozine for Claudio's,
575   Th'offence pardons itself. Dear Isabel,
I have a motion much imports your good,
Whereto if you'll a willing ear incline,
What's mine is yours and what is yours is mine.
So, bring us to our palace, where we'll show
580   What's yet behind, that's meet you all should know.

[*Exeunt*]

---

558 **cuckold** man with an unfaithful wife   560 **therewithal** in addition   561 **Remit** pardon
forfeits punishments   562 **pleasure herein executed** wishes fulfilled   563 **pressing to death**
one who refused to plead guilty or innocent was pressed with heavy weights until he pleaded
or died (plays on the sense of "death by sexual exertion")   566 **restore** make amends to
(by marriage)   568 **confessed her** been her confessor   570 **behind** to come   **gratulate**
pleasing/expressive of thanks   576 **motion . . . good** proposal that greatly concerns your
benefit   579 **bring** accompany   580 **yet behind** still to be revealed   **meet** fitting

TEXTUAL NOTES

F = First Folio text of 1623, the only authority for the play
F2 = a correction introduced in the Second Folio text of 1632
Ed = a correction introduced by a later editor
SD = stage direction
SH = speech heading (i.e. speaker's name)

List of parts *based on "Names of All the Actors" (reordered) at end of* F *text*

1.1.74 relish *spelled* rallish *in* F **80 SD** *Exit* = F2. F *places SD after line* 79
1.2.55 SH MISTRESS OVERDONE = Ed. F = *Bawd. (throughout)* **77 SH POMPEY** = Ed. F = *Clo. or Clow. (throughout)*
1.3.19 morality = Ed. F = *mortality*
1.4.11 and witless = F2. F = *witlesse* **22 fourteen** = F *Some eds emend to* nineteen **28 Becomes more** = Ed. F = *More* **46 in** = F. *Some eds emend to* me *or* it **50 me** = Ed. F *omits*
1.5.2 SH FRANCISCA = Ed. F = *Nun* **58 giving-out** = F. *Some eds emend to* givings-out
2.1.13 your = Ed. F = *our*
2.2.75 back again = F2. F = *againe* **118 now** = F. *Some eds emend to* new *or* raw **121 ere** = Ed. F = *here* **135 ne'er** = F2 F = *neuer*
2.4.9 seared = Ed. F = *feard* **57 or** = Ed. F = *and* **84 me be** = F2. F = *be*
3.1.29 sire = Ed. F = *fire* **54 me ... them** = Ed. F = *them to hear me* **74 Though** = Ed. F = *Through* **99 enew** = Ed. F = *emmew* **143 penury** = F2. F = *periury* **225 by oath** = F2. F = *oath* **297 eat, array** = Ed. F = *eate away* **311 Free from** = F2. F = *From* **409 dearer** = Ed. F = *deare* **434 now ... yet** = F. *Some eds emend to* not past it yet. **469 See** = Ed. F = *Sea* **474 it is** = Ed. F = *as it is*
4.1.24 well come = F. *Some eds emend to* welcome **62 quests** = F2. F = *Quest*
4.2.42–44 = F. *Some eds assign the speech to Abhorson* **94 Happily** *Spelled* Happely *in* F **100** *Assigned to the Provost* =Ed. F *assigns to the Duke* **lordship's** = Ed. F = *Lords* **101** *Assigned to the Duke* =Ed. F *assigns to the Provost*
4.3.14 Forthright = Ed. F = *Forthlight* **Shoe-tie** *spelled* Shootie *in* F **86 yonder** = Ed. F = *yond* **128 convent** *spelled* Couent *in* F
4.4.4 redeliver = Ed. F = *re-liuer*
4.5.6 Flavius' = Ed. F = *Flavia's* **8 Valentius** = Ed. F = *Valencius*
5.1.14 me = Ed. F = *we* **188 her** = F2 F = *your* **455 confiscation** = F2. F = *confutation* **580 that's** = F2. F = *that*

SCENE-BY-SCENE ANALYSIS

ACT 1 SCENE 1

The themes of law, power, and justice are established as the Duke of Vienna appoints Angelo as his substitute in his absence. This begins a series of character pairings and exchanges, generating questions on the nature of identity, linked to the theme of "disguise." Escalus expresses the "worth" of Angelo, which raises issues of the monetary or social "value" of individuals. Angelo arrives and the duke places him in charge of "Mortality and mercy in Vienna," a phrase that reflects the main concerns of the play, suggesting that this is not a conventional comedy. Angelo asks to be given some lesser test of his "mettle," but the duke insists that he has chosen Angelo and must leave at once. The theme of secrecy/concealment is evident, as the duke's destiny is unclear and his departure is deliberately private from his people.

ACT 1 SCENE 2

A second set of characters who generate much of the play's low, bawdy humor is introduced. Their setting is the taverns and brothels inhabited by pimps and prostitutes, a constant reminder of the theme of sex. The presence of prostitution also raises issues concerning human "worth," particularly that of women and their status and power within society.

Lucio is engaged in banter with two gentlemen when Mistress Overdone interrupts them to say that Claudio has been arrested for getting Juliet pregnant, thereby breaking Vienna's laws on premarital sex. Pompey, a bawd, comes to tell Mistress Overdone of a proclamation that all the brothels in Vienna are to be "plucked down," another sign of the changes under Angelo's rule. Mistress Overdone worries what will become of her, but Pompey reassures her that, though she changes her place, she "need not change [her] trade"—

a bawdy quip, but perhaps also a reference to the constancy of identity beneath the various disguises/assumed identities throughout.

ACT 1 SCENE 3

The Provost leads Claudio to prison accompanied by Juliet, Lucio, and the gentlemen. Claudio protests at being shown "to th'world," but the Provost explains that these are Angelo's orders, an ironically public display of justice that contrasts with his later, concealed offenses. Lucio asks Claudio what he has done, and Claudio replies, "What but to speak of would offend again," raising the theme of speech and the potential power of words. He explains to Lucio that Juliet is pregnant but that they are "upon a true contract." They have been prevented from marrying because Juliet's relatives oppose the match and have retained her dowry, a circumstance that reinforces the pecuniary element to relationships, in marriage as well as prostitution. Claudio describes how laws of Vienna that were forgotten under the duke have been resurrected. This means he could face the death penalty for Juliet's pregnancy.

He asks Lucio to ask his sister, Isabella, who is about to enter a convent, to plead with Angelo on his behalf. He is confident in her ability to persuade him because of her youth and skill in the use of the "prosperous art" of language. Isabella's choice of chastity sets her apart from the other women in the play in sexual terms, and this reference to her command over language forms a stark contrast to Juliet, who has remained silent, perhaps a visual symbol of her powerlessness. Her pregnancy also serves as a thematic visual representation: the presence of both an impending birth and execution during the play provide constant reminders of the themes of life and death.

ACT 1 SCENE 4

The duke asks Friar Thomas for "secret harbour" at the monastery. He explains that his love of a reclusive existence has meant that the "strict statutes and most biting laws" of Vienna have been allowed to slip and the city has become a corrupt place where "liberty plucks justice by the nose." He feels that it would be hypocrisy to try to enforce these laws himself, having given his people their liberty in the first place, and so he is leaving it to Angelo. He asks to be disguised as a friar, so that he can return to Vienna and secretly watch Angelo's progress: he wishes to see the effects of power on the "precise" (meaning puritanical) Angelo. This demonstrates the complicated characterization of the duke: he acknowledges his weak leadership and is addressing this, but in a way that absolves him of responsibility for any consequences. There also seem to be personal motives behind his behavior, with his "experiment" concerning the effects of power on the individual. The duke's exchange of roles reinforces the themes of switched identities and disguise.

ACT 1 SCENE 5

Isabella questions Francisca about life in the convent, expressing her desire for a life of "strict restraint," creating an ironic parallel with the self-disciplined Angelo. Lucio calls out, and Francisca sends Isabella to the door to learn why he is there. Lucio explains that Claudio is in prison for getting Juliet "with child." He describes Angelo in terms that support his characterization so far: his blood is "snow-broth" and he "never feels / The wanton stings and motions of the sense." He tells Isabella that "All hope is gone," unless she can "soften Angelo," as a warrant has been issued for Claudio's execution. He urges her to use her "power," although, ironically, it is a power that seems to come from female submission: the moving image of a "maiden" who "weep[s] and kneel[s]." Isabella agrees.

ACT 2 SCENE 1

Lines 1–43: Angelo argues that the law should not become a "scarecrow" for criminals to "perch" on rather than fear. Escalus agrees, but suggests that they could be more lenient, pleading on Claudio's behalf. He asks Angelo to remember that, at some point in his life, he may have "Erred" in the same way, but Angelo is unmoved, declaring that " 'Tis one thing to be tempted, Escalus / Another thing to fall." He adds that if he should ever commit the same crime as

Claudio, then he would expect the same punishment. He orders that Claudio is executed by nine o'clock the next morning.

Lines 44–265: Elbow brings Pompey and Froth before Angelo and the scene takes a comic turn, contrasting with the preceding conversation. The themes remain the same, however: sex, corruption, and the law, emphasizing the fine line between comedy and tragedy. Humor is generated through the character of Elbow, a figure of fun with limited understanding and confusing habits of speech—malapropisms such as "benefactors" instead of "malefactors," for example. The confusion he creates is compounded by the foolishness of Froth and the innuendo and wordplay of Pompey, who is scornful of Elbow and his vague accusations. After a frustrating attempt to understand Elbow's purpose and conversation, Angelo leaves Escalus to deal with them. Escalus' attempts at interrogation are hindered by their nonsense and Pompey's increasingly bawdy humor. He eventually dismisses Froth and Pompey with a warning and instructs Elbow to bring him some names of other men who might become constables. The scene ends on a serious note as he grieves over Claudio's sentence.

ACT 2 SCENE 2

Lines 1–191: The Provost waits to speak with Angelo, musing on the harsh nature of Claudio's punishment. He asks Angelo to reconsider, but Angelo tells him to do his "office" or lose his job. The Provost wishes to know what to do with "the groaning Juliet," who is "very near her hour," one of an increasing number of references to the progression of time which create tension. Angelo commands that Juliet be taken to "some more fitter place." Lucio and Isabella are shown in. Conflict is evident in Isabella's character as she acknowledges that she abhors Claudio's crime, but must plead on his behalf, describing herself "At war 'twixt will and will not," one of many phrases that reinforce the idea of balance raised by the play's title. Angelo refuses to change his mind and Lucio says that Isabella is "too cold," urging her to kneel and "hang upon his gown."

The power of Isabella's eloquence is shown in an exchange that highlights the complexities of law and power and establishes the difference between human and divine justice. She asks Angelo what would happen if God were to judge as he does, but he remains unmoved. Urged by Lucio, Isabella continues to argue her point. Aside, Angelo ambiguously acknowledges to himself that Isabella speaks "such sense / That my sense breeds with it," showing awareness of her reason, but also his stirring sexual attraction to her. He is about to leave when Isabella offers him a bribe: she will pray for his soul. Angelo gives no direct response, but tells her to return tomorrow "any time 'fore noon."

Lines 192–217: Angelo's soliloquy reveals his sexual attraction to Isabella. This seems to stem from her virtue: he desires her "foully for those things / That make her good." His internal struggle is evident as he experiences the emotions that he judges harshly in others.

ACT 2 SCENE 3

The duke, now disguised as a Friar, claims that he has come to minister to the prisoners. The Provost points out Juliet and the duke/ "Friar" asks her if she repents, which she does. He argues that her sin was "heavier" than Claudio's, showing that society places more moral weight on the sexual purity of women than men. He tells her that he is going to see Claudio, informing her of his imminent execution. Juliet is in despair.

ACT 2 SCENE 4

Alone, Angelo considers his feelings, and dwells on the difference between speech, thought, and action: while he gives "empty words" to heaven, his thought "Anchors on Isabel." A servant announces Isabella and Angelo struggles to control his feelings. She tells him that she has come to know his "pleasure," a word that he freely misinterprets. Angelo says that Claudio will die, but ambiguously adds that it may be that he will "live awhile." Isabella is confused. Angelo puts a question to her: would she commit a sin to save her brother's life? Isabella misunderstands him, taking the "sin" in question to mean that of pleading for Claudio and his being forgiven. Frustrated, Angelo asks directly whether she would "lay down the treasures of [her] body" to save Claudio. Isabella declares that she would rather die than give her body "up to shame." Angelo tells her that he loves her and that Claudio's life will be spared if she will have sex with him. Disgusted, Isabella accuses him of hypocrisy and threatens to "tell the world aloud." He replies that no one will believe her because of his "unsoiled name" and, giving her until the next day to answer him, leaves. Alone, Isabella realizes that he is right: no one would believe her. She goes to tell Claudio, confident that her brother's "mind of honour" means that he would rather die "Before his sister should her body stoop / To such abhorred pollution."

ACT 3 SCENE 1

Lines 1–55: The duke, still disguised as a Friar, visits Claudio in prison and counsels him to prepare to die, arguing that death is better than life, which is full of difficulty and pain. Claudio thanks him and claims that he is ready to die. Isabella arrives and asks to see Claudio. The duke hides to overhear their conversation.

Lines 56–188: Isabella tells Claudio that he must die. He asks if there is "no remedy," and she explains that the only alternative will "fetter" him until his death. Claudio believes that she means life imprisonment, emphasizing his focus on the physical/bodily aspects of existence, in contrast to Isabella's concerns with the soul. He is further confused when she explains that she means a life imprisonment outside of jail. When Claudio demands to know what she means, Isabella is afraid to tell him, suggesting that she is not as confident in her brother as she was at the end of the previous scene. He assures her that he is not afraid of death, and she explains that the "outward-sainted deputy," Angelo, will grant Claudio's freedom in exchange for her virginity. Claudio says that she "shalt not do't," and Isabella is relieved. Claudio comments on Angelo's hypocrisy, but then tells Isabella that he is afraid to die, "To lie in cold obstruction and to rot," again emphasizing his concerns with the body rather than the soul. He asks her to agree to Angelo's demands, arguing that the sin would become a virtue because she would be saving his life. Angry and disgusted, Isabella says that it is best that he should die. The duke interrupts and asks to speak to Isabella privately. She goes aside, and the duke speaks quickly to Claudio, telling him that he overheard their conversation. Pretending that he is Angelo's confessor, he says that Angelo was only testing Isabella and that Claudio will die anyway. Claudio goes to ask Isabella's pardon.

Lines 189–275: Isabella speaks to the duke, believing him to be a Friar, and says that she would rather that her brother died than she have an illegitimate child by Angelo. The duke claims to have a solution that will both save Claudio and Isabella's virtue, and also help "a poor wronged lady." He tells Isabella about Mariana, who was betrothed to Angelo, but between the "time of the contract and limit of the solemnity" her brother died in a shipwreck, and her dowry was lost with him. Angelo then rejected Mariana without a dowry, pretending that he had discovered she was unfaithful. This revelation reinforces issues concerning human "worth," but also raises further questions about the duke's motivations: if he has known this all along, then he knows that the popular image of Angelo is untrue and his appointment of Angelo as deputy is difficult to understand. The duke suggests that Isabella agree to Angelo's demands, but asks that their meeting take place in "shadow and silence" so that Mariana, who still loves Angelo, can take her place. Isabella agrees.

Lines 276–352: Elbow brings in Pompey, who sees Lucio and hopes he will pay his bail. The duke is disgusted by their bawdy conversation, which creates a comic contrast to the scene so far. Lucio refuses to pay, and Pompey is led away to prison.

Lines 353–441: Lucio, unaware of the disguise, asks the "Friar" if he has any news of the duke. Dramatic irony is sustained as Lucio criticizes the duke for leaving and putting Angelo in charge. He suggests that Angelo could be more lenient toward "lechery," and says that the duke would have been more sympathetic, as he enjoyed "the sport" himself. Lucio slanders the duke as drunk and lecherous. The duke, in disguise, can do nothing, but threatens to report Lucio when the duke "returns."

Lines 442–532: Escalus and the Provost escort Mistress Overdone to prison for running a brothel. She claims that Lucio has informed on her and reveals that he has a child by a woman he promised to marry, but didn't. Escalus tells the Provost that Angelo will not change his mind about Claudio, who is to die the next day. The duke's soliloquy reveals his anger with Angelo, who "weeds" the vice in the city but lets his own grow.

ACT 4 SCENE 1

A Boy sings a melancholy song to Mariana, but she dismisses him when the duke/"Friar" arrives. As Isabella approaches, the duke asks Mariana to leave them for a while. Isabella says that Angelo has given her two keys and instructions to meet in a garden that night. In turn, she has told Angelo that they must remain in the dark and that she can only stay a short while. The duke calls Mariana and tells Isabella to explain matters to her. They return after a short while and Mariana agrees to the plan if the duke advises it. He states that Angelo is Mariana's "husband on a pre-contract" and therefore it can be no sin for her to have sex with him, an argument which seems to contradict the law under which Angelo has imprisoned Claudio, raising a subtle distinction between "crime" and "sin."

ACT 4 SCENE 2

The Provost asks Pompey to act as executioner's assistant, creating an unusual juxtaposition of comedy and tragedy. Claudio and Barnardine, another prisoner, are called, but Claudio arrives alone and explains that Barnardine is asleep. The Provost shows him the warrant for his execution and tells him to go and prepare himself. The duke arrives, still in disguise, and asks if anyone has come with a pardon for Claudio, knowing that Mariana has kept Isabella's half of the bargain with Angelo. A Messenger comes, but instead of a pardon, Angelo has sent instructions that Claudio is to be executed by four o'clock and his head delivered to Angelo by five. Realizing that Angelo has not kept his word, the duke improvises an alternative plan. He asks about Barnardine, and, learning that he is a drunkard who "apprehends death no more dreadfully but as a drunken sleep," suggests that they execute him early and send his head to Angelo in place of Claudio's, another exchange of identities. The Provost is unsure until shown a letter with the duke's seal on it and is assured that he is acting on the duke's behalf.

ACT 4 SCENE 3

Dark humor is generated as Barnardine refuses to be executed, arguing that he has been drinking all night and needs more time to prepare himself. The Provost suggests an alternative: they can send the head of yet another prisoner, the pirate Ragozine, who has died of natural causes. Once alone, the duke reveals his intention to write to Angelo, telling him he will soon be returning and that he intends to enter the city "publicly." Isabella arrives, wanting to hear whether Angelo's pardon for Claudio has arrived. The duke decides to tell her that Claudio has been executed, although once again his motives are unclear. He tells her that "The duke comes home tomorrow" and that Angelo and Escalus are to meet him at the gates. Explaining that he cannot be there himself, he sends Isabella with a letter to Friar Peter, who will accompany Isabella and Mariana to accuse Angelo in front of the duke. Lucio enters, expressing sympathy for Isabella and criticizing the duke, unaware that he is speaking to him.

ACT 4 SCENE 4

Angelo and Escalus discuss the duke's instructions and make arrangements to meet him at the gate with various people of importance from the city. They also reveal that he has told them to proclaim "that if any crave redress of injustice, they should exhibit their petitions in the street." This emphasizes that the duke's return will be public, unlike the other events of the play. Angelo's soliloquy reveals that he is relying on Isabella's "tender shame" to prevent her speaking out and says that he executed Claudio out of fear that he would have revenged his sister.

ACT 4 SCENE 5

The duke, no longer disguised, makes arrangements with Friar Peter.

ACT 4 SCENE 6

Isabella is nervous, but Mariana tells her that she must obey the "Friar," who has said that she must continue the pretense that Angelo has taken her virginity. Friar Peter arrives to take them to meet the duke.

ACT 5 SCENE 1

In keeping with generic expectations of a comedy, the various deceptions and misunderstandings are made public and rectified, although this is not straightforward: the duke deliberately delays the revelation of certain facts and, even when order is restored, several questions remain unanswered.

Lines 1–187: The duke greets Angelo and Escalus as Friar Peter leads in Isabella. She kneels before the duke and asks him for "justice, justice, justice, justice!" Angelo claims that Isabella is unstable due to the execution of her brother, but she accuses him of being "an adulterous thief, / An hypocrite" and "a virgin-violator." She urges the duke to "make the truth appear where it seems hid" and explains Angelo's offense against her, assisted (unasked) by Lucio, who continues to interrupt throughout the scene, often to comic effect. The duke pretends not to believe Isabella and, when she starts to leave, has her arrested for slandering Angelo. He claims that it must be a plot and asks Isabella who knew of her intentions, and she tells him about "Friar Lodowick" (the duke's assumed identity). Lucio interrupts, saying that he met "Friar Lodowick" and that he slandered the duke, but Friar Peter says that this is not true and neither are Isabella's claims against Angelo. Isabella is led away and the duke asks Angelo to be the "judge / Of [his] own cause."

Lines 188–302: Mariana enters, veiled. The duke asks her to show her face but she refuses to do so until her husband bids her. The duke asks whether she is married, a "maid," or a widow, but she denies all three, and he responds, "Why, you are nothing then," emphasizing the value/status of women in a society in which their position is determined entirely in relation to men. Mariana claims that Angelo is her husband and that he has "known" her body, even though he thinks that he has not. Angelo asks to see her face and she unveils herself, a visual representation of the revelations in this scene. Mariana tells Angelo that it was she, not Isabella, he had sex with. Angelo confesses he knows Mariana and explains their broken engagement, but claims that she and Isabella are mad and merely "instruments" in someone else's plan. He asks to be allowed to "find this practice out," and the duke agrees. The Provost is sent to find "Friar Lodowick" and the duke explains that he must leave for a while. Escalus asks Lucio about "Lodowick" and Lucio repeats his claim that he slandered the duke. Escalus asks him to remain until "Lodowick" is brought before them and calls for Isabella.

Lines 303–406: The duke returns, disguised as a Friar again, claiming that he is an outsider and has watched "corruption boil and bubble" in Vienna. Angelo questions Lucio about the "Friar" and Lucio claims that he slandered the duke. Escalus commands that the "Friar" be taken to prison but, as the Provost seizes him, Lucio pulls the duke's hood off only to reveal his true identity. The duke has Lucio arrested and takes Angelo's seat, emphasizing his return to power. Angelo confesses his crime and asks to be sentenced to death, but the duke sends him away to be married at once to Mariana.

Lines 407–518: The duke apologizes to Isabella for Claudio's death, saying that he could not reveal his identity before, and that Claudio died sooner than he expected. Angelo and Mariana are brought back in, married. The duke orders that Angelo should be executed as Claudio was: "Like doth quit like, and measure still for measure." Mariana protests and asks Isabella to join her in pleading for Angelo's life, and, despite the duke reminding her that Angelo should pay for Claudio's death, she agrees. Isabella argues that Angelo's intentions were sincere until he met her. The duke refuses to listen, then turns to the Provost and asks why Claudio was beheaded at an "unusual hour" and fires him for acting without a special warrant from himself. The Provost argues that he thought it was wrong, and kept Barnardine alive "For testimony whereof." The duke summons Barnardine.

Lines 519–580: Barnardine is brought in, along with Juliet and Claudio, whose face is hidden. The duke pardons Barnardine and the Provost reveals that the muffled man is Claudio. The duke pardons him as well and asks Isabella to marry him, apparently forgetting her intention to become a nun. He pardons Angelo and punishes Lucio by ordering him to marry the woman that he made pregnant, despite Lucio's protests that she is a "whore." However, the text gives no clues as to the various characters' responses to the duke; in particular, Isabella's answer to his proposal. Despite the "tidy" resolution, therefore, the end of the play creates a problematic tension between the generic requirements of comedy and the dark events that have occurred.

MEASURE FOR MEASURE IN PERFORMANCE: THE RSC AND BEYOND

The best way to understand a Shakespeare play is to see it or ideally to participate in it. By examining a range of productions, we may gain a sense of the extraordinary variety of approaches and interpretations that are possible—a variety that gives Shakespeare his unique capacity to be reinvented and made "our contemporary" four centuries after his death.

We begin with a brief overview of the play's theatrical and cinematic life, offering historical perspectives on how it has been performed. We then analyze in more detail a series of productions staged over the last half-century by the Royal Shakespeare Company. The sense of dialogue between productions that can only occur when a company is dedicated to the revival and investigation of the Shakespeare canon over a long period, together with the uniquely comprehensive archival resource of promptbooks, program notes, reviews, and interviews held on behalf of the RSC at the Shakespeare Birthplace Trust in Stratford-upon-Avon, allows an "RSC stage history" to become a crucible in which the chemistry of the play can be explored.

Finally, we go to the horse's mouth. Directors and actors know the plays from the inside: we interview the director of a distinguished RSC production and actors who have played the parts of Isabella and the duke to high acclaim.

FOUR CENTURIES OF MEASURE FOR MEASURE: AN OVERVIEW

Measure for Measure has enjoyed a patchy stage history since its first recorded performance at Whitehall before James I on St. Stephen's night (December 26) 1604. Based on internal evidence, the play is thought to have been written earlier that same year and was most likely performed by the King's Men, the acting company with which Shakespeare was associated, at the Globe playhouse. There are no further records of its performance before the closure of the theaters in 1642 and their reopening in 1660.

The Restoration period introduced moving scenery and women onto the stage. Many of Shakespeare's plays were revived, having been "improved" in various ways. Restoration productions of *Measure* were heavily adapted in order to eliminate those elements considered indecorous—the low-life scenes and the emphasis on sex—in order to produce a play in keeping with contemporary sensibilities. William Davenant's adaptation, *The Law Against Lovers*, performed by the Duke of York's Servants at Lincoln's Inn Fields in 1662, incorporates Beatrice and Benedick from Shakespeare's *Much Ado About Nothing*. Benedick becomes Angelo's younger brother and leads an insurrection against the prison to free Claudio. Beatrice is a wealthy heiress, sister to Juliet, and Angelo's ward. Mariana is eliminated, but there is a younger third sister, Viola, who dances a sarabande (passionate dance) with castanets, a performance much enjoyed by Samuel Pepys.[1] Angelo, disgusted by the low morals of women in his society, claims to have been merely testing Isabella, whom he finally marries. Benedick marries Beatrice, and the duke, most likely played by Thomas Betterton, the leading actor of the period, retires to a monastery. Despite its muddle and eccentricity, Davenant's adaptation does resolve in its own way some of the issues that have troubled later critics. It recognizes that there is a problem in the union of the duke and Isabella, that the "bed trick" is a sleazy device, and that Angelo and Isabella seem temperamentally suited.

Charles Gildon's *Measure for Measure, or Beauty the Best Advocate* (1700) was produced at the height of the vogue for inserting masques into plays. Gildon incorporated Purcell's *Dido and Aeneas* with a libretto by Nahum Tate, rearranged into four musical entertainments devised by Escalus to celebrate Angelo's birthday. Purcell's work was the first sung-through opera in English, and Gildon's deployment of the work was equally innovative. He used it to turn his play into a dramatic opera in which the story of Dido and Aeneas is integrated into the main plot and used to comment on Mariana's story. No contemporary scores survived, and Purcell's haunting music would have been lost had it not been for the play's survival.

Shakespeare's play was revived in 1720 at Lincoln's Inn Fields with James Quin as the duke. He continued to play the role in revivals until his retirement in 1750. From 1737 onward he was successfully partnered by Susannah Cibber, who played Isabella to great acclaim. Other notable actresses to play the part were Mrs. Yates and Peg Woffington. Mrs. Fitzhenry created a success in the part opposite Henry Mossop at Dublin's Smock Alley theater. Sarah Siddons was undoubtedly the most famous historical Isabella though, playing the part from 1783 to 1812, most often with her brother, the handsome and dignified John Philip Kemble, as the duke. Later their younger brother Charles joined the distinguished cast to play Claudio. Kemble's acting version, which cut sexual and bawdy references and thinned many of the longer speeches, continued in use for fifty years. In her 1808 edition of the play, Mrs. Inchbald writes that "Mrs Siddons's exquisite acting, and beautiful appearance in Isabella, are proverbial . . . Mrs Yates was admired in the part—both her person and voice were favourable for the representation—but Mrs Siddons had not at that time appeared."[2]

The play continued to be revived periodically in increasingly heavily bowdlerized texts. One Victorian critic explained that there was "no other play of Shakespeare's in which so much of the dialogue is absolutely unspeakable before a modern audience."[3] Samuel Phelps staged it periodically at Sadler's Wells between 1846 and 1857, with himself as the duke and Laura Addison as Isabella, again using a bowdlerized text. The only important production in the following decades was Adelaide Neilson's at the Haymarket theater in 1876 and 1878. In 1888 the Polish-born Helena Modjeska produced and starred in a one-night revival at New York's Fourteenth-Street Theatre to general critical acclaim:

> A very large portion of the original text has been retained, but the comic scenes have been vigorously cut, and though Pompey, Elbow and Froth appear, their vivacity is kept within decent bounds. The performance, which was brilliant in an

artistic sense and of rare beauty so far as Mme. Modjeska was concerned, was otherwise even and interesting.[4]

William Poel, the English actor-manager, was one of the leading theatrical figures in the reaction against over-elaborate Victorian staging who advocated a return to the fast-paced fluid action of the Elizabethan theater, inspired by the recent discovery of the Dutch traveler and student Johannes de Witt's drawing of the Swan theater made on his visit to London in 1596. Accordingly, the Shakespeare Reading Society staged *Measure for Measure* in 1893 within a reconstruction of a seventeenth-century playhouse inside London's Royalty Theatre. The attempt to recreate Elizabethan staging received a mixed reception:

> The performance might fairly be described as a reading of the play by the members of the society in costume on virtually a bare stage, or, at least, a stage representing . . . a "scene individable." Usually it is assumed that in such circumstances the imagination of the onlooker would be so stimulated as to conjure up streets and palaces surpassing the art of the modern *metteur-en-scène*. The present writer must confess that he had no such experience. In fact, though following the action closely, he had no picture of the scene before his mind at all.[5]

The 1908 revival of the production at the Gaiety Theatre, Manchester, was on the whole more warmly received:

> Mr Poel did wonders, but he could not get rid of the proscenium arch. What he gave us was not an Elizabethan stage as it was to Elizabethan playgoers, but a picture of an Elizabethan stage seen through the frame of a modern proscenium. So we gained a good visual idea of a Shakespearean stage, but not the Elizabethan sensation of having an actor come forward to the edge of a platform in the midst of ourselves and deliver speeches from the position almost like that of a speaker from a pulpit or from a front bench in Parliament, with only the nar-

rowest scope for theatrical illusion, with no incentive to natu-
ralism, and with every motive for putting his strength into
sheer energy and beauty of declamation, giving his performance the special qualities of fine recitation as distinct from
those of realistic acting. But, without that, we got a good deal.[6]

Although Poel's own performance as Angelo was singled out for
praise, criticism was made of the still heavily bowdlerized text used.
The play's time had not yet come.

There were a number of productions in the early twentieth century, including Oscar Ashe's at the Adelphi in 1906. His wife, Lily
Brayton, played Isabella but, like Poel, Ashe himself chose to play
Angelo rather than the duke. The amateur production in the same
year by the Oxford Union Dramatic Society aroused hostility among
the townsfolk on the grounds of the play's "indecency," as did Poel's
production at the Stratford Memorial Theatre in 1908. There were
four revivals at the Old Vic between 1918 and 1937. In the earliest
of these, Sybil Thorndike played the part of Lucio, owing to the
shortage of male actors; according to critic Gordon Crosse, "Her
man-about-town swagger was a real triumph."[7] The 1933 production boasted a distinguished cast, with Charles Laughton as Angelo,
Flora Robson as Isabella, Roger Livesey as the duke, and James
Mason as Claudio. Laughton's Angelo was later described by Tyrone
Guthrie as "not angelic, but a cunning oleaginous monster, whose
cruelty and lubricity could have surprised no one, least of all himself."[8]

It was Peter Brook's 1950 production at the Shakespeare Memorial Theatre in Stratford which was finally to establish the play in the
modern repertoire:

Mr Peter Brook's intelligent production very successfully establishes the ambience of out-at-elbows evil. His settings are at
once ingenious and practical, and his use of detail is unobtru-
sively felicitous—the tarboosh [fez] on a gaolbird's head to
remind us that the frontiers of Asia are not so far away, the
domesticated pheasants in the moated grange bequeathed not

so long ago by the Romans . . . The play, rarely done at all, can rarely have been done better.[9]

The performances of Harry Andrews as the duke, John Gielgud as Angelo, and the nineteen-year-old Barbara Jefford as Isabella were warmly received. Brook's production was innovative in a number of ways. Kenneth Tynan mentions the "grisly parade of cripples and deformities which Pompey introduces in that leprous Viennese gaol," in which "All the ghastly comedy of the prison scenes was summed up in this horridly funny piece of intention."[10] It was the fifth act, however, that was "Brook's triumph," in which he "used another of his charged and daring pauses";

> this time before Isabella at "Look, if it please you, on this man condemn'd" knelt to plead for the life of Angelo. He asked Barbara Jefford to pause each night until she felt that the audience could stand it no longer. The silence lasted at first for about thirty-five seconds. On some nights it would extend to two minutes. "The device," Brook said, "became a voodoo-pole— a silence in which all the inevitable elements of the evening came together, a silence in which the abstract notion of mercy became concrete for that moment to those present."[11]

Cecil Clarke presented the play in the Stratford, Ontario, Shakespeare Festival's production of 1954 "as a sober probing into the complexities and inconsistencies of human nature—with a generous injection of low and often bawdy comedy."[12] Anthony Quayle's production at Stratford in 1956 built on Brook's success, with the production centered on Anthony Nicholls' benign duke and strong support from Margaret Johnston's austere Isabella, Emlyn William's Angelo, Alan Badel's Lucio, and Patrick Wymark's Pompey. The American Shakespeare Festival staged a production the same year in which the directors

> John Houseman and Jack Landau apparently determined to prove that . . . this reputedly dark and difficult piece could

1. 1950, Peter Brook production. Harry Andrews as the duke, surrounded by prisoners, a "grisly parade of cripples and deformities" which added to the "ghastly comedy."

be turned into very light comedy. By decking it out in late nineteenth-century costumes and playing it like a Strauss operetta, they managed to avoid the central acting and interpretive problems and to present an entertainment which was greeted kindly by some reviewers, if not by Shakespeare enthusiasts.[13]

In the American director Margaret Webster's 1957 production at London's Old Vic, Anthony Nicholls reprised the role of the duke and Barbara Jefford the part of Isabella, with John Neville playing Angelo. The duke was the central figure; "Miss Webster sees that it is not Angelo's conscience but the Duke's Wolfenden survey* which is the crux of the play, and if you can make the Duke seem a true sociologist and not a mere Arabian Nights *farceur* the usually intractable and tedious second half will come fully alive."[14] In the early 1960s, productions

> began, increasingly, to present the duke as the semi-allegorical, God-like figure that some theatrical reviewers had been looking for in the mid-1950s and that literary critics had been discussing since the 1930s. And, even more emphatically than Quayle's production of 1956 or Webster's production of 1957, these presentations made Duke Vincentio the leading character in the play.[15]

In Michael Elliott's 1963 production at the Old Vic, James Maxwell's duke appeared as a "mysterious, semi-divine personage."[16] In the final act the duke was "robed in Cardinal's red, entering triumphantly to ecclesiastical music in front of a great sun, with onlookers falling prostrate before him."[17]

In the program notes to his 1966 production at the Bristol Old Vic, Tyrone Guthrie argues that,

> I suspect he is meant to be something more than a glorified portrait of royalty. Rather he is a figure of Almighty God; a stern and crafty father to Angelo, a stern but kind father to Claudio, an elder brother to the Provost . . . and to Isabella, first a loving father and, eventually the Heavenly Bridegroom to whom at the beginning of the play she was betrothed.[18]

Many of the critics were unconvinced by Guthrie's ideas, or rather John Franklin Robbin's performance of them. The London *Times'*

---

* Baron Wolfenden, a British educationalist, was best known for chairing the Wolfenden Report, which conducted a survey into sexual relations in the UK in the late 1950s and recommended the decriminalization of homosexuality.

reviewer thought that without Guthrie's program note "one might not have guessed that this jovially eccentric figure, whirling his crucifix like a propeller, was intended to possess metaphysical significance."[19]

Productions of the eighteenth and nineteenth centuries all took the need for a happy ending for granted and altered the play in various ways in order to achieve this. Quin and Kemble omitted the last lines of the duke's final speech, adding lines of their own. Such efforts seem to point to a perceived need to make the union between the duke and Isabella more acceptable by adding elements of romantic courtship and wooing. In 1970 John Barton's RSC production (discussed in detail below) ended with Isabella alone on stage, without any sign of having accepted the duke's proposal of marriage. 1970 thus represents a watershed for the play.

Because of the controversial nature of the issues it deals with, *Measure for Measure* has been a play on which directors have been keen to impose strong readings and interpretations. Those qualities that condemned the play for a Victorian audience, the themes of sexual corruption and hypocrisy by an establishment of powerful men, have recommended it to late twentieth- and twenty-first-century audiences. Interpretations of the play have been influenced by Freudian ideas about sexuality, and feminist analyses of gender and the workings of patriarchy. Robin Phillips set his production for the Stratford Festival, Ontario, in 1975 "not in the mystic Vienna chosen by Shakespeare but in the realistic Vienna of Franz Josef at the beginning of this century."[20] While praising Brian Bedford's "magnificently dry Angelo" and Martha Henry's "quivering passion" and "frenzy of Puritan zeal and its concomitant suggestion of sexuality," critics were most impressed/disturbed by William Hutt's "urbanely authoritative Duke—a man in this production with a taste for young women, young boys, mischief, and religiosity—and Richard Monette's powerfully, ingratiatingly sinister Lucio" seen as "something new":

Normally Lucio is seen as a rascal—Mr. Phillips makes him, rather than the Duke, the conscience of the play, the ironic, Brechtian commentator, who stands at the center of the action, all-knowing, all-seeing, half-shocked and half-amused.[21]

In the same year Charles Marowitz produced an adaptation which, differing from his usual "collage" technique of cutting, pasting, and redistributing lines, used what he calls "narrative guile" to persuade the audience that what they were seeing was a conventional production, before radically reworking the plot: "It was only at that point where most people felt reassured that this was *Measure* as they knew it that one began to switch rails."[22] The most shocking difference in Marowitz's version was paradoxically the absence of the "bed trick." The duke does not disguise himself as "Friar Lodowick" and the rest of the revised narrative unfolds from that. As in earlier adaptations, the low-life characters were eliminated, which had the effect of darkening the play still further—with no space at all for a comic/romantic reading. The surreal dreamlike and recorded voice sequences intensified its nightmare quality.

Michael Rudman's decision to transpose the play to a post-colonial Caribbean island for the National's 1981 production at the Lyttelton Theatre was ultimately vindicated, despite the "risk of being labeled as a white political snob":

> Some scenes are stunningly effective—our first glimpse of Eileen Diss's set, a colonial capital with its familiar traces of being a Western playground, gambling dens and tarts—the interrogation of Oscar James's Pompey which fails because of Elbow's illiteracy—the final street scene where the Duke (Stefan Kalipha) unmasks Angelo and so publicly proposes to Isabella (Yvette Harris). For once, too, we can believe that Isabella actually wants to marry the Duke, the correct interpretation. She is honoured, she does blush at the prospect and that dedicated religiosity (which has already been dented by her experiences) crumbles away.[23]

In the event, Mark Lamos' keenly anticipated 1989 production at the Lincoln Center's Mitzi E. Newhouse Theater in New York was to prove a disappointment:

> The beginning of Mr. Lamos's inventiveness, unfortunately, also proves to be its sum. While his "Measure for Measure"

remains in present-day costume . . . the production never achieves a specificity that might conjure up the atmosphere of the gritty world we live in. The play languishes instead in an antiseptic void: the standard-issue vacuum of Modern Dress Theater.[24]

Critic Frank Rich goes on to ask, "Why stage this fascinating play—whose so-called problems are challenges to theatrical exploration—if one has nothing burning to say about it?"[25] Many directors since have been keen to explore theatrically the challenges and problems that the play poses, including Libby Appel's 1998 production for the Oregon Shakespeare Festival, which used a total of seven actors, "each playing both a higher and lower character. Vilma Silver, for instance, played both Isabella and Mistress Overdone."[26] Jerry McAllister's 1999 production incorporated the city streets in his New York production, set not in Vienna "but Times Square right now."[27] Mary Zimmerman's 2001 production in Central Park featured the park itself: "In focusing on a grand scheme that makes fools of prudes and tyrants, and choosing the comic over the grim whenever possible, the production makes Shakespeare's notoriously unpleasant play pass by quite pleasantly."[28]

In 2004 Simon McBurney's Théâtre de Complicité's production was staged at the Royal National Theatre in London. Described as an "in-yer-face" production in which the "sanctimonious pirate, that went to sea with the Ten Commandments" (1.2.7–8) was George W. Bush, whose face flashed up on large television screens overshadowing the stage.[29] The production advertised its contemporary resonance with the Viennese prisoners wearing Camp X-Ray-like orange jumpsuits. As theater historian Stuart Hampton-Reeves comments, "Rarely had a production been so keyed to its moment. It caught the mood of audiences who were minded, it seemed, to embrace a play in which authority and manipulation are treated so ambivalently."[30] The narrative focus was "Angelo's psychological journey, which ended with a dramatic breakdown." David Troughton as the duke was "too cruel a character to be the main centre of dramatic tension," whereas Naomi Frederick's Isabella was "too abused to fill that role."[31] In the final scene, the duke offered Isabella his hand,

and then stepped back to reveal a small chamber at the rear of the stage in which was a brightly lit white bed. Isabella was at the front of the stage, kneeling, her head turned back, her mouth gaping, so enacting the silence that Shakespeare wrote for her (and Angelo doing the same). The Duke was in the middle left, stooping, his hand stretched out towards the bed. The Olivier is a big stage . . . so these spatial differences created a real impact: suddenly attention was thrown on the bed in the distance, the Duke isolated in the middle of the stage, the rest of the cast sharing the audience's view of these two lonely scenes, the Duke and his empty bed.[32]

The play's contentious subject matter did not recommend it to early filmmakers. Prints of an Italian film version from the 1940s are "believed lost."[33] In 2006 the well-known cinematographer Bob Komar directed an updated film version set on a British army base. With a running time of eighty minutes, the text is heavily cut, eliminating the low-life scenes, but it does incorporate a short dialogue from *Romeo and Juliet*. There are strong central performances from Josephine Rogers as Isabella, Daniel Roberts as Angelo, and Simon Phillips as the duke. Peter Brook filmed his French adaptation with the Bouffes du Nord company for television, *Mesure pour mesure*, in 1979, the same year in which the BBC television Shakespeare was shown.

Measure for Measure was one of the earliest plays to be recorded in the BBC television Shakespeare series. It was directed by Desmond Davis and starred Kate Nelligan as Isabella, Tim Piggott-Smith as Angelo, and Kenneth Colley as the duke.[34] The remit of this series was straight, no-frills Shakespeare. Colley's pleasant but lightweight duke is no match for Piggott-Smith's intense and brooding deputy, nor for Nelligan's serious-minded Isabella. Clad in a white habit throughout and made to appear deliberately sexless, she made a convincing nun. Her scenes with Angelo were compelling and Angelo's proposition seemed shocking and perverse. Piggott-Smith's performance suggested real, repressed passion and innate violence. Nelligan's portrayal of Isabella makes her acquiescence in the "bed trick" seem highly unlikely, however, as does her silent acceptance of the duke as a husband at the end, signaled by taking his hand and exiting with him. As is to be expected with the BBC, there is a splendid cast of low-life characters, led by John McEnery's engaging Lucio and Frank Middlemass's wonderfully gothic Pompey. Television's intense, melodramatic focus meant that the most successful scenes were bound to be the debates between Angelo and Isabella, and they were.

David Thacker's 1994 production for BBC2's *Bard on the Box* series, with Tom Wilkinson as the duke, Corin Redgrave as Angelo, and Juliet Aubrey as Isabella, was a braver and more challenging production. Set in an indeterminate, slightly futuristic period, Wilkinson's duke was world-weary, fleshy, greasy-haired, and drinking heavily, a middle-aged man in a midlife crisis. As the production starts, he is watching CCTV footage of sleazy street scenes of pimps and prostitutes, and pornographic videos, alone in a darkened room surrounded by a chaotic clutter of books and debris. This is a fast-paced production full of televisual awareness. The pace is achieved by heavy cutting—over one thousand lines, so that just less than two thirds survives with textual thinning throughout and some redistribution of lines. The low-life scenes are eliminated except insofar as they relate to the main plot, although Henry Goodman gives a bravura performance as a Spanish Pompey. The story this adaptation tells is of a sordid, modern, postindustrial city, presided over by gray-haired men in gray suits, and how two of these middle-aged men come to life again, awakened by the power of a young, lovely, and innocent girl. It seems to align *Measure for Measure* in a curious way with another "problem" play, *All's Well That Ends Well*, but instead of the king allowing Helena the husband of her choice, he suggests marriage to himself instead. This society is a real wasteland in which the old are rejuvenated at the expense of the young.

AT THE RSC

John Mortimer wrote that "a great play doesn't answer questions, it asks them,"[35] and *Measure for Measure*, possibly more than any other play in Shakespeare's canon, leaves us with more questions and debate about characters, their motivation, and its resonance for our times, than most modern dramas. Reviewers, actors, and directors are consistently astonished by its modernity in this regard. Where the perspectives on the institutions of the state and the Church may seem antiquated and beyond our understanding, this play, which questions the very fabric of society through the *assumed* moral high ground of its leaders, has a direct relevance to contemporary society, which directors are keen to explore.

The RSC's productions of this play clearly demonstrate a shift in how society thinks about the world. As Nigel Wood explained, "*social context*, time and place will radically influence the text's interpretation and presentation to accord with the current fashions of criticism—feminist, Marxist, psychological . . . together with the current forms of theater style."[36]

Judi Dench, who played Isabella in 1962, believed that:

There are many things in it that a modern audience can recognise very easily about corruption in a city on every level throughout government, throughout society as a whole. Corruption is not just confined to pimps and prostitutes . . . this kind of corruption is a cancer. It's something that will break out again and again . . . who can tell what might happen after the curtain comes down on that particular city with its seemingly redeemed society?[37]

Noting how the critical and cynical view of politicians in postwar generations had altered our interpretation of the play, critic Irving Wardle suggested that, "Intellectually fashionable since the end of the war, *Measure for Measure* has undergone a total reversal of meaning from a parable on divine justice to a fable of social oppression. It is clearly central to the prevailing moral climate."[38]

In its radical Brechtian rereading, Keith Hack's 1974 production launched "an indiscriminate attack on all forms of authority."[39] Featuring a photograph of Richard Nixon, and saucy seaside-postcard-type illustrations, the program notes for this production included an alternative analysis of the play by controversial playwright Edward Bond, whose work had obviously influenced the director:

It is ironic that the academic theatre and the critics take the Duke at his face value, and remain caught up in the whole pretence of "seeming" that Shakespeare attacked. In fact, our politics are still run by Angelos, made publicly respectable by Ducal figure-heads and theories, supported by hysteria (Isabella), and mindlessly obeyed by dehumanised forces (the Provost and Abhorson).[40]

The Watergate scandal and the messy conclusion of the Vietnam War obviously informed this angry and impassioned reading of the play. "All the world's a tatty stage, and no one in authority is to be trusted."[41] The collision and corruption of respected society and the Viennese "stew" was implied in casting and costume decisions: Mistress Overdone (played by a large Dan Meaden) was a "ginger-wigged drag act" who also doubled as a conspicuous nun, and Lucio wore "finery so shabby that his stockings are full of holes." The acting area was surrounded at the back by a wire grid through which Hogarthian grotesques would gaze at the action. Reminiscent of an insane asylum, "The resultant ambiguity was intentional. Who was in the cage—onlookers or actors (or audience)?"[42]

Many of the directors who have chosen to produce *Measure for Measure* have done so because they, like Keith Hack, have a burning desire to tackle issues directly relevant to their own time. When invited to direct a Shakespeare play for the RSC, director Nicholas Hytner decided to stage *Measure* because it seemed to him "a play about how individuals relate to government as well as to each other."[43] At the tail end of the Thatcherite era, Hytner suggested that "a society is sick where rulers and ruled speak different languages, and that self-knowledge is the prime requisite of those who exercise power."[44]

The British government of the late 1980s promoted the moral values of the family unit, while some of its number were discovered to be conducting adulterous affairs and indulging in deviant sexual behavior. The word "sleaze" became synonymous with "politician." Reflected in Mark Thompson's setting for Hytner's production, "Soaring industrial towers, vaguely reminiscent of the Centre Pompidou or the new Lloyds Bank building in the City, swivel round to usher us into a dark underworld."[45] To Roger Allam, who played the duke in Hytner's production, it was

> significant that much of the play is set in a prison, the ultimate embodiment of the state's desire for control . . . We move from the court into the world of pimps and whores, a public street-life teeming with vitality, but one that is corrupt [through fourteen years of non-government]. We stressed this very strongly in our production. The grey cut-away coats and knee-breeches of the court gave way to outrageous cycling shorts and Doc Marten boots. Most of our whores were rent-boys, run by Pompey, working a gents' toilet that rose from the floor. This was our attempt to de-anaesthetise the clichéd presentation of prostitutes in Shakespeare's plays, and thus shock and awaken our audience anew to the meaning of the scene . . . We could only have come up with our particular view of the text at our point in history, that is, post-feminist, post-Aids, and post-Thatcherism . . . Fifteen to twenty years ago many people viewed the state and its public institutions as corrupt, or useless, or repressive. After all the Thatcher privatisations, many of those same people look back with nostalgia and regret to those times of greater consensus.[46]

Trevor Nunn, in 1991, focused on the psychological drama inherent in the play. This created "a coherent, exciting, but deliberately narrow path through the play's vastness."[47] His setting was fin-de-siècle Vienna:

> To locate *Measure for Measure* in Freud's heartland, with psychoanalytic quotations in the programme, is to emphasise how eerily the play anticipates Freud. Nunn, in this admired production . . . interprets the unconscious mind, with desires refusing to be repressed, as the play's [motivating] force.[48]

The production was staged in The Other Place studio theater in order to "put Shakespeare's celebrated 'problem play' under the moral microscope."[49] By doing so, Nunn created a tension and intimacy that was palpable to the audience:

> In The Other Place, no projection is required. The actors are in the same situation as in a television studio or before a film camera. The audience can hear them breathing and believes it can hear them thinking. All kinds of unexpected truths begin to emerge, all kinds of details and fluctuations of language and philosophical complexities and nuances of character.[50]

Nunn also found profound contemporary relevance in his innovative psychological focus:

> Think of the Guildford Four or the Birmingham Six.* An eminent judge can argue that it doesn't matter if innocent individuals suffer as long as the idea of the law is upheld and kept pure. Well, the distinction between law and justice is on every page of Measure for Measure . . . Or think of the immediate scepticism that greets Isabella when she accuses Angelo in the last scene. You can't open a newspaper without it being asked whether the victim of a rape can be believed when she says she did nothing to encourage it. And then of course there's the whole issue of the permissive society. It is extraordinary that Shakespeare should actually use the word "permissive" . . . You think, "I do not believe that this play was written in 1605."[51]

Through the examination of three pivotal areas we can see how directorial choices can alter the whole meaning of the play. The rest of this discussion will focus on the duke's motivation, Angelo's reaction to Isabella's plea, and Isabella's response to the duke's proposal. By exploring how the RSC has made sense of Measure's central characters we will discover some solutions to a play that provides no easy answers.

---

* Irish citizens erroneously convicted of terrorism in the 1970s.

The Duke's Motives

Measure for Measure, like any other Shakespeare play but perhaps a little more than some, presents a vast area of choice to the director, not least in that great area of mystery, human and superhuman, surrounding the duke.[52]

Critics constantly refer to the word "enigmatic" when describing the character of the duke. He remains more elusive than most Shakespearean characters because he is a man who acts and schemes but rarely soliloquizes. We never hear why he does what he does. Actors playing the part, unlike readers of the play, have to make a solid decision as to the motivation of the duke in order to perform the role with any sort of coherency. Michael Pennington, who played the part in 1978, explained: "the part of the Duke is so enormous that you cannot take it on unless you have an attitude towards him. You have to suggest there is some kind of journey for him during the play which is both physical and spiritual."[53]

To show how "enigmatic" Shakespeare's text is with regards to the duke's character we will look at three extremely different readings from productions in 1974, 1987, and 1991.

Barrie Ingham's Duke for Keith Hack's 1974 production was presented as "the grand sexual manipulator and designer of the whole action."[54] This *Measure for Measure*, which one reviewer referred to as "no better than an insult thrown in the face of the audience,"[55] wallowed in the degeneracy of the ruling classes. A "garishly perverted sexuality was in league with an established church and the chief ally of the corruption,"[56] the arch "melodramatic" manipulator of the action was the duke:

> Mr Hack presents him as a morally discredited fraud wearing the mask of justice. The structure of the production, in fact, is to show the forces of law and order and the underworld victims as two sides of the same coin.[57]

> Hack . . . saw a sexual basis to the political hypocrisies of the Viennese state. Thus the Duke was a lecher fondling Isabella

whilst pretending to comfort her, lustfully encompassing her in the folds of his cloak. The sexuality of this Duke was more perverse than that of Angelo, Lucio's words being taken at face value, "He had some feeling of the sport, he knew the service" [3.1.380–81].[58]

This extreme version of the play left no doubt as to the duke's nature, "a posturing role-player, one intoxicated with the joys of manipulating his subjects. In a corrupt Vienna, nothing was more corrupt than the motives of the Establishment."[59] In his manipulation and pursuit of Isabella the duke became the "ultimate deviant of the play."[60]

This reading of the character came in for heavy criticism by critics who felt the director had altered the meaning of Shakespeare's text too much to suit his own vision. Many actors also felt that playing the duke as an amoral manipulator was to seriously misread the text:

There is a great deal of plotting and scheming, it is true, but, behind the scheming, there is, always, the drive of high moral purpose. And to those who would argue that he is unnaturally obsessed with the necessity to make his scheme succeed, I would answer that he is playing for the highest stakes, playing indeed for his life and the moral regeneration of his city and his subjects . . . A gesture as immense as handing over the reins of power to a young and relatively inexperienced Angelo must go hand in hand, I felt, with some sort of psychological crisis.[61]

In Daniel Massey's evaluation of the duke there is an implied motivation for public good, but also one of self-discovery.[62] Roger Allam, in Nicolas Hytner's 1987 production, took this "psychological crisis" as the main motivation for the duke's actions:

[the duke] seemed to be in the midst of a deep personal crisis about the value of life itself . . . Does the experience and responsibility of power change your belief in how to live, even if you seem absolutely certain? [This] relates to the Duke as much as to Angelo. He needs to discover how power has changed his own purpose . . . Angelo is used because he seems certain, not because he is suspected of being a hypocrite . . . above all the Duke is testing himself [by using a surrogate]. The Duke constantly uses other people, Angelo, Claudio, Isabella, even Lucio, as a means of self-knowledge.[63]

Allam emphasized that the duke was at a turning point. At the start of the play, reviewers described him as being in the throes of a mental breakdown. The following action dictated whether he decided to go on living or chose death:

I felt strongly that if Angelo had not proved a hypocrite the Duke would never have returned to Vienna. He would either have entered "some monastery" or, remembering the despair of "be absolute for death," would have committed suicide . . . A series of chances and "ifs" has occurred to pull the Duke back from despair.[64]

Through the "obliteration of public persona"[65] the duke "dons a friar's habit almost as an act of therapy":[66]

Being a Duke would still mean paralysis, whereas as the Friar he has become someone who can use his intellect to solve problems, make judgements, and act upon them immediately whilst responding to events as they occur. He is, as it were, living. He is also speaking prose rather than verse.[67]

The formal constrictions of language and costume discarded, the duke discovers the freedom to understand that "life is all there is, so we might as well live it as best we can; that being human is not a given but something we have to strive for. That the reason we are here is to live and that this involves making many difficult judgements."[68]

Trevor Nunn's 1991 production included a piece of stage business and manipulation of the text to expose the duke's motives:

the lights went up on Philip Madoc's middle-aged, bespectacled, bearded Duke, sitting on a couch examining some scraps of paper in a folder—press cuttings they were, several of them, and they would appear again later as the Duke told Isabella the story of Angelo and Mariana and their broken betrothal. Retrospectively, one saw how the Duke was very deliberately engaged in a psychological investigation of Angelo. The couch, the choice of period, even, to some extent, Madoc's appearance, were all part of this Freudian allusion.[69]

Trevor Nunn transposed lines from Act 3 to the start of the play, "He who the sword of heaven will bear / Should be as holy as severe." Upon these words Escalus then entered and the normal play text began. In order to emphasize that the duke's interest in Angelo was also a concern to others, another adjustment was made when the duke goes to ask for the Friar's disguise. Initially very reluctant to lend the duke religious garments, the Friar seeks out the duke's true motivation. The words "Lord Angelo is precise" [meaning a puritan] "palpably struck an immediate chord with the Friar, as who should say: 'Now you're talking; I don't trust the slimy creep either. How many habits was it you said you'd like? What about the sandals?'"[70]

Isabella and Angelo acted out their neuroses on a minimal set dominated by a Freudian couch: "If Nunn finds an overall theme in *Measure for Measure*, it is the 'painful acquisition of self-knowledge' mentioned in the programme. Never has a revival left me so aware that all three main characters are undergoing an emotional education forced to accept the darkness within."[71]

Angelo: Awakening the Beast

"Angelo is someone who lives in a world of ideas"[72]: the embodiment of the law, who believes in it to such a degree that he will enforce it regardless of who the offender is, or indeed from what class they come. John Mortimer described him as:

a cold blooded judge who regards the law as a kind of perfect computer to be operated without human feelings . . . [The law against fornication] fails to pass the test of natural justice because it quite fails to take into account the reality of human nature. But for the cold-blooded Judge Angelo, it's the law and that's enough."[73]

Angelo's safe and certain world is shattered by the most devastating and life-changing of discoveries—the awakening of his sexuality. Unfortunately for Isabella, the object of his desire, this awakening happens when she is in need of his compassion, and he is in the first flush of power. The scene in which Angelo's emotions uncontrollably erupt (Act 2 Scene 4) is one of the most electrifying and disturbing in the Shakespearean canon. The potent mix of emotions ignited between these two repressed characters is very revealing, and shifts the play from "the question of the criminal's guilt to that far more interesting matter, the guilt of the judge."[74]

Michael Pennington, who played Angelo in Keith Hack's 1974 production, suggested,

In the case of Angelo, you are dealing with someone who is obviously a very efficient and competent career man but who knows nothing at all about himself sexually and is very much out of touch with that side of his personality. So that when his sexuality is triggered off it is of a very adolescent and uncertain kind. He is very much like Isabella. They're both absolutists, very proud and with great concern about self-image.

In the set of mirrors which reflects the world of *Measure*, it is possible to see Isabella and Angelo as siblings, as partners, because they do use the same kind of language. We wanted to try and catch the similarity between them. Perhaps in another world they might be lovers. There was a sexual potential between them that I wanted to catch, and I also felt very strongly that Angelo's crime is not what he thinks it is. He thinks it is desiring a saint, whereas it is a political crime, it is a monstrous abuse of his position, so that I think the crux of his downfall is political.[75]

Ian Richardson played Angelo as someone "highly sexed . . . and aware of all things sensual" but who chose to suppress his desires.

With the loosening of censorship laws in 1970 Richardson saw an opportunity to provide a more sexually deviant reading of the part:

> I physically abused her and pressed my hands firmly up her skirts. I also felt that Angelo's sexuality was rather sinister, so I asked Estelle [Kohler] if we could do some business where I pulled her hair . . . perhaps a kind of sadist who has met a masochist, and this rubbed off on Sarah Kestelman who played Mariana, who felt that if this was so . . . then she must play the part as someone who really rather goes in for that kind of thing. It was an exciting and good production.[76]

2. 1970, John Barton production. Ian Richardson as Angelo, Estelle Kohler as Isabella. "Angelo's sexuality was rather sinister" and he performed "some business where [he] pulled her hair."

In this production Angelo's disgust at his own behavior and the possibilities of his darker nature were exposed only after the scene: "In the coldly perverted interview he advanced to her butting her with his groin. Only in solitude was he able to relax his act as he broke down in tears at the thought of his apostasy and inherent weaknesses."[77]

David Haig, who played Angelo in 1991, pointed out that,

If Angelo's channelled his feelings and drives into the law, she's channelled them into her faith. It could have sexual roots, this kind of diversionary tactic . . . [He believed that] those two encounters between Angelo and Isabella in which she deploys her considerable brainpower constitute probably the first time he's been intellectually engaged by somebody of the opposite sex. Here are two minds that are meeting equally . . . she drags him in from his containment because of the forcefulness of her ideas and her passion. Part of her appeal to him is that she's drawn him into her intellectual sphere.[78]

The physical brutality of Angelo, first explored by Ian Richardson, was again evident in David Haig's performance: "When Isabella twigs to his meaning and threatens to expose him, this Angelo reacts with a chilling, frenzied violence, slamming her down on his sofa and shaking her as though she were some rag-doll."[79] Critics were quick to recognize the implications of the production:

What [Trevor] Nunn is at pains to explore are the locked-in demons which lurk behind this demeanour of upright rectitude. And what we take away with us is a shattering analysis of a potential wife beater, rapist or worse . . . Put a woman at his mercy, ask him to show her human compassion and he can relate only by proving himself the dominant male. The sinister quality in all this is heightened by David Haig's obsessively neat beard, a jaw-framing affair reminding one instinctively of the Yorkshire Ripper [a notorious serial killer of the time].[80]

Angelo's self-knowledge has been portrayed as being catastrophic for the character himself. In an unusual but affectingly sympathetic reading, Alex Jennings in 1994 played Angelo as:

> a man of iron control and impeccable religiosity who views his own moral disintegration with something approaching panic. He consistently harps on the word "evil" and, rather than paw and claw Isabella, throws himself at her feet in abject humiliation. Once exposed he craves death, as if he knows he can never reconstruct his sense of identity.[81]

In 1978 Jonathan Pryce brought out the sexual frustration that underlies Angelo's appetite for order. He played the part as a man who ultimately cannot face living with the knowledge of the darker self that dwells within him. His performance was so effective that it had the very odd result of making him the "sympathetic centre of the play. [At the end] the attention is held by [Angelo], completing a superbly rounded interpretation, with a vacant and terrified stare of panicky regret while awaiting final adjudication."[82] As John Mortimer pointed out:

> We are all born with the same imperfections, call it human frailty if you are an Atheist or original sin if you happen to be a Christian. Judges are wise men, perhaps, but as prey to lust and envy and prejudice as those they have to try . . . Is any man or woman fit to sit in judgement on a fellow human being? . . . is judgement on our fellow human beings at best any more than hypocrisy?[83]

Isabella's Choice

Irony attaching to plot and character is given its most powerful expression in the denouement when the duke, in his Friar's gown, and Isabella, in her novice's habit, dissociate themselves from the particular obligations which those habiliments symbolize and belatedly emerge as hero and heroine of a romantic comedy.[84]

Productions have variously ended with Isabella happily accepting the duke's proposal, completely shocked to the point of madness, making a downright refusal of his offer, or in total indecision. The portrayal of the duke and his motives will, of course, affect the final outcome, but some productions have also implied that the duke's social position leaves Isabella with no option but to accept him, regardless of her own feelings.

Isabella's faith, humanity, and identity go through a test of fire during the play and in the end she is left with a choice: to accept the man who has put her through this ordeal, or to return to a world removed from the company of men. Isabella's choice in productions of *Measure for Measure* will often depend on whether the actress portrays her as an innocent but strong woman of faith and integrity who is brought to an understanding of herself and mercy, or as someone neurotically repressed, "a prig . . . running away from the world into the convent because she's frightened of her own sexuality."[85]

Anne Barton, in the program notes to the RSC's 1970 production, asks the time-honored question: why does Isabella not make any verbal reply to the duke's proposal? And suggests: "It is at least possible that this silence is one of dismay."[86] Judi Dench, who played Isabella in 1962, thought:

There seems to be no explanation for the way she suddenly renounces her vocation to become a nun, but I think that she has learnt about weakness. It's as if she was, at the beginning of the play, a very young girl, who sees everything as either positive or negative, good or bad, white or black. Her character is flawed because of this but during the play she learns about human weakness, not only from the Duke, but also from Angelo. The change that Shakespeare intends her to undergo is that she should see that everything is not so simple and straightforward and that there are shades of grey. She learns to be compassionate and to make allowances for other people . . . By the end of the play, Isabella, like Angelo, has been made to face reality and has even questioned her decision to become a nun. So the acceptance of the Duke doesn't come as such a surprise and is perhaps a marriage of minds anyway.[87]

3. 1962, John Blatchley production. Judi Dench as Isabella believed she was a woman who "has [learned] about human weakness."

But changing attitudes to sexual politics by 1970 questioned this reasoning. Referred to as a "feminist" production, John Barton's gave the RSC its first in which Isabella appeared to flatly refuse the proposal of the duke:

> He shrugs slightly, saddened, and leaves the stage . . . But I'm confident that Shakespeare meant "so" to mean "now that's done" rather than "too bad," which is the way [Sebastian] Shaw pronounces it. Does Barton mean to imply that Isabella finds the Duke as Machiavellian as everyone else, or what?

It isn't clear, hasn't been prepared for, and (I suspect) isn't justified.[88]

In 1983, "both the political and the theatrical climate had changed . . . chastity was being reclaimed as a sexual option."[89] Where Estelle Kohler had played Isabella's character as a "collision of sexual nausea and cold Puritanism,"[90] Juliet Stevenson rejected the idea that Isabella was retreating from the world due to some sort of sexual neurosis. She saw Isabella's decision to go into a convent as a positive one, a means of bringing goodness into the world through prayer. The trial in the last act exposed the "seemers" for what they really were, and Isabella's test had revealed a sensuality that did not detract from her faith. The emphasis was on a meeting of minds:

> unless the Duke takes on the trial of himself, which involves bringing himself to let Lucio off the hook, to exercise forgiveness, he hasn't learned the capacity for mercy from Isabella, and there is no justification for a happy ending. Nothing mutual has been established between them. He watched me watching, turned back to Lucio, and reprieved the death sentence . . . I used to take a long, long pause, in which I looked at everyone—drawing in the collective experience in a way. Then I took the Duke's hand . . . Shakespeare gives Isabella no words at the end. Maybe because she doesn't know what to say to the Duke's proposal. It's often the case with female protagonists: discounting the Epilogue, Rosalind doesn't speak for the last twenty minutes of As You Like It.[91]

Other productions favored an ambiguous ending:

> I stammered hesitantly on the first [proposal] . . . trying to show the Duke's realization of the anguish and pain he has put Isabella through . . . Josette [Simon] gave me a long appraising stare, and still did not consent. The play stops rather than ends, leaving many possibilities in the air . . . In our production we tried to show this open, unresolved ending by putting a wordless coda after the text has finished. In Mark Thompson's set

the huge city gates had been drawn up to reveal a kind of idyllic pastoral never-never land beyond . . . Isabella goes towards the pastoral scene at the back, stops, and turns back towards the city and the Duke as the lights go down. People often used to ask me whether they married or not, annoyed at our denying them a happy ending, or suspicious at our being overoptimistic. We thought probably they did, but only after a very long conversation.[92]

In a darker reading, the disturbing nature of the duke's manipulations on Isabella's psyche were played out in the final scene of Steven Pimlott's 1994 production:

at the end, Stella Gonet's Isabella fetches the Duke (Michael Feast) a stinging slap across the chops when he makes his tactless, last-minute pitch to become an item with her. No sooner has she hit him than she's passionately kissing him better . . . then she has second thoughts about that response too,

4. 1994, Steven Pimlott production. Stella Gonet as Isabella, Michael Feast as the duke. The final scene showed Isabella "still clearly in shock from the emotional turmoil his scheming has caused."

abruptly recoiling with little sobs, still clearly in shock from the emotional turmoil his scheming has caused.[93]

The marriage of the duke and Isabella, should it occur, points to a resolution that would bring a possible healing to their ruptured and chaotic society. In the latter part of the twentieth century our inherent mistrust of leaders and politicians made that happy ending less acceptable and the resulting future of the characters and their state less certain or secure. Isabella's choice is personal *and* political. In the face of collapsing values and beliefs, she, with the duke, through their learned understanding, compassion, and mercy, have a chance to restore order and to enact the laws of that society with a justice that is tempered by the understanding of human fallibility.

PLAYING *MEASURE FOR MEASURE*

Sir Trevor Nunn is the most successful and one of the most highly regarded of modern British theater directors. Born in 1940, he was a brilliant student at Cambridge, strongly influenced by the literary close reading of Dr. F. R. Leavis. At the age of just twenty-eight he succeeded Peter Hall as artistic director of the RSC, where he remained until 1978. He greatly expanded the range of the company's work and its ambition in terms of venues and touring. He also achieved huge success in musical theater and subsequently became artistic director of the National Theatre in London. His productions are always full of textual insights, while being clean and elegant in design. Among his most admired Shakespearean work has been a series of tragedies with Ian McKellen in leading roles: *Macbeth* (1976, with Judi Dench, in the dark, intimate space of The Other Place), *Othello* (1989, with McKellen as Iago and Imogen Stubbs as Desdemona), and *King Lear* (2007, in the Stratford Complete Works Festival, on world tour, and then in London). He talks here about his 1991 RSC production of *Measure for Measure* in the intimate studio space of The Other Place in Stratford-upon-Avon.

Josette Simon OBE (born 1960) is a British actress of Antiguan descent. She trained at the Central School of Speech and Drama in

London and has performed frequently with the Royal National Theatre and Royal Shakespeare Company, as well as appearing regularly on television and in film. As a black actor, she has been at the forefront of "color-blind casting," frequently taking roles traditionally considered white. Her RSC repertoire includes roles in *Macbeth*, *Antony and Cleopatra*, *Much Ado About Nothing*, *The Tempest*, *The Merchant of Venice*, *Love's Labour's Lost*, and *A Midsummer Night's Dream*. She talks here about playing Isabella in Nicholas Hytner's 1987 production for the RSC in Stratford and London.

Roger Allam (born in 1953) is an English actor, known primarily for his stage career, although he has performed in film and television. He has been nominated three times for the Laurence Olivier Award for Best Actor, winning once. He has also been nominated for, and won, the Laurence Olivier Award for Best Supporting Actor. He played Inspector Javert in the original RSC production of the stage musical *Les Misérables*. He first joined the RSC in 1981 and his roles have included Mercutio in *Romeo and Juliet*, Theseus/Oberon in *A Midsummer Night's Dream*, Clarence in *Richard III*, Brutus in *Julius Caesar*, Sir Toby Belch in *Twelfth Night*, Macbeth, and the duke in Nicholas Hytner's 1987 production of *Measure for Measure*, which he talks about here.

Trevor Nunn: Directing *Measure*

I did a very particular production of *Measure for Measure* as part of a venture that presented Shakespeare's play in repertoire with a stage adaptation of *The Blue Angel* [the famous 1930 film by Josef von Sternberg, starring Marlene Dietrich]. Therefore, in my mind, the Vienna of Shakespeare's play became the Vienna of Freud and the study of sexual aberration, obsession, and fantasy in psychological terms. The duke became, relatively easily, a Freud-like intellectual who was intent on conducting an experiment to provide himself with a case history. This study was focused on a youngish authoritarian administrator, Angelo, to find out whether his extreme judgmental behavior might have a root in sexual repression.

Given that this was a small theater production, created to open the spanking new Other Place Theatre in Stratford, but also to tour to nontheater venues around the British Isles, the design was very simple and not at all pictorially descriptive of the different locations the play requires. However, the intention, through the use of a few elements of furniture and bold lighting and detailed costumes, was to provide a sense of very real spaces, and therefore the production was not burdened by an overarching or symbological design concept.

My experience was that audiences didn't find Isabella in any way unbelievable, even though her priorities and decisions are alarming. I think this was because it became very clear, very quickly in the production that Isabella was an obsessive personality, that her determination to remove herself from the world and spend her life as a celibate nun was, in her case, both maladjusted and extreme. Isabella is not a "heroine" in any traditional sense. She is a troubled and unbalanced character whom we observe slowly moving toward self-knowledge as she is confronted with the awareness of her sexuality. Shakespeare encapsulates Isabella's condition in the phrase, "More than our brother is our chastity." It's a shocking statement, but it exemplifies her extreme state of mind.

In this production, Isabella was clearly very young, still in late teenage, impressionable, full of the urgency and intolerance of youth, and unaware, to a great extent, of her impact on others. As a novice, she was dressed severely, but not yet in the robes and cowl of a nun who had already taken her vows. Once alone with Angelo, she was fervent and spontaneous and, consumed with the same zeal as in her religious faith, she pursued Angelo to the point where she was touching him, taking his hand, coming into "his space," breaking that invisible barrier we all instinctively observe in normal social contact. Thus Angelo was immensely affected by her vigor, her whirlwind passionate appeal, and was very understandably aroused by her proximity.

In this production, Angelo, too, was clearly sexually repressed, of an age when he was no longer romantically eligible, he was nonetheless obviously somebody who both could and should be sexually active, but who had taken the decision that, for "moral" and intellectual reasons, he must abstain.

The title *Measure for Measure* is proverbial, and clearly applies to the kind of justice that is delivered at the end of the story (with

5. 1991, Trevor Nunn production. Claire Skinner as Isabella. "Isabella is not a 'heroine' in any traditional sense. She is a troubled and unbalanced character."

Angelo being "punished" with the restoration of his relationship with Mariana, with Lucio punished with marriage to one of his whores, etc.), but the title is also a phrase about balance. Shakespeare provides us with central characters who are essentially *unbalanced* and pushes them into circumstances where they are forced to confront their extreme behavior and thereby possibly recognize that there is a better balance that could be either restored or discovered.

The play is a humanist masterpiece, and was clearly only a "problem play" in ages that required a clear "moral" purpose in drama or, at the very least, clear category distinctions of "tragedy" and "comedy." It is about flawed people, about how human nature is essentially flawed, contradictory, muddled, and, in post-psychological jargon, "mixed up." Accordingly, it is a play that accentuates just how crude and inappropriate are the human institutions of the law, the Church, the government, and, perhaps above all, the concept of the death penalty.

"[M]an, proud man, / Dressed in a little brief authority" is Isabella's anguished outburst against her tormentor, but it stands emblematically as the observation that is most fundamental to Shakespeare's intention in this play. It's not a surprise, therefore, to discover that Shakespeare is also concerned not only with understanding and self-knowledge, but with forgiveness. The last scene of the play prefigures the ideas of forgiveness and reconciliation that we find so potently in the "late plays" like *Cymbeline* and *The Tempest*. Isabella, under the gaze of her guide and mentor, the duke, is given the decision to take of whether or not Angelo shall be in receipt of her mercy.

In my production (though I know for certain this also happened in Peter Brook's production of the play), the silence before Isabella spoke was very long, almost intolerably long. It was the silence during which her struggle with the extremes of her nature is being waged. As she finds that possibility of forgiveness in herself, the battle is won, her change toward a greater humanity and balance has begun, and, in turn, it takes Angelo to a place where, for the first time, the world seems to be different from what he had come to believe it to be.

This brings us to the question of what it is that happens finally between Isabella and the duke. It became fashionable, a generation or so ago, to play the final moments of *Measure for Measure* as evidence that *all* authority is corrupt and hypocritical, and thus in this reading, the duke, whom we had supposed was an enlightened man of conscience, cynically uses his power to force the much abused Isabella to his own bed. Since Shakespeare leaves her silent at the point of the duke's proposal, it is entirely possible to interpret this as evidence that the girl is aghast, speechless in horror, frozen with the realization that all men are the same and that there is now really nobody to whom she can complain. But I argued that such interpretation was entirely unfounded in the text, and that the opposite conclusion is not only more coherent, unifying the many themes of the play, but richly and rewardingly playable by the protagonists.

Isabella, alone in the world with her brother under sentence of death, has found one person she can turn to, rely on, and share with. She believes him to be a priest, but her increasing contact with him brings about increasing understanding and dependence. The discovery, in the final scene, that her mentor and friend is not a priest, but the much loved and much lamented duke, is for her as exciting as it is bewildering.

In this production then, Isabella's silence was tearful and profoundly happy, a charged emotional state that was too full to allow speech. In going to him, and he to her, she was aware that she was relinquishing her zeal to spend her life as a nun, that she was now wanting to live within the world, not outside it, and that she was instinctively committing to a future based on spiritual kinship, mutual respect, and a meeting of minds—to which we should admit no impediment. The point of the conclusion is that their future will not be based on or exhausted by sex.

So often we discover Shakespeare has a theme or a subject, every aspect of which he intends to explore, especially its opposite. Here in *Measure for Measure*, the subject is sex, but by that same token it is also an exploration of frigidity, or a holiness that eschews, through celibacy or decree, the functions of our bodies. And, as so often is also true, Shakespeare doesn't arrive at a proselytizing conclusion or a moral tag, he arrives at a sense of the need for humans to find the middle way, or the balance, or the measure that equals the measure.

Josette Simon: Playing Isabella

Did you work out a rationale for why Isabella wants to be a nun at the beginning of the play?

I didn't particularly have a negative rationale for her. I explored that. Especially because she and Claudio are (it seems) orphans and how that may have impacted on her and her emotional life. I felt that, for her, it was a very positive decision. I think that because it's such a strict and extraordinary thing to do, it's felt to be a negative decision:

something sinister must have happened to her that she wants to lock herself away from the world. But I felt that for her it was a positive choice, I felt she was very happy to go in there. I didn't work out a complete rationale at that time but I felt that as part of the character of Isabella, she believed it was a positive step in her life.

She seems to want the conditions placed upon the nuns to be even stricter than they are—does that suggest that she has a certain fanatical quality herself?

That's right. I think the thing about her is that she's an absolutist. She's absolutely passionate about everything she does and she's absolute in everything she does. She has to do things to extremes. The order of Saint Clare's is a very strict order anyway; to want it to be even stricter may be bizarre but it absolutely fits with her character. She does things to the nth degree, and the fact is she isn't satisfied until she's absolute.

And is that maybe one of the things that attracts Angelo to her?

Yes, though not on its own. I think it attracts Angelo because he recognizes that quality, and also her passion, of course. There's something very attractive about her anyway; there's something extraordinary about somebody with that much passion and that much belief. Angelo is a dispassionate person. He's so rigid, so repressed that I think the combination of Isabella's qualities excites him. I think it is the absolute nature of her personality and her extraordinary passion, which is alien to him, that when combined together excites him.

Nuns are traditionally quiet women, and yet Isabella has superb powers of argument. Does she take pleasure in her debates with Angelo?

I certainly did when playing her. I don't think Isabella's enjoyment of her speeches is solely why she's able to argue so well, but I think she definitely gets transported. She has an extraordinary intellect, an extraordinary power of argument, and facility with language. Her words are exquisite, and I think she does enjoy the arguments, but not in a conscious way. I don't think she thinks "I love the feeling that I'm getting from doing this." I think the argument itself is what drives her and her aptitude with language. She enjoys trying to explain to Angelo exactly what she means.

For me, yes, the language is extraordinary. I remember at the time that the enjoyment of the language and the power of her argument always ran alongside an anxiety that as a performer you're drawing as much out of the language as you could. But you never can with Shakespeare; on the very last day you're still not satisfied, there's still more to go, and that's what's so joyous about it.

Is it uncomfortable for her to have Lucio around as her intermediary?

No, I don't think so. I think if she'd met Lucio before the dilemma of her brother's plight had been put to her, she would have found him uncomfortable to be around. I think that there's a feature of Isabella that she's able to square certain slightly dodgy dealings with her own sense of righteousness. I think that with Lucio, the fact that she loves her brother so much and would do almost anything for him means she's able to qualify it—in order, she thinks, to get him off. I think Lucio being his friend is a much stronger resonance for her than what else he's capable of. Because she's trying to save his life I think she doesn't go into it too deeply; if she did, I don't think she would want to be anywhere near Lucio. But he fulfills a purpose and she's able to square that purpose within the boundaries of her humanity.

The line "More than our brother is our chastity" can be difficult for a modern, sexually free-and-easy society to accept: what was your take on this key point of principle?

I have to say that when Nick [Hytner—director] asked me to play Isabella, one of the first things that practically every single person said to me was, "How are you going to do that line?" I'm sure it happens today when an actor is asked to play her. It's sort of a Becher's

Brook at the Grand National. Like approaching a very large fence. But actually, it's only one line!

Whenever you do the classics, you're always accompanied by many years of past performances that have been deemed "definitive," so you're always up against people's perceptions of how you're going to do a part, or how you're going to do *that* line. My answer whenever I approach the classics is to pretend it's never happened before. No one's ever seen the play, I don't know anything about it; I try to banish every single thing from my mind, because those preconceptions are not the criteria under which to try to breathe life into a part or fulfill the truth of a line. You can't approach it having that baggage in your head. So the line becomes something to do with the whole mining of the character of Isabella. It's also to do with you and the director and Shakespeare, fulfilling what you think Isabella is about, where she's at when she says that line. If in performance you come at it thinking, "Oh my God, I'm approaching that line!" then your head is already in the wrong place, because you should be trying to inhabit, in body, Isabella to such a degree that you *know* why she's saying that line. You believe it. You have the character's best interests at heart, so therefore, if you are embedded as deeply as you can possibly get yourself into that part, you will understand why you say that line, and that's all that matters.

Having said that, of course it is the most extraordinary line. And in this day and age, as you rightly say, it's very hard for an audience to go with that. But as I said, in a sense I didn't care what the audience was thinking, I cared what she was thinking. And in terms of caring what she thinks, she *absolutely* believes it. It's natural: it's part of her extraordinary character. It's part of the thing that excites Angelo. Who is this person? This is someone quite unlike anybody he, we, you, or anybody else has ever met. She's intriguing. It's telling that you don't just think she's a silly, prissy, repressed old cow! There's something endearing about her that she can hold such an absolute belief. I think in this day and age you can still go with that, and the answer lies absolutely in the belief of the person playing Isabella; not asking an audience to believe the same thing, but to understand why she believes it. For me, that line became part of the resolve to fully inhabit Isabella as a whole.

In your production, did Angelo come close to a sexual assault upon your Isabella?

Absolutely, he was very physical. He was violent and it was very scary for me. Obviously I knew what was happening, but you do get so deeply enmeshed with the person you're playing that it always came as a shock to me. The thing about it is you try to live in the moment, even though, of course, you are doing it every night. When he suddenly grabbed me I was thinking, as Isabella was, that the fact he wanted to see her again was that he'd been swayed. She was moving closer to Claudio's life being saved. He grabbed her with such violence, sexual violence, and although he didn't actually then do anything after that, hitherto he'd been very contained, so she had no idea what was going on inside of him. At that point, in our production, you feared for her life as well as her sexuality. I think it's a moment where he's so out of control that anything could have happened.

Is there anything problematic about Isabella's willingness to set up the "bed trick" with Mariana?

As I said earlier, she's able somehow to qualify things. Because Mariana was betrothed to Angelo, I think that *just about* qualifies it. If she was just a woman who was taking part in this "bed trick" then Isabella wouldn't do it; she couldn't countenance that at all. But I think the fact of the betrothal somehow squared it, just about. She finds something she can live with. The other thing to remember, of course, is that Claudio has had sex with his girlfriend before marriage: there are all of these things she's confronted with that in theory in the cold light of day she absolutely would not let pass. But there are certain qualifications that she's able to just about make and I think this is important in the whole of her journey.

I think that when I came to look at the journey Isabella had gone on there's a sense of compassion that she has learned. She starts the play incredibly passionate and absolute, and totally committed to her beliefs. She does of course contain a massive amount of humanity, but she doesn't particularly have a worldly humanity: in a sense, she was shutting herself off. Out of the world. Away from the world.

6. Josette Simon as Isabella, Sean Baker as Angelo. Angelo's "sexual assault": "he was very physical. He was violent and it was very scary for me."

But, having experienced the world, she couldn't live in the same way that she was when she started the play. I think she came to understand people, human frailty and fallibility, and I think she learned a lot about the wider world and her own place in it—about her own way of thinking about the world, being in the world, and about other people.

Were there any intimations of the duke's marriage proposal before it actually came?

No. There were no intimations at all. Isabella is very focused, she has tunnel vision, she's absolutely committed to whatever it is she's fighting for. She doesn't see it coming. Not that his intentions were obvious; they weren't. It is a surprise to everybody. Including the audience.

And how did you respond to it when it did?

I remember during the rehearsal period we didn't make any decisions about it and quite late on still hadn't decided how it was going to end. And I realized that therein lay the answer: she hadn't decided. As we all know, Shakespeare doesn't do anything without a reason; there's always a reason when you're mining that script, you're like a detective looking for clues. Her last speech is to ask for Angelo's life to be spared and after that she says absolutely nothing at all for two and a half pages. She never speaks again. And there's a reason: he can't leave her for two and a half pages at the end of the play with nothing to say without some reason. That reason, it seemed to us, was that she didn't know whether she wanted to marry him or not. For me it was completely wrong that she should say "yes." Why should she say "yes"? Because it's right at the end of the play, we all go home happy and satisfied and think how wonderful, they go off together, they suit each other . . . no, no, no. You have to ask why she is not speaking for all that time. So at the end of our production he asked her and she walked upstage to the exit: it was a very, very long walk upstage just before blackout, and a moment before the blackout, she turned around and looked at him.

So you don't know what she decided. I loved that we did that because I think for me that was the absolute truth. Shakespeare gives you the answers: for me he gave the answer that she didn't speak.

Roger Allam: Playing the Duke

Why does the duke vacate his role at the beginning of the play?

> . . . if our virtues
> Did not go forth of us, 'twere all alike
> As if we had them not. . . .
> (Act 1 Scene 1)

> We have strict statutes and most biting laws,
> . . .
> Which for this fourteen years we have let slip.
> (Act 1 Scene 4)

The duke has been a recluse, has "ever loved the life removed," and through his inaction, over a period of fourteen years, has let Vienna fall into moral and political decay. In our production, directed by Nicholas Hytner at Stratford in 1987, the street life of Pompey, Lucio, and Mistress Overdone was lively and filled with vitality. But it is corrupt, a world of pimps and whores. The world of the court was sclerotic, seized up through fourteen years of a kind of non-government. The duke is in a personal crisis just as the state is in a public crisis. He has thought himself into complete paralysis. He has to do something drastic before he has a complete breakdown, so he runs away: he leaves the identity of being a duke and governing, and disguises himself so he can see how the state is run by Angelo.

Why did he choose Angelo?

Angelo seems certain of how to live his own life and govern other people's. He will be strict and govern according to a fundamentalist Christian view of life and human foibles, whereas the more liberal Escalus would not. Angelo has been given the power of life and death in Vienna, and complete scope to enforce the letter of the law or to qualify it. "Hence shall we see, / If power change purpose, what our seemers be." Perhaps the duke was once as certain as Angelo seems now. Through disguise and spying on the results of Angelo's prescriptive certainty, the duke will gain self-knowledge. Will power change Angelo's purpose? Did it once change the duke's? He doesn't really know. We felt that the duke in these early stages of the play was a desperate man on the run, clutching at straws to prevent himself from completely retiring from the world to a monastery, or perhaps even becoming suicidal.

Did you find that Lucio was a particular thorn in your side? There's some truth in his claim that you are the "duke of dark corners," isn't there?

Our duke took himself very seriously and most certainly lacked a sense of humor about his public position, his predicament, and his reclusive nature. It amused me that although Lucio has accused the duke of being lecherous—"Ere he would have hanged a man for the getting a hundred bastards, he would have paid for the nursing a thousand"—the thing that really angers and provokes the duke to a furious response is when Lucio suggests that he lacks wisdom and is a "superficial, ignorant, unweighing fellow." So yes, Lucio is a particular thorn in his side, who flusters him and pricks his pomposity, though by becoming the object of humor he is humanized in the audience's eyes. He learns from Lucio that being in shadow as a recluse can very easily be misconstrued in the most gossipy way. Also, yes, he is in disguise and spying on his own city, so very much the duke of "dark corners."

Is there something uncomfortable about the way the duke takes on the disguise of a Friar and starts hearing people's confessions, something you are not supposed to do when you haven't taken vows yourself?

The duke certainly uses his disguise to gain knowledge and advantage for himself and he gives advice to others, but he never formally takes confession and offers absolution of sins, so I don't think he is compromising vows he has not taken.

What did you discover in the great central encounter with Claudio?

"Be absolute for death" is actually not bad advice to give to someone facing execution, but it seemed to us to be as much, if not more, about the duke himself and his own despairing state of mind. Throughout the speech he describes life itself as worthless: "a thing / That none but fools would keep." Life is "Servile to all the skyey influences," it is "death's fool," it is "not noble" but "nursed by baseness." "Thou art not thyself, / For thou exists on many a thousand grains / That issue out of dust . . . Thou art not certain." The duke's own sense of himself has fragmented so that he is not "certain" of how to live, to act, to govern, to judge, to measure. For the duke at this point in the play, life equals being dead but having to live. It is his lowest point, his nadir, the very depths of his despair. The speech articulates why he has run away. We made Act 3 one continuous scene, set in a huge prison. By the end of it the duke is a changed man. Claudio's view of life and death is the opposite of his. For Claudio, death equals living but having to die. But more importantly, there is the revelation of Angelo's hypocrisy, the fact that he is only "well seeming." This comes as a complete bombshell and stimulates the duke into action. Solving Isabella's predicament becomes the means by which he can solve his own. Not that he necessarily knows this, but he becomes alive and uses his intellect in an active way on Isabella's behalf. He also starts speaking mainly in prose rather than verse, which seemed to us a further indication of the great changes taking place within him. At the end of Act 3 the duke has a short soliloquy which has three lines that were of special significance to us: "He who the sword of heaven will bear / Should be as holy as severe," and later in the speech, "Craft against vice I must apply." For me, the duke begins to formulate here the idea that bearing the sword of heaven, being absolute and certain, is a way of life that should not be imposed on people, and that vice is better dealt with by "craft": by using your intellect to make judgments rather than being guided by abstract fixed beliefs.

7. Roger Allam. The duke's central encounter with Claudio: "We made Act 3 one continuous scene, set in a huge prison. By the end of it the duke is a changed man."

At what point did you begin to think that you might like to marry Isabella yourself? And what was her response?

"The hand that hath made you fair hath made you good." Isabella's physical beauty obviously strikes him from the first time he sees her. Throughout the play the duke observes and experiences Isabella go through an enormous emotional journey. Her religious and moral certainty is tested to extremes. She remains true to it but is flexible and pragmatic enough to embrace the duke's plan to outwit Angelo. Angelo's double treachery, however, means that the duke has to employ the Ragozine plan, and cannot tell Isabella that Claudio is alive. He does this primarily, I think, to keep the dangerous secret between himself and the Provost, and making her "heavenly comforts of despair" is a gloss put on necessity. This interpretation was made possible by keeping the Provost onstage in Act 4 Scene 3 to hear Isabella's "Peace, ho, be here!" so that the snatched, hurried decision not to tell her was in some ways a mutual one. On hearing this news Isabella flung her arms around me in despair. This had an enormous impact on my duke. He not only realizes how much he has hurt her, but he has a beautiful woman in his arms, probably for the first time in his life. The play explores the tensions between our physical and sexual desires, and our attempts to repress them. Angelo sentences people to death for giving in to them. The only way they can be controlled and somehow made safe and all right is through marriage, the traditional happy ending for a comedy. It was from this point that my duke wanted to marry Isabella, but he did not know quite how things were going to work out. In the last scene he witnesses Isabella have the extraordinary generosity of spirit to plead for Angelo's life; thereby embodying the very best aspects of religious conviction, mercy, and forgiveness. In the end, as he marries off Lucio to his "punk" and Angelo to Mariana, the duke blurts out his own proposal, stammering nervously. In the light of the extra anguish she has been put through over Claudio, Isabella would stare at me in disbelief at the sheer crassness. After the second proposal, leaving Angelo and Mariana on one side of the stage with Claudio, Juliet, and their baby on the other, she would go upstage to where the city gates looked out onto a pastoral landscape, stop, and turn back toward me as the lights went down.

SHAKESPEARE'S CAREER IN THE THEATER

BEGINNINGS

William Shakespeare was an extraordinarily intelligent man who was born and died in an ordinary market town in the English Midlands. He lived an uneventful life in an eventful age. Born in April 1564, he was the eldest son of John Shakespeare, a glove maker who was prominent on the town council until he fell into financial difficulties. Young William was educated at the local grammar in Stratford-upon-Avon, Warwickshire, where he gained a thorough grounding in the Latin language, the art of rhetoric, and classical poetry. He married Ann Hathaway and had three children (Susanna, then the twins Hamnet and Judith) before his twenty-first birthday: an exceptionally young age for the period. We do not know how he supported his family in the mid-1580s.

Like many clever country boys, he moved to the city in order to make his way in the world. Like many creative people, he found a career in the entertainment business. Public playhouses and professional full-time acting companies reliant on the market for their income were born in Shakespeare's childhood. When he arrived in London as a man, sometime in the late 1580s, a new phenomenon was in the making: the actor who is so successful that he becomes a "star." The word did not exist in its modern sense, but the pattern is recognizable: audiences went to the theater not so much to see a particular show as to witness the comedian Richard Tarlton or the dramatic actor Edward Alleyn.

Shakespeare was an actor before he was a writer. It appears not to have been long before he realized that he was never going to grow into a great comedian like Tarlton or a great tragedian like Alleyn. Instead, he found a role within his company as the man who patched up old plays, breathing new life, new dramatic twists, into tired repertory pieces. He paid close attention to the work of the university-educated dramatists who were writing history plays and tragedies for the public stage in a style more ambitious, sweeping, and poetically grand than anything that had been seen before. But he may also have noted that what his friend and rival Ben Jonson would call "Marlowe's mighty line" sometimes faltered in the mode of comedy. Going to university, as Christopher Marlowe did, was all well and good for honing the arts of rhetorical elaboration and classical allusion, but it could lead to a loss of the common touch. To stay close to a large segment of the potential audience for public theater, it was necessary to write for clowns as well as kings and to intersperse the flights of poetry with the humor of the tavern, the privy, and the brothel: Shakespeare was the first to establish himself early in his career as an equal master of tragedy, comedy, and history. He realized that theater could be the medium to make the national past available to a wider audience than the elite who could afford to read large history books: his signature early works include not only the classical tragedy *Titus Andronicus* but also the sequence of English historical plays on the Wars of the Roses.

He also invented a new role for himself, that of in-house company dramatist. Where his peers and predecessors had to sell their plays to the theater managers on a poorly paid piecework basis, Shakespeare took a percentage of the box-office income. The Lord Chamberlain's Men constituted themselves in 1594 as a joint stock company, with the profits being distributed among the core actors who had invested as sharers. Shakespeare acted himself—he appears in the cast lists of some of Ben Jonson's plays as well as the list of actors' names at the beginning of his own collected works—but his principal duty was to write two or three plays a year for the company. By holding shares, he was effectively earning himself a royalty on his work, something no author had ever done before in England. When the Lord Chamberlain's Men collected their fee for performance at court in the Christmas season of 1594, three of them went along to the Treasurer of the Chamber: not just Richard Burbage the tragedian and Will Kempe the clown, but also Shakespeare the scriptwriter. That was something new.

The next four years were the golden period in Shakespeare's

career, though overshadowed by the death of his only son Hamnet, aged eleven, in 1596. In his early thirties and in full command of both his poetic and his theatrical medium, he perfected his art of comedy, while also developing his tragic and historical writing in new ways. In 1598, Francis Meres, a Cambridge University graduate with his finger on the pulse of the London literary world, praised Shakespeare for his excellence across the genres:

> As Plautus and Seneca are accounted the best for comedy and tragedy among the Latins, so Shakespeare among the English is the most excellent in both kinds for the stage; for comedy, witness his *Gentlemen of Verona*, his *Errors*, his *Love Labours Lost*, his *Love Labours Won*, his *Midsummer Night Dream* and his *Merchant of Venice*: for tragedy his *Richard the 2*, *Richard the 3*, *Henry the 4*, *King John*, *Titus Andronicus* and his *Romeo and Juliet*.

For Meres, as for the many writers who praised the "honey-flowing vein" of *Venus and Adonis* and *Lucrece*, narrative poems written when the theaters were closed due to plague in 1593–94, Shakespeare was marked above all by his linguistic skill, by the gift of turning elegant poetic phrases.

PLAYHOUSES

Elizabethan playhouses were "thrust" or "one-room" theaters. To understand Shakespeare's original theatrical life, we have to forget about the indoor theater of later times, with its proscenium arch and curtain that would be opened at the beginning and closed at the end of each act. In the proscenium arch theater, stage and auditorium are effectively two separate rooms: the audience looks from one world into another as if through the imaginary "fourth wall" framed by the proscenium. The picture-frame stage, together with the elaborate scenic effects and backdrops beyond it, created the illusion of a self-contained world—especially once nineteenth-century developments in the control of artificial lighting meant that the auditorium could be darkened and the spectators made to focus on the lighted stage. Shakespeare, by contrast, wrote for a bare platform stage with a standing audience gathered around it in a courtyard in full daylight. The audience were always conscious of themselves and their fellow spectators, and they shared the same "room" as the actors. A sense of immediate presence and the creation of rapport with the audience were all-important. The actor could not afford to imagine he was in a closed world, with silent witnesses dutifully observing him from the darkness.

Shakespeare's theatrical career began at the Rose Theatre in Southwark. The stage was wide and shallow, trapezoid in shape, like a lozenge. This design had a great deal of potential for the theatrical equivalent of cinematic split-screen effects, whereby one group of characters would enter at the door at one end of the tiring-house wall at the back of the stage and another group through the door at the other end, thus creating two rival tableaux. Many of the battle-heavy and faction-filled plays that premiered at the Rose have scenes of just this sort.

At the rear of the Rose stage, there were three capacious exits, each over ten feet wide. Unfortunately, the very limited excavation of a fragmentary portion of the original Globe site, in 1989, revealed nothing about the stage. The first Globe was built in 1599 with similar proportions to those of another theater, the Fortune, albeit that the former was polygonal and looked circular, whereas the latter was rectangular. The building contract for the Fortune survives and allows us to infer that the stage of the Globe was probably substantially wider than it was deep (perhaps forty-three feet wide and twenty-seven feet deep). It may well have been tapered at the front, like that of the Rose.

The capacity of the Globe was said to have been enormous, perhaps in excess of three thousand. It has been conjectured that about eight hundred people may have stood in the yard, with two thousand or more in the three layers of covered galleries. The other "public" playhouses were also of large capacity, whereas the indoor Blackfriars theater that Shakespeare's company began using in 1608—the former refectory of a monastery—had overall internal dimensions of a mere forty-six by sixty feet. It would have made for a much more intimate theatrical experience and had a much smaller capacity, probably of about six hundred people. Since they paid at least six-pence a head, the Blackfriars attracted a more select or "private" audience. The atmosphere would have been closer to that of an indoor performance before the court in the Whitehall Palace or at Richmond. That Shakespeare always wrote for indoor production at court as well as outdoor performance in the public theater should make us cautious about inferring, as some scholars have, that the opportunity provided by the intimacy of the Blackfriars led to a sig-nificant change toward a "chamber" style in his last plays—which, besides, were performed at both the Globe and the Blackfriars. After the occupation of the Blackfriars a five-act structure seems to have become more important to Shakespeare. That was because of artifi-cial lighting: there were musical interludes between the acts, while the candles were trimmed and replaced. Again, though, something similar must have been necessary for indoor court performances throughout his career.

Front of house there were the "gatherers" who collected the money from audience members: a penny to stand in the open-air yard, another penny for a place in the covered galleries, sixpence for the prominent "lord's rooms" to the side of the stage. In the indoor "private" theaters, gallants from the audience who fancied making themselves part of the spectacle sat on stools on the edge of the stage itself. Scholars debate as to how widespread this practice was in the public theaters such as the Globe. Once the audience were in place and the money counted, the gatherers were available to be extras on stage. That is one reason why battles and crowd scenes often come later rather than early in Shakespeare's plays. There was no formal prohibition upon performance by women, and there certainly were women among the gatherers, so it is not beyond the bounds of possi-bility that female crowd members were played by females.

The play began at two o'clock in the afternoon and the theater had to be cleared by five. After the main show, there would be a jig—which consisted not only of dancing, but also of knockabout comedy (it is the origin of the farcical "afterpiece" in the eighteenth-century theater). So the time available for a Shakespeare play was about two and a half hours, somewhere between the "two hours' traffic" men-tioned in the prologue to *Romeo and Juliet* and the "three hours' spectacle" referred to in the preface to the 1647 Folio of Beaumont and Fletcher's plays. The prologue to a play by Thomas Middleton refers to a thousand lines as "one hour's words," so the likelihood is that about two and a half thousand, or a maximum of three thousand lines, made up the performed text. This is indeed the length of most of Shakespeare's comedies, whereas many of his tragedies and histories are much longer, raising the possibility that he wrote full scripts, possibly with eventual publication in mind, in the full knowledge that the stage version would be heavily cut. The short Quarto texts published in his lifetime—they used to be called "Bad" Quartos—provide fascinating evidence as to the kind of cutting that probably took place. So, for instance, the First Quarto of *Hamlet* neatly merges two occasions when Hamlet is overheard, the "Fishmonger" and the "nunnery" scenes.

The social composition of the audience was mixed. The poet Sir John Davies wrote of "A thousand townsmen, gentlemen and whores, / Porters and servingmen" who would "together throng" at the public playhouses. Though moralists associated female playgoing with adultery and the sex trade, many perfectly respectable citizens' wives were regular attendees. Some, no doubt, resembled the modern groupie: a story attested in two different sources has one citizen's wife making a post-show assignation with Richard Burbage and ending up in bed with Shakespeare—supposedly eliciting from the latter the quip that William the Conqueror was before Richard III. Defenders of theater liked to say that by witnessing the comeuppance of villains on the stage, audience members would repent of their own wrongdoings, but the reality is that most people went to the theater then, as they do now, for entertainment more than moral edification. Besides, it would be foolish to suppose that audiences behaved in a homogeneous way: a pamphlet of the 1630s tells of how two men went to see *Pericles* and one of them laughed while the other wept. Bishop John Hall complained that people went to church for the same reasons that they went to the theater: "for company, for custom, for recreation . . . to feed his eyes or his ears . . . or perhaps for sleep."

Men-about-town and clever young lawyers went to be seen as much as to see. In the modern popular imagination, shaped not least by *Shakespeare in Love* and the opening sequence of Laurence Olivier's *Henry V* film, the penny-paying groundlings stand in the yard hurling abuse or encouragement and hazelnuts or orange peel at the actors, while the sophisticates in the covered galleries appreciate Shakespeare's soaring poetry. The reality was probably the other way around. A "groundling" was a kind of fish, so the nickname suggests the penny audience standing below the level of the stage and gazing in silent open-mouthed wonder at the spectacle unfolding above them. The more difficult audience members, who kept up a running commentary of clever remarks on the performance and who occasionally got into quarrels with players, were the gallants. Like Hollywood movies in modern times, Elizabethan and Jacobean plays exercised a powerful influence on the fashion and behavior of the young. John Marston mocks the lawyers who would open their lips, perhaps to court a girl, and out would "flow / Naught but pure Juliet and Romeo."

THE ENSEMBLE AT WORK

In the absence of typewriters and photocopying machines, reading aloud would have been the means by which the company got to know a new play. The tradition of the playwright reading his complete script to the assembled company endured for generations. A copy would then have been taken to the Master of the Revels for licensing. The theater book-holder or prompter would then have copied the parts for distribution to the actors. A partbook consisted of the character's lines, with each speech preceded by the last three or four words of the speech before, the so-called "cue." These would have been taken away and studied or "conned." During this period of learning the parts, an actor might have had some one-to-one instruction, perhaps from the dramatist, perhaps from a senior actor who had played the same part before, and, in the case of an apprentice, from his master. A high percentage of Desdemona's lines occur in dialogue with Othello, Lady Macbeth's with Macbeth, Cleopatra's with Antony, and Volumnia's with Coriolanus. The roles would almost certainly have been taken by the apprentice of the lead actor, usually Burbage, who delivers the majority of the cues. Given that

8. Hypothetical reconstruction of the interior of an Elizabethan playhouse during a performance.

apprentices lodged with their masters, there would have been ample opportunity for personal instruction, which may be what made it possible for young men to play such demanding parts.

After the parts were learned, there may have been no more than a single rehearsal before the first performance. With six different plays to be put on every week, there was no time for more. Actors, then, would go into a show with a very limited sense of the whole. The notion of a collective rehearsal process that is itself a process of discovery for the actors is wholly modern and would have been incomprehensible to Shakespeare and his original ensemble. Given the number of parts an actor had to hold in his memory, the forgetting of lines was probably more frequent than in the modern theater. The book-holder was on hand to prompt.

Backstage personnel included the property man, the tire-man who oversaw the costumes, call boys, attendants, and the musicians, who might play at various times from the main stage, the rooms above, and within the tiring-house. Scriptwriters sometimes made a nuisance of themselves backstage. There was often tension between the acting companies and the freelance playwrights from whom they purchased scripts: it was a smart move on the part of Shakespeare and the Lord Chamberlain's Men to bring the writing process in-house.

Scenery was limited, though sometimes set pieces were brought on (a bank of flowers, a bed, the mouth of hell). The trapdoor from below, the gallery stage above, and the curtained discovery space at the back allowed for an array of special effects: the rising of ghosts and apparitions, the descent of gods, dialogue between a character at a window and another at ground level, the revelation of a statue or a pair of lovers playing at chess. Ingenious use could be made of props, as with the ass's head in *A Midsummer Night's Dream*. In a theater that does not clutter the stage with the material paraphernalia of everyday life, those objects that are deployed may take on powerful symbolic weight, as when Shylock bears his weighing scales in one hand and knife in the other, thus becoming a parody of the figure of Justice, who traditionally bears a sword and a balance. Among the more significant items in the property cupboard of Shakespeare's company, there would have been a throne (the "chair of state"), joint stools, books, bottles, coins, purses, letters (which are brought on stage, read or referred to on about eighty occasions in the complete works), maps, gloves, a set of stocks (in which Kent is put in *King Lear*), rings, rapiers, daggers, broadswords, staves, pistols, masks and vizards, heads and skulls, torches and tapers and lanterns which served to signal night scenes on the daylit stage, a buck's head, an ass's head, animal costumes. Live animals also put in appearances, most notably the dog Crab in *The Two Gentlemen of Verona* and possibly a young polar bear in *The Winter's Tale*.

The costumes were the most important visual dimension of the play. Playwrights were paid between £2 and £6 per script, whereas Alleyn was not averse to paying £20 for "a black velvet cloak with sleeves embroidered all with silver and gold." No matter the period of the play, actors always wore contemporary costume. The excitement for the audience came not from any impression of historical accuracy, but from the richness of the attire and perhaps the transgressive thrill of the knowledge that here were commoners like themselves strutting in the costumes of courtiers in effective defiance of the strict sumptuary laws whereby in real life people had to wear the clothes that befitted their social station.

To an even greater degree than props, costumes could carry symbolic importance. Racial characteristics could be suggested: a breastplate and helmet for a Roman soldier, a turban for a Turk, long robes for exotic characters such as Moors, a gabardine for a Jew. The figure of Time, as in *The Winter's Tale*, would be equipped with hourglass, scythe, and wings; Rumour, who speaks the prologue of *2 Henry IV*, wore a costume adorned with a thousand tongues. The wardrobe in the tiring-house of the Globe would have contained much of the same stock as that of rival manager Philip Henslowe at the Rose: green gowns for outlaws and foresters, black for melancholy men such as Jaques and people in mourning such as the Countess in *All's Well That Ends Well* (at the beginning of *Hamlet*, the prince is still in mourning black when everyone else is in festive garb for the wedding of the new king), a gown and hood for a friar (or a feigned friar like the duke in *Measure for Measure*), blue coats and tawny to distinguish the followers of rival factions, a leather apron and ruler for a carpenter (as in the opening scene of *Julius Caesar*—and in *A Midsummer Night's Dream*, where this is the only sign that Peter Quince is a carpenter), a cockle hat with staff and a pair of sandals for a pilgrim or palmer (the disguise assumed by Helen in *All's Well*), bodices and kirtles with farthingales beneath for the boys who are to be dressed as girls. A gender switch such as that of Rosalind or Jessica seems to have taken between fifty and eighty lines of dialogue—Viola does not resume her "maiden weeds," but remains in her boy's costume to the end of *Twelfth Night* because a change would have slowed down the action at just the moment it was speeding to a climax. Henslowe's inventory also included "a robe for to go invisible": Oberon, Puck, and Ariel must have had something similar.

As the costumes appealed to the eyes, so there was music for the ears. Comedies included many songs. Desdemona's willow song, perhaps a late addition to the text, is a rare and thus exceptionally poignant example from tragedy. Trumpets and tuckets sounded for ceremonial entrances, drums denoted an army on the march. Background music could create atmosphere, as at the beginning of *Twelfth Night*, during the lovers' dialogue near the end of *The Mer-*

chant of Venice, when the statue seemingly comes to life in *The Winter's Tale*, and for the revival of Pericles and of Lear (in the Quarto text, but not the Folio). The haunting sound of the hautboy suggested a realm beyond the human, as when the god Hercules is imagined deserting Mark Antony. Dances symbolized the harmony of the end of a comedy—though in Shakespeare's world of mingled joy and sorrow, someone is usually left out of the circle.

The most important resource was, of course, the actors themselves. They needed many skills: in the words of one contemporary commentator, "dancing, activity, music, song, elocution, ability of body, memory, skill of weapon, pregnancy of wit." Their bodies were as significant as their voices. Hamlet tells the player to "suit the action to the word, the word to the action": moments of strong emotion, known as "passions," relied on a repertoire of dramatic gestures as well as a modulation of the voice. When Titus Andronicus has had his hand chopped off, he asks "How can I grace my talk, / Wanting a hand to give it action?" A pen portrait of "The Character of an Excellent Actor" by the dramatist John Webster is almost certainly based on his impression of Shakespeare's leading man, Richard Burbage: "By a full and significant action of body, he charms our attention: sit in a full theater, and you will think you see so many lines drawn from the circumference of so many ears, whiles the actor is the centre. . . ."

Though Burbage was admired above all others, praise was also heaped upon the apprentice players whose alto voices fitted them for the parts of women. A spectator at Oxford in 1610 records how the audience were reduced to tears by the pathos of Desdemona's death. The puritans who fumed about the biblical prohibition upon crossdressing and the encouragement to sodomy constituted by the sight of an adult male kissing a teenage boy on stage were a small minority. Little is known, however, about the characteristics of the leading apprentices in Shakespeare's company. It may perhaps be inferred that one was a lot taller than the other, since Shakespeare often wrote for a pair of female friends, one tall and fair, the other short and dark (Helena and Hermia, Rosalind and Celia, Beatrice and Hero).

We know little about Shakespeare's own acting roles—an early allusion indicates that he often took royal parts, and a venerable tradition gives him old Adam in *As You Like It* and the ghost of old King Hamlet. Save for Burbage's lead roles and the generic part of the clown, all such castings are mere speculation. We do not even know for sure whether the original Falstaff was Will Kempe or another actor who specialized in comic roles, Thomas Pope.

Kempe left the company in early 1599. Tradition has it that he fell out with Shakespeare over the matter of excessive improvisation. He was replaced by Robert Armin, who was less of a clown and more of a cerebral wit: this explains the difference between such parts as Lancelet Gobbo and Dogberry, which were written for Kempe, and the more verbally sophisticated Feste and Lear's Fool, which were written for Armin.

One thing that is clear from surviving "plots," or storyboards of plays from the period is that a degree of doubling was necessary. *2 Henry VI* has over sixty speaking parts, but more than half of the characters only appear in a single scene and most scenes have only six to eight speakers. At a stretch, the play could be performed by thirteen actors. When Thomas Platter saw *Julius Caesar* at the Globe in 1599, he noted that there were about fifteen. Why doesn't Paris go to the Capulet ball in *Romeo and Juliet*? Perhaps because he was doubled with Mercutio, who does. In *The Winter's Tale*, Mamillius might have come back as Perdita and Antigonus been doubled by Camillo, making the partnership with Paulina at the end a very neat touch. Titania and Oberon are often played by the same pair as Hippolyta and Theseus, suggesting a symbolic matching of the rulers of the worlds of night and day, but it is questionable whether there would have been time for the necessary costume changes. As so often, one is left in a realm of tantalizing speculation.

THE KING'S MAN

On Queen Elizabeth's death in 1603, the new king, James I, who had held the Scottish throne as James VI since he had been an infant, immediately took the Lord Chamberlain's Men under his direct patronage. Henceforth they would be the King's Men, and for the rest of Shakespeare's career they were favored with far more court performances than any of their rivals. There even seem to have been rumors early in the reign that Shakespeare and Burbage were being considered for knighthoods, an unprecedented honor for mere actors—and one that in the event was not accorded to a member of the profession for nearly three hundred years, when the title was bestowed upon Henry Irving, the leading Shakespearean actor of Queen Victoria's reign.

Shakespeare's productivity rate slowed in the Jacobean years, not because of age or some personal trauma, but because there were frequent outbreaks of plague, causing the theaters to be closed for long periods. The King's Men were forced to spend many months on the road. Between November 1603 and 1608, they were to be found at various towns in the south and Midlands, though Shakespeare probably did not tour with them by this time. He had bought a large house back home in Stratford and was accumulating other property. He may indeed have stopped acting soon after the new king took the throne. With the London theaters closed so much of the time and a large repertoire on the stocks, Shakespeare seems to have focused his energies on writing a few long and complex tragedies that could have been played on demand at court: *Othello*, *King Lear*, *Antony and Cleopatra*, *Coriolanus*, and *Cymbeline* are among his longest and poetically grandest plays. *Macbeth* only survives in a shorter text, which shows signs of adaptation after Shakespeare's death. The bitterly satirical *Timon of Athens*, apparently a collaboration with Thomas Middleton that may have failed on the stage, also belongs to this period. In comedy, too, he wrote longer and morally darker works than in the Elizabethan period, pushing at the very bounds of the form in *Measure for Measure* and *All's Well That Ends Well*.

From 1608 onward, when the King's Men began occupying the indoor Blackfriars playhouse (as a winter house, meaning that they only used the outdoor Globe in summer?), Shakespeare turned to a more romantic style. His company had a great success with a revived and altered version of an old pastoral play called *Mucedorus*. It even featured a bear. The younger dramatist John Fletcher, meanwhile, sometimes working in collaboration with Francis Beaumont, was pioneering a new style of tragicomedy, a mix of romance and royalism laced with intrigue and pastoral excursions. Shakespeare experimented with this idiom in *Cymbeline* and it was presumably with his blessing that Fletcher eventually took over as the King's Men's company dramatist. The two writers apparently collaborated on three plays in the years 1612–14: a lost romance called *Cardenio* (based on the love-madness of a character in Cervantes' *Don Quixote*), *Henry VIII* (originally staged with the title *All Is True*), and *The Two Noble Kinsmen*, a dramatization of Chaucer's "Knight's Tale." These were written after Shakespeare's two final solo-authored plays, *The Winter's Tale*, a self-consciously old-fashioned work dramatizing the pastoral romance of his old enemy Robert Greene, and *The Tempest*, which at one and the same time drew together multiple theatrical traditions, diverse reading, and contemporary interest in the fate of a ship that had been wrecked on the way to the New World.

The collaborations with Fletcher suggest that Shakespeare's career ended with a slow fade rather than the sudden retirement supposed by the nineteenth-century Romantic critics who read Prospero's epilogue to *The Tempest* as Shakespeare's personal farewell to his art. In the last few years of his life Shakespeare certainly spent more of his time in Stratford-upon-Avon, where he became further involved in property dealing and litigation. But his London life also continued. In 1613 he made his first major London property purchase: a freehold house in the Blackfriars district, close to his company's indoor theater. *The Two Noble Kinsmen* may have been written as late as 1614, and Shakespeare was in London on business a little over a year before he died of an unknown cause at home in Stratford-upon-Avon in 1616, probably on his fifty-second birthday.

About half the sum of his works were published in his lifetime, in texts of variable quality. A few years after his death, his fellow actors began putting together an authorized edition of his complete *Comedies, Histories and Tragedies*. It appeared in 1623, in large "Folio" format. This collection of thirty-six plays gave Shakespeare his immortality. In the words of his fellow dramatist Ben Jonson, who contributed two poems of praise at the start of the Folio, the body of his work made him "a monument without a tomb":

And art alive still while thy book doth live
And we have wits to read and praise to give . . .
He was not of an age, but for all time!

SHAKESPEARE'S WORKS: A CHRONOLOGY

1595–97	*Love's Labour's Won* (a lost play, unless the original title for another comedy)
1595–96	*A Midsummer Night's Dream*
1595–96	*The Tragedy of Romeo and Juliet*
1595–96	*King Richard the Second*
1595–97	*The Life and Death of King John* (possibly earlier)
1596–97	*The Merchant of Venice*
1596–97	*The First Part of Henry the Fourth*
1597–98	*The Second Part of Henry the Fourth*
1598	*Much Ado About Nothing*
1598–99	*The Passionate Pilgrim* (20 poems, some not by Shakespeare)
1599	*The Life of Henry the Fifth*
1599	"To the Queen" (epilogue for a court performance)
1599	*As You Like It*
1599	*The Tragedy of Julius Caesar*
1600–01	*The Tragedy of Hamlet, Prince of Denmark* (perhaps revising an earlier version)
1600–01	*The Merry Wives of Windsor* (perhaps revising version of 1597–99)
1601	"Let the Bird of Loudest Lay" (poem, known since 1807 as "The Phoenix and Turtle" [turtledove])
1601	*Twelfth Night, or What You Will*
1601–02	*The Tragedy of Troilus and Cressida*
1604	*The Tragedy of Othello, the Moor of Venice*
1604	*Measure for Measure*
1605	*All's Well That Ends Well*
1605	*The Life of Timon of Athens*, with Thomas Middleton
1605–06	*The Tragedy of King Lear*
1605–08	? contribution to *The Four Plays in One* (lost, except for *A Yorkshire Tragedy*, mostly by Thomas Middleton)

1606	*The Tragedy of Macbeth* (surviving text has additional scenes by Thomas Middleton)
1606–07	*The Tragedy of Antony and Cleopatra*
1608	*The Tragedy of Coriolanus*
1608	*Pericles, Prince of Tyre*, with George Wilkins
1610	*The Tragedy of Cymbeline*
1611	*The Winter's Tale*
1611	*The Tempest*
1612–13	*Cardenio*, with John Fletcher (survives only in later adaptation called *Double Falsehood* by Lewis Theobald)
1613	*Henry VIII (All Is True)*, with John Fletcher
1613–14	*The Two Noble Kinsmen*, with John Fletcher

FURTHER READING
AND VIEWING

CRITICAL APPROACHES

Bennett, Robert S., *Romance and Reformation in the Erasmian Spirit of Shake-speare's Measure for Measure* (2000). Lively, detailed discussion of the play's genre, ethics, and construction.

Bloom, Harold, ed., *William Shakespeare: Measure for Measure*, Modern Critical Interpretations (1987). Excellent selection of influential twentieth-century essays.

Chedgzoy, Kate, *William Shakespeare: Measure for Measure*, Writers and Their Work Series (2000). Good introduction covering history, context, and performance.

Geckle, George L., ed., *Measure for Measure*, Shakespeare: The Critical Tradition Series (2001). Comprehensive collection of essays from 1783 to 1920, including Hazlitt, Coleridge, and Swinburne.

Hawkins, Harriet, " 'The Devil's Party': Virtues and Vices in *Measure for Measure*," *Modern Critical Interpretations: William Shakespeare's Measure for Measure*, edited by Harold Bloom (1987), pp. 81–93. Lively, discursive, relates to popular culture.

Jamieson, Michael, "The Problem Plays, 1920–1970: A Retrospect," *Shakespeare Survey* 25 (1972), pp. 1–10. Useful introductory account of the history of the so-called "problem plays."

Knight, G. Wilson, "*Measure for Measure* and the Gospels," in *The Wheel of Fire: Interpretations of Shakespearian Tragedy* (1949), pp. 73–96. Detailed account of the play's religious allusions.

Riefer, Marcia, " 'Instruments of Some More Mightier Member': The Constriction of Female Power in *Measure for Measure*," *Shakespeare Quarterly* 35 (1984), pp. 157–69. Strong feminist reading.

Rowe, M. W., "The Dissolution of Goodness: *Measure for Measure* and Classical Ethics," *International Journal of the Classical Tradition* 5 (1998), pp. 20–46. Powerful reading arguing that the play shows the superiority of classical, notably Aristotelian, ethics over "puritan" conceptions of morality.

Seiden, Melvin, *Measure for Measure: Casuistry and Artistry* (1990). Catholic discussion of the play's problems.

Shuger, Debora Kuller, *Political Theologies in Shakespeare's England: The Sacred and the State in Measure for Measure* (2001). Detailed historical account of the relationship between Tudor/Stuart politics and religion.

Stead, C. K., ed., *Shakespeare: Measure for Measure*, Casebook Series (1971). Useful collection of early and influential twentieth-century essays.

Tennenhouse, Leonard, "Representing Power: *Measure for Measure* in Its Time," in *Shakespeare and History*, ed. Stephen Orgel and Sean Keilen (1999), pp. 321–38. Reads the play in conjunction with other disguised ruler plays as a transitional text from Tudor to Jacobean periods.

Watt, Gary, *Equity Stirring: The Story of Justice Beyond Law* (2009), pp. 218–25. Exceptionally interesting, placing the play in the context of the emergence of the concept of "equity" in English law.

Wood, Nigel, ed., *Measure for Measure*, Theory in Practice Series (1996). Theoretically informed selection of essays exploring history, politics, and performance.

THE PLAY IN PERFORMANCE

Barton, John, and Gareth Lloyd Evans, "Directing Problem Plays," *Shakespeare Survey* 25 (1972), pp. 63–71. Fascinating account arguing that the production offers a richer, more complex version of the play than a critic can.

Berry, Ralph, "Measure for Measure: Casting the Star," *Shakespeare in Performance: Castings and Metamorphoses* (1993), pp. 119–25. Original look at the play in performance.

Coursen, H. R., "Why Measure for Measure?," in *Shakespeare on Television: An Anthology of Essays and Reviews*, ed. J. C. Bulman and H. R. Coursen (1998), pp. 179–84. Favorable discussion of BBC production.

Hampton-Reeves, Stuart, *Measure for Measure*, Shakespeare Handbooks Series (2007). Useful introduction to the play and history of performance.

Jackson, Russell, and Robert Smallwood, eds., *Players of Shakespeare 2* (1988), pp. 13–31. Daniel Massey on playing the duke in *Measure for Measure*: thoughtful actor's account.

Jackson, Russell, and Robert Smallwood, eds., *Players of Shakespeare 3* (1993). Roger Allam on playing the duke, pp. 21–41.

McCandless, David, *Gender and Performance in Shakespeare's Problem Comedies* (1997), pp. 108–22. Academic's account of directing a radical student production.

Nicholls, Graham, "*Measure for Measure* Before 1970," in *Measure for Measure: Text & Performance* (1986), pp. 50–53. Part 1: a good introductory account; part 2: discusses four productions in detail—RSC 1970, Marowitz 1975, RSC 1978, BBC 1979.

Parsons, Keith, and Pamela Mason, *Shakespeare in Performance* (1995). Basic introduction by Mike Paterson, pp. 131–35, lavishly illustrated.

Rocklin, Edward L., "Measured Endings: How Productions from 1720 to 1929 Close Shakespeare's Open Silences in *Measure for Measure*," *Shakespeare Survey* 53 (2000) pp. 213–32. Useful, detailed discussion of different approaches to the last scene.

Rutter, Carol, *Clamorous Voices: Shakespeare's Women Today* (1988). Chapter 2, "Isabella: Virtue Betrayed?," pp. 26–52. Actresses who've played the part discuss the role and the play.

AVAILABLE ON DVD

Measure for Measure, directed by Desmond Davis for BBC Shakespeare (1979, DVD 2005). Tim Piggott-Smith and Kate Nelligan are excellent as Angelo and Isabella; typically splendid BBC cast of low-life characters.

Measure for Measure, directed by David Thacker (1994, DVD 2007) with Tom Wilkinson, Corin Redgrave, Juliet Aubrey, and Henry Goodman. Updated setting, sophisticated televisual awareness—terrific performances, touching and disturbing.

Measure for Measure, directed by Bob Komar (DVD 2007). Updated, heavily cut and set in British army barracks, with Josephine Rogers as Isabella, Daniel Roberts as Angelo, and Simon Phillips as the duke.

REFERENCES

1. Robert Latham and William Matthews, eds., *The Diary of Samuel Pepys*, Vol. 3 (1970), p. 32. This diary entry may have referred to the premiere on 15 February 1662 or a later performance on 17 December in the same year.
2. Mrs. Inchbald, *Measure for Measure* (1808), p. 5, quoted in Rosalind Miles, *The Problem of Measure for Measure* (1976), p. 305.
3. William Archer, *The Theatrical "World" for 1893* (1894), pp. 266–73.
4. *New York Times*, 7 February 1888.
5. *The Times*, London, 11 November 1893.
6. C. E. Montague, "The Art of Mr Poel," in his *Dramatic Values* (1925), pp. 222–43.
7. Gordon Crosse, *Shakespearean Playgoing 1890–1925* (1953), p. 54.
8. Tyrone Guthrie, *A Life in the Theatre* (1961).
9. Peter Fleming, *The Spectator*, Vol. 184, No. 6351, 17 March 1950, pp. 337–38.
10. Kenneth Tynan, *He That Plays the King: A View of the Theatre* (1950), pp. 138–52.
11. J. C. Trewin, "Moon and Stars: 1950–1952," in his *Peter Brook: A Biography* (1971), pp. 50–65.
12. Jack Karr, *Toronto Star*, 29 June 1954, quoted in Jane Williamson, "The Duke and Isabella on the Modern Stage," in *The Triple Bond: Plays, Mainly Shakespearean in Performance*, ed. Joseph G. Price (1975), pp. 149–69.
13. Williamson, "The Duke and Isabella on the Modern Stage," pp. 149–69.
14. *Time and Tide*, 30 November 1957.
15. Williamson, "The Duke and Isabella on the Modern Stage," pp. 149–69.
16. *The Times*, London, 4 April 1963.
17. Williamson, "The Duke and Isabella on the Modern Stage," pp. 149–69.
18. Tyrone Guthrie, note in *Measure for Measure* RSC Programme, 1966.
19. *The Times*, London, 4 March 1966.
20. Clive Barnes, *New York Times*, 13 June 1975.

21. Ibid.
22. Charles Marowitz, *The Marowitz Shakespeare* (1978), p. 20.
23. John Elsom, *The Listener*, Vol. 105, No. 2709, 23 April 1981.
24. Frank Rich, *New York Times*, 10 March 1989.
25. Ibid.
26. Nancy Taylor, *Theatre Journal*, Vol. 51, No. 1 (March 1999), pp. 73–76.
27. D. J. R. Bruckner, *New York Times*, 20 August 1999.
28. Ben Brantley, *New York Times*, 18 June 2001.
29. Stuart Hampton-Reeves, *Measure for Measure*, Shakespeare Handbooks Series (2007), p. 124.
30. Ibid.
31. Ibid., p. 125.
32. Ibid., pp. 128–9.
33. Ibid., p. 130.
34. This is one of the productions discussed in detail in Graham Nicholls, *Measure for Measure: Text and Performance* (1986).
35. John Mortimer, "Measure for Measure," in *Shakespeare in Perspective*, Vol. 1, ed. Roger Sales (1982).
36. Nigel Wood, "Measure for Measure," in *Performing Measure for Measure*, ed. Peter Corbin (1996).
37. Judi Dench, "Measure for Measure," in Sales, *Shakespeare in Perspective*, Vol. 1.
38. Irving Wardle, *The Times*, London, 5 September 1974.
39. Benedict Nightingale, *New Statesman*, 13 September 1974.
40. Keith Hack, note in *Measure for Measure* RSC Programme, 1974.
41. Peter Thomson, *Shakespeare Survey* 28 (1975).
42. Ibid.
43. Nicholas Hytner, interview with Janet Watts, *Observer*, 8 November 1987.
44. Michael Billington, *Country Life*, 12 November 1987.
45. Ibid.
46. Roger Allam, "The Duke in Measure for Measure," in *Players of Shakespeare 3*, ed. Russell Jackson and Robert Smallwood (1993).
47. Robert Smallwood, *Shakespeare Quarterly* (1992).
48. Nicholas de Jongh, *Evening Standard*, 11 March 1992.
49. Matt Wolf, *City Limits*, 19 March 1992.
50. Interview with Trevor Nunn by Benedict Nightingale, *The Times*, London, 27 August 1991.
51. Ibid.

52. Smallwood, *Shakespeare Quarterly*.
53. " 'But man, proud man, dress'd in a little brief authority . . . ,' Angelo and the Duke," in Judith Cook, *Shakespeare's Players* (1983).
54. Michael Scott, *Renaissance Drama for a Modern Audience* (1982), p. 61.
55. B. A. Young, *Financial Times*, 5 September 1974.
56. Peter Thomson, *Shakespeare Survey* 28 (1975).
57. Wardle, *The Times*, London, 5 September 1974.
58. Scott, *Renaissance Drama for a Modern Audience*, p. 61.
59. Ralph Berry, *Changing Styles in Shakespeare* (1981).
60. Peter Ansorge, *Plays and Players* (October 1974).
61. Daniel Massey, "The Duke in *Measure for Measure*," in *Players of Shakespeare 2*, ed. Russell Jackson and Robert Smallwood (1988).
62. Daniel Massey played the Duke for the RSC in 1983.
63. Allam, "The Duke in Measure for Measure."
64. Ibid.
65. Michael Coveney, *Financial Times*, 13 November 1987.
66. Michael Billington, *Country Life*, 12 November 1987.
67. Allam, "The Duke in Measure for Measure."
68. Ibid.
69. Robert Smallwood, *Shakespeare Quarterly* (1992).
70. Robert Smallwood, *Shakespeare Quarterly* (1991).
71. Benedict Nightingale, *The Times*, London, 12 March 1992.
72. Daniel Evans on Angelo for the RSC Online Play Guides, *Measure for Measure*.
73. John Mortimer, "Measure for Measure," in Sales, *Shakespeare in Perspective*.
74. Ibid.
75. Michael Pennington, in Cook, *Shakespeare's Players*. Michael Pennington played Angelo in the RSC's 1974 production directed by Keith Hack.
76. Ian Richardson, in Cook, *Shakespeare's Players*.
77. Scott, *Renaissance Drama for a Modern Audience*, p. 61.
78. David Haig in interview with Ceridwen Thomas, *Plays and Players*, October 1991.
79. Paul Taylor, *Independent*, 12 March 1992.
80. Jack Tinker, *Daily Mail*, 13 March 1992.
81. Michael Billington, *Guardian*, 22 October 1994.
82. Michael Coveney, *Financial Times*, 28 June 1978.
83. Mortimer, "Measure for Measure."
84. J. M. Nosworthy, "Introduction" to *Measure for Measure* (1969), p. 44.

85. Juliet Stevenson, "Isabella: Virtue Betrayed," in Carol Rutter, *Clamorous Voices* (1988).

86. Anne Barton, "But man, proud man . . . ," note in *Measure for Measure* RSC Programme, 1970.

87. Dench, "Measure for Measure."

88. Benedict Nightingale, *New Statesman*, 10 April 1970.

89. Carol Rutter, "Isabella: Virtue Betrayed," in her *Clamorous Voices*.

90. Scott, *Renaissance Drama for a Modern Audience*.

91. Stevenson, "Isabella: Virtue Betrayed."

92. Allam, "The Duke in Measure for Measure."

93. Paul Taylor, *Independent*, 22 October 1994.

ACKNOWLEDGMENTS AND PICTURE CREDITS

Preparation of "*Measure for Measure* in Performance" was assisted by a generous grant from the CAPITAL Centre (Creativity and Performance in Teaching and Learning) of the University of Warwick for research in the RSC archive at the Shakespeare Birthplace Trust.

Thanks as always to our indefatigable and eagle-eyed copy editor Tracey Day and to Ray Addicott for overseeing the production process with rigor and calmness.

Picture research by Michelle Morton. Grateful acknowledgment is made to the Shakespeare Birthplace Trust for assistance with picture research (special thanks to Helen Hargest) and reproduction fees.

Images of RSC productions are supplied by the Shakespeare Centre Library and Archive, Stratford-upon-Avon. This Library, maintained by the Shakespeare Birthplace Trust, holds the most important collection of Shakespeare material in the UK, including the Royal Shakespeare Company's official archive. It is open to the public free of charge.

For more information see www.shakespeare.org.uk.

1. Directed by Peter Brook (1950). Angus McBean © Royal Shakespeare Company
2. Directed by John Barton (1970). Reg Wilson © Royal Shakespeare Company
3. Directed by John Blatchley (1962). Joe Cocks Studio Collection © Shakespeare Birthplace Trust
4. Directed by Steven Pimlott (1994). Malcolm Davies © Shakespeare Birthplace Trust
5. Directed by Trevor Nunn (1991). Joe Cocks Studio Collection © Shakespeare Birthplace Trust

6. Directed by Nicholas Hytner (1987). Joe Cocks Studio Collection © Shakespeare Birthplace Trust
7. Directed by Nicholas Hytner (1987). Joe Cocks Studio Collection © Shakespeare Birthplace Trust
8. Reconstructed Elizabethan playhouse © Charcoalblue

Modern Library is online at
www.modernlibrary.com

MODERN LIBRARY ONLINE IS YOUR GUIDE TO CLASSIC LITERATURE ON THE WEB

THE MODERN LIBRARY E-NEWSLETTER

Our free e-mail newsletter is sent to subscribers, and features sample chapters, interviews with and essays by our authors, upcoming books, special promotions, announcements, and news. To subscribe to the Modern Library e-newsletter, visit **www.modernlibrary.com**

THE MODERN LIBRARY WEBSITE

Check out the Modern Library website at
www.modernlibrary.com for:

- The Modern Library e-newsletter
- A list of our current and upcoming titles and series
- Reading Group Guides and exclusive author spotlights
- Special features with information on the classics and other paperback series
- Excerpts from new releases and other titles
- A list of our e-books and information on where to buy them
- The Modern Library Editorial Board's 100 Best Novels and 100 Best Nonfiction Books of the Twentieth Century written in the English language
- News and announcements

Questions? E-mail us at **modernlibrary@randomhouse.com**.
For questions about examination or desk copies, please visit
the Random House Academic Resources site at
www.randomhouse.com/academic

HB 03 05 2019 0541